Hideaway

A novel

D. B. Crawford

PublishAmerica
Baltimore

First printing

ISBN: 1-4137-6242-5
PUBLISHED BY PUBLISHAMERICA, LLLP
www.publishamerica.com
Baltimore

Printed in the United States of America

For Charles and Paul

Chapter One

Joanne Blake knew this was not going to be one of the best Mondays of her life. She had awakened early with a dull pain somewhere in her entrails, a pain that seemed to be constantly with her now as winter, decidedly irritable, was making its way to a losing confrontation with spring.

The pain sharpened as she impatiently maneuvered her car through the morning rush hour. Cars were inching along despite the fact that the snow-removal crews had done a good job of clearing the accumulation of the past weekend. The culprit was the cold sun, which, in a playful mood, was delighting in reflecting its rays off the fresh banks bordering the street straight into drivers' fields of vision. To make matters worse, water had accumulated on the salted pavement, and windshields needed continual cleaning.

As she once more pressed the button for a spray of fluid to be swept by the wipers, Joanne wondered why she lived in such a climate. Her job and the house no longer offered her the luxury of time to spend on the ski slopes. *Or are they just excuses*, she wondered. Skiing had lost the attractiveness and purpose, it once had when she was younger.

After devoting years of effort and sacrifice to reach an enviable world-class ranking on the ski team, not the very top, but close enough for comfort, she had met Roger and her life had veered in a new direction. She had celebrated her twenty-third birthday the previous fall, and, without fully acknowledging it at first, she knew she wanted to transfer her devotion for the sport to the tall young man with dark eyes and curly black hair.

The season's competitions were over when she first saw Roger by the fireplace in the lodge at White Mountain in March. The attraction had been instantaneous on her part when he smiled at her. Too shy to make any direct move, she had simply returned the smile. Her group sat away from the fireplace, near the window, and she had stolen many glances in his direction, certain he was doing the same, although she involuntarily turned her attention back to her friends as soon as he moved his eyes.

Noticing the roving eyes, one of the fellows in her group had gone over to Roger's table to bring him back and introduce him all around. Roger sat beside Joanne and impressed her with his wit and his charm. For some unknown reason, she tried to minimize her reputation as a skier, only to be rebuked by Dennis Mercer, the group's top skier, who set the record straight for Roger.

Later, she quickly accepted Roger's invitation to be driven home. As he controlled his VW Beetle easily on the snow-covered pavement, he told her he was cramming for his bar exam and that he would, in the coming summer, be joining the firm of McBride and Porteous, one of the city's most respected law partnerships. She told him about her work in market research for the pharmaceutical giant Scalls-Morton and the creative painting courses she was taking in the evening. He had made no secret of the fact that he was amazed at her ability to combine it all.

"It's simply a matter of being organized and orderly. Besides, painting's just a hobby at best. My mother was an artist. When I was little, I used to sit beside her when she was painting and try to imitate her. I thought it was fun. I still do, although I know I'm not too good."

"I would like to see one of your paintings sometime," Roger said, "to judge for myself."

"You may regret it," she replied, and he had laughed in amusement.

"You said your mother *was* an artist..." he began.

"My mother died when I was twelve."

"I'm sorry."

She was certain the simple words were sincere.

At her house, he helped her with her skis, but, to her disappointment, declined an invitation for a cup of coffee. He did, however, ask her to join him on the slopes the following weekend.

Until the end of the season, they spent as much time as possible skiing. She pushed him to new heights as they sped down the mountain, exhilarated by each new turn and mesmerized by each other. He soon got into the habit of stopping halfway down the steepest hills, beckoning her to him and kissing her. Somehow his lips were always warm despite the cold, and she responded with ardor, oblivious to the whistles and jeers of the other skiers as they whizzed by. On the last day they were to ski together that season, she was well aware that they spent more time kissing on the lifts and on the slopes than they did actually skiing. When she pointed this out to Roger, he simply smiled and asked her if she minded. She did not. Not in the least.

The following summer, she told her coach that she had decided to give up competitive skiing. He had tried to make her reconsider, but to no avail. Competition had lost its urgency for Joanne. She would never become the best skier in the world; she had, however, proven herself and was very satisfied with her accomplishments. The medals and the memories she had accumulated would last her a lifetime. It was time to grow up, to move on.

A year later, Joanne and Roger were married. Her father insisted on a large wedding and she had reluctantly agreed. She would have preferred a small affair, but the older man had insisted. Who else was he going to spend his money on? It would be the family's only wedding; why not make it something to remember with pride and joy? She could not deny him his wish, he who had faced tragedy, pain, and loneliness with bravery and courage.

In the months leading up to what was to be a perfect wedding day, her father would engage in long discourses on the law with Roger. She was sure her dad, a police sergeant with an impressive record, kept some sort of tab on the cases he *won* over his future son-in-law. Joanne liked that they enjoyed each other's company. They were to be the best of friends, sharpening each other's wits for twelve years until the policeman's heart gave out.

Joanne's reverie came to an abrupt end when her car was narrowly missed by a taxi, the driver obviously believing she and the others were moving much too slowly for his liking. He sped suddenly on her right, the side of his vehicle climbing part of the way up the snowbank before cutting sharply in front of her. She cursed under her breath as much to the inconsiderate driver as to the pain, which had suddenly reappeared somewhere under her fastened seat belt.

It was still there when Joanne saw the hospital come into view. Inside she saw the same personnel she had dealt with on her previous visit less than two weeks earlier. The second set of tests she was undergoing took longer than the first. Doctors, nurses, and assistants seemed very intent on avoiding even the slightest error—if error had been committed the first time. It was, after all, as far as any of them could remember, Joanne overheard, the first request by Dr. Calder for such tests to be duplicated on a patient. Everyone had obviously been a little shaken. Their reputations, even perhaps their jobs, were on the line.

Joanne Blake quietly followed the instructions given to her, drinking chalky liquid and allowing endless X-rays, then remaining motionless for some time, while a scanner studied her body. Even though it made her feel nauseated despite the mild sedation, she accepted that a long, slim instrument be pushed down her throat so a tiny sample could be extracted from her stomach. Through it all she did not complain. Dr. Calder was an excellent physician, and she appreciated that he wanted to be doubly sure of the damage to her stomach before deciding on a course of treatment.

It was nearly noon before her ordeal was over.

Chapter Two

It was exactly noon when Peggy, Joanne Blake's secretary, glanced at her watch. She was trying to decide whether to go to lunch or wait for her boss to return when she saw Peter Malton, president and chief executive officer of Scalls-Morton, round the corner and walk swiftly toward her. She knew he would greet her briefly on his way to Joanne's office where the sight of the orderly desk would make him inquire about Joanne's whereabouts. Peggy's predictions were right-on.

"Joanne's not in?" the president asked, although he already knew the answer.

"No, sir. She said she would be late today."

"Where is she?"

"I really don't know, sir. She said she had some personal business to attend to, but she should be in shortly," Peggy told him truthfully.

"You mean, she's not been in all morning? Is she ill?"

"I'm sure she's not. She'd have told me if something was wrong." Peggy disliked the man's inquisitive tone, and wished he would go away. "She just had something to do. I'll call you as soon as she comes in if you wish."

"You mean, Joanne's not in? She's never around when you're looking for her."

Both Peter and Peggy turned at the sound of Harvey Mack's voice. The production manager had appeared from nowhere, his fiery eyes matching his red hair. *He is in a rotten mood, as usual,* Peggy thought.

"Where is she? I need to talk to her now." Mack spoke the words to both Peter and Peggy in a tone that held them jointly responsible for his irritation.

"I'm right here," Joanne said, coming down the hall with a faint smile on her face. "What seems to be the problem?" she asked, and without waiting for an answer from either man, turned to her secretary. "Good morning, Peggy. Any messages?"

"Yes, right here," the woman replied, obviously relieved, and handed her boss half a dozen small slips.

Turning to the two men, Joanne said casually, "So, you want to see me, gentlemen? Please come in."

Her coat removed, her tailored beige suit seemed made for the brown leather of her large chair. *She looks tired and weary,* Peter thought. *I don't like it.*

Harvey was the first to speak. "I want to know why there was nothing in the paper this morning to set the record straight about the fire last week. You were supposed to do something. Right now the media has us looking like we don't give a damn about the safety of our employees."

Joanne closed her eyes for a second. She really didn't feel up to another confrontation with Harvey Mack. "By us you mean you, don't you, Harv?"

Harvey turned to the president for support. "Peter, are you going to let her get away with this? We had agreed that there was to be an all-out PR effort to counteract the bad publicity we've been getting." Turning to Joanne, but still speaking to Peter Malton, he added, "Of course, she's hardly ever around lately, so how can she..."

Joanne interrupted him sharply. "Wait a second. I'm never around? Well, Harv, if you had attended the executive meeting Friday afternoon, you'd know that it was decided, at my suggestion, that we do nothing at the moment." Harv opened his mouth to say something, but Joanne put up her hand and continued. "It was just a small fire. No injuries, and damage was slight, relatively speaking. By now, everyone has forgotten about it. This week, next week, whenever it seems appropriate, we'll give the media something positive about the company. I feel it'll be much more effective than trying to defend ourselves now, which is what we'd be doing."

"What's wrong with that? Once again the media's after us. We have to defend ourselves." Harvey's usually red face was getting redder by the minute.

"Harv, the trouble here is that you feel you're getting bad publicity because one of your men actually started the fire. You want to be vindicated, but I don't feel it's an appropriate position for the company at this time. The executive agreed with me. I should think the case would be closed."

"Well, I don't think it is." Turning again to the president, who had remained quiet throughout the exchange, Harvey said, "I want another meeting. My department's at stake; I think I should have some say in the matter. I don't think it's fair that a decision like that was taken without my vote."

Peter Malton spoke in an even tone. "Harv, I agree that this is the best course of action. It'll be much better for all of us in the long run. Why don't you let it ride this time, okay?"

Harvey's anger was reaching a crescendo. The man had always been an aggravation for Joanne, and she disliked his paranoid attitude, his outbursts whenever Scalls-Morton had to face special challenges, including being the target of legal action. Instead of being concerned about saving the reputation of the company, Harvey Mack tended to scream up and down that whatever the problem, it was a fabrication bent on discrediting him and his department. Today, true to form, he was viewing the small fire of a few days earlier as a personal affront. And Joanne could sense that he could barely refrain from confronting Peter Malton for siding with her because she was his personal friend.

However Harvey did control himself, which is more than he would have done if Peter had not been in the room, Joanne knew. He spoke again after a few seconds, his voice low but strong. "Well, I'd better see something 'positive' as you put it, very soon. Not next week, but this week."

"I'll see what I can do, Harv," Joanne replied, tired from the encounter and the dull pain inside her. Harvey got up and left without further comment.

"That man aggravates me, Peter," Joanne said as soon as the door had closed.

"I know, but he's…"

She interrupted him. "The best production man around. I'm fully aware of that, but you should consider sending him to charm school!"

Peter Malton smiled. "His manner may be rough, but he's a good man. You two will never get along, and I'll be damned if I know why."

"The problem began when we first met and has been gradually getting worse. He disliked me from the start. I've tried, but I just don't understand the man."

"It's all part of the game of working with people, JoJo."

"So, what did you want to see me about?"

"Is everything okay, JoJo?"

"Of course, why do you ask?"

"Well, you seem to be spending a lot of time away from the office these days. I'm worried about you."

The pain in Joanne's stomach had been building up since her visit to the hospital and it made her feel irritable. "Peter, after all the evenings and weekends I've spent working for this company over the years, you mean to tell me that I cannot take a few hours off for some personal business?"

Peter felt the sharpness in her voice, and it convinced him all was not right. "Of course not, JoJo. It's just that I think something's wrong and I would like to help if I can, that's all."

"Nothing's wrong, Peter, so please don't worry."

"You look tired and you've been losing weight. I don't like it."

For a second Joanne felt like telling Peter that her ulcer had gotten the better of her and she would probably need time off for an operation. She was resigned to that fact. However, her orderly mind convinced her that she should only approach the subject when she was completely certain of the medical intervention that would be needed. In an effort to save Peter Malton from further worry, she kept the conversation light.

"Peter, did you ever think that maybe, just maybe, I'm having an affair with a man who's only free during the day?"

Peter saw in her eyes a mischievousness he had not seen in a long time. "Well, I suppose that's your business, JoJo," he said, then added in a tone that he tried, not too successfully, to make appear stern. "But, you'll have to make up for the lost time. I don't allow time off during business hours for lust."

Joanne smiled.

Peter spoke again. "Well, here's what I really came in here for. Are you going to be available for a long lunch on Thursday?"

"Thursday?" Joanne quickly glanced at her appointment book. "I have an early meeting outside the office but I should be back here by ten or so."

"Good. Our Japanese friends are coming in to visit our lab and look over our operations. I'll be taking them to lunch to discuss the preliminary details of our proposed joint venture. I think it's important you join us. You're good at selling the company and your intuition isn't bad. I want you to get to know them at the outset. It would be to our advantage. What do you say?"

"Sure. No problem. I certainly want to get involved in the project as much as I possibly can."

"Good. Then it's settled." Peter got up to leave, but he was not fully satisfied. He knew Joanne was avoiding discussing with him whatever was troubling her.

It bothered him. Perhaps the office was not the right setting for personal discussions.

"JoJo, how about dinner with Mary and me later this week? Let's say Friday?"

"Sounds good. I haven't seen her for some time. It'll be fun to catch up."

"Mary will call you."

Peter Malton was very fond of Joanne. He worried about her the same way he worried about his own children, and would have liked her to be happy. She definitely was not at the present time. Whatever was bothering her, she was keeping to herself, or at least not sharing it with him. She might, however, share it with his wife Mary.

Peter had first seen Joanne when she was eleven years old. He and Mary had been married for a couple of years when they moved into their first home in a well-kept, middle-class neighborhood next door to Joanne's parents, Joe and Kate Alcott. Mary soon befriended Kate, an artist some fifteen years older than she, fascinated by her unique style of large, bold strokes. She enjoyed watching the deft hands turn a blank canvas into a superb tableau rich in detail and color. As Kate painted, the two women talked, the older woman offering invaluable advice that could only come from years of experience in managing a household. In exchange, Mary was more than willing to take care of little Joanne when the need arose.

Mary had liked the girl from the start. She reminded her of her own younger sister she left behind when she moved to get married. Joanne was often at the Malton house, talking with Mary about anything and everything, when Peter came home from work. She would relate the exploits of her father in fighting crime, embellishing whenever possible Peter was certain, discuss her school friends and her teachers, and ask questions about life that Mary was on occasion at a loss to answer.

After Kate was diagnosed as having cancer, she underwent treatments that left her worn out, and she eventually gave up painting. On days when Kate was especially lacking in energy, Joanne was invited to dinner at the Maltons'. At first she would chat happily, but soon grew more silent and withdrawn. Mary Malton tried to encourage the child to talk, but it was obvious she could feel the tragedy unfolding at her house, although she had been told by her father that everything would be fine and that her mother would be well again.

While Kate was hospitalized for a couple of months in the fall, Joanne celebrated her twelfth birthday. The Maltons organized a party that all her friends and her father attended, but Joanne was quiet and distant. By then, the adults knew there was no hope for Kate. The Maltons' courageous efforts to offer a cheerful atmosphere were lost on the policeman and his young daughter. Mary saw that Joanne kept looking at Joe in an effort to understand what was happening to the man who had once been so buoyant and happy, but who, by then, had become withdrawn and sad.

When Kate came home from the hospital, a nurse was hired to see to her needs and an aunt moved in to take care of the house. For a while, Joanne seldom visited the Maltons. After school, she would come home and read to her mother. It became a familiar scene for Mary Malton who was spending a lot of time next door. The little girl would read rapidly as if afraid that her mother's frail body would deteriorate to a further degree of fragility if she stopped. When her mother had lapsed into a coma-like sleep induced by painkillers, the nurse would gently motion to Joanne that it was useless to carry on, and she would run to her room and lock the door.

As Christmas approached that year, Kate's health seemed to miraculously improve. She was able to spend several hours each day supervising the preparations for the holidays. JoJo, as her mother affectionately called her, once more became a bubbly, contented child. She brought out the decorations and took a great deal of pride in following her mother's directions on how and where to put them. The house was once more what a home should be. On Christmas Eve, Mary Malton heard Joanne tell her aunt that Dr. Calder had promised to cure her mother's illness and that he had kept his word. Despite her better judgment, Mary began to believe that Joanne might be right after all.

The Maltons had Christmas dinner at the Alcotts' home after canceling plans to visit Mary's parents because of the long car ride. Mary was then nearly seven months pregnant.

The Maltons would always remember that day as a day of hope. The woman who had been condemned was a new person. She had been able to bring up a full vessel of strength deep from within the well of dwindling vitality. She had laughed with them and had even sipped a glass of wine. The transformation seemed so natural and easy that even the adults considered that a medical error would soon be merely a painful retrospection in future conversations. The woman who was said to have cancer was recovering.

But Dr. Calder did not keep his promise to Joanne. Her mother passed away quietly during a cold night in early January, mercifully while the child was asleep.

In the months that followed, Mary Malton took little Joanne under her wing as she had willingly promised the dying mother and, later at the funeral, the grieving father. She often took her shopping and let her decide on the clothes for the new Malton baby; she let her choose the wallpaper for the nursery walls and, what JoJo enjoyed most, she let her feel the baby's kicks inside its protective womb.

Both Mary and Peter encouraged JoJo to cry over the great loss in her life whenever she felt like it. At first these episodes were numerous but, little by little, they diminished. On February 29 of that year, Mary delivered a healthy baby boy. A beaming Peter Malton took JoJo to the hospital to see the feisty little creature, who was obviously angry at being forced to face life. JoJo, her nose against the glass wall, was in awe. She asked Peter a host of questions which he patiently answered, but he had to laugh when JoJo told him, "It's too bad he's going to have birthdays only every four years."

Joanne often visited the baby, but as she and her father resumed their lives, her visits became less frequent. In the years that followed, the Maltons were very pleased to see her blossom into a well-adjusted teenager despite the tragedy she had lived, and came to rely on her as a babysitter for their son as well as for their daughter, born two years later. JoJo enjoyed taking care of the children, and Peter knew instinctively that she would be a dedicated mother.

Peter Malton's responsibilities increased over the years as did his financial status. While Joanne was busy traveling with the ski team, the Maltons moved to a new home in a more affluent part of the city, but always they were to remain friends. When a marketing research job opened up at Scalls-Morton, he made sure Joanne was among the frontrunners. She was hired and spurred by Peter's advice and help, her career with the company progressed nicely over the years as she gained experience in various capacities. She was director of public relations for the company by the time Peter became president.

JoJo and Peter were friends, but Joanne was more at ease with Mary in whom, Peter knew, she confided many of the joys and problems of daily living. If Mary was not a mother to JoJo, she was certainly a very close older sister. Peter counted on that very special relationship to help his employee and friend in her time of crisis.

Alone in his office, Peter dialed the familiar number and spoke to his wife.

Chapter Three

It was well past six o'clock when Joanne Blake unlocked the front door of her home. Wiping her boots on the mat, she entered and closed the door quickly behind her. The temperature had been dropping all day and, as was her habit, she wanted as little cold air as possible worming itself inside.

As she was removing her coat and boots in the entrance foyer, the smell of roasted chicken hit her nostrils making her slightly nauseated. The pain in her stomach had disappeared sometime during the afternoon and she hoped she would not have to pay by feeling queasy most of the evening, as frequently happened these days. She could hear her children arguing about who had the most homework, while on the television screen a newscaster was competing for attention with his review of the world's latest problems and disasters.

"I'm home," she called from the hall where she had stopped to look over the day's mail. Both her children replied an automatic, "Hi, Mom." Deciding the letter carrier had not brought anything of great importance, she sauntered into the large kitchen. Her fifteen-going-on-sixteen-year-old daughter, Terri, and her thirteen-year-old son, Jason, were seated at the round table, enjoying their evening meal prepared by Mrs. Lucas.

Mrs. Lucas took care of the cleaning and most of the laundry for Joanne, and prepared the evening meal three times a week. Joanne left her notes on what had to be done and it was always well carried out. *I have not seen Mrs. Lucas for some time*, she thought suddenly. She left her pay in an envelope, and Mrs. Lucas always left the empty envelope on the counter after scribbling "Thank you" on it. Joanne made a mental note that she should come home early one evening soon to talk to the woman who was quite an invaluable help in her life.

"We went ahead. We didn't know at what time you'd be home," Terri was saying. Dark curls framed her pretty oval face, and Joanne was once more stuck by her resemblance to her father. Her clear skin and rosy glow gave her a healthy, pure look.

"That's quite all right," Joanne said, after making a point of turning off the blaring television on the counter. "How's the chicken?"

"Great," Jason replied, too busy with his meal to look up. His brown hair had a slight auburn sheen matching Joanne's, and his round face still showed no sign of puberty.

"Anything happen today?" Joanne asked as she got a plate from the cupboard and joined her children at the table,

"Not much," Terri said. "Until the break, it's study, study for the mid-terms."

"You'll do fine," Joanne encouraged, carving herself a small piece of white meat from the fowl, which she complemented with half a baked potato.

"Is that all you're eating?" Terri asked. "No wonder you're losing weight!"

"I'm not very hungry."

"You work too hard. You should take some time off. Susan's mother has stopped working for a year, just to rest. That's what you should do."

It was not the first time that Terri was voicing concern for her mother's health. It worried Joanne. But since an operation seemed inevitable, perhaps she would seriously think about taking a long leave of absence.

"You could get into serious painting," Terri commented, "and maybe finish that portrait of Jason and me."

"I'll think about it," Joanne replied. She had started a portrait of her children months earlier, but there never seemed to be enough time or she was too tired to work on it. A medical leave from work would be a great opportunity to do some of the things she enjoyed but somehow never managed to get around to. Perhaps the ulcer was coming at a good time after all.

"Dad called tonight," Jason said suddenly, lifting his face from his plate. "He wants to take us skiing in Colorado during the break. He wants you to call him to make sure it's okay."

"We can go, can't we?" Terri asked.

"I don't see any problems with it. Where are you going to stay?"

"Dad got this condo in Vail from one of his clients," Jason said.

"Vail. Well, well. Not too shabby," Joanne exclaimed.

"Mom, why don't you come with us? You could take a week off, couldn't you?" Terri asked. After a short pause, she added, "The condo has four bedrooms. We could each have our own space."

"I'll think about it," Joanne replied with a slight smile. *I have to admit it sounds inviting. A week on the slopes, at my favorite spot.*

They finished their meal with the discussion centering on the children's school work. As she ate, Joanne felt a little hungrier and took a second helping.

"May I be excused?" Jason asked, pushing his chair away from the table.

"Where are you going?" Joanne asked.

"It's Monday night. I have hockey. Remember?"

"Right," Joanne said although she had forgotten. "Want me to drive you?"

"No. Mr. Mitchell's going to stop by."

Joanne decided she'd better be out of sight when he came to the door. Gordon Mitchell had asked her out so many times, and she had refused so many times, that she was running out of excuses.

Jason got up and was looking at his mother. "You should go out with him. Then maybe he would stop all these questions about you!"

"I don't want to go out with him, Jason. He's not my type. If he keeps bugging you, just tell him I've got a boyfriend. Okay?"

"Okay."

She patted his arm as he left the room. She felt sorry for her son having to face the man's barrage of inquisitive questions. Gordon Mitchell was not the kind of man who took no for an answer. He owned a sporting goods store in the neighborhood shopping mall and was very involved in sports activities of all kinds. He coached the hockey league to which his two sons and Jason belonged. He loved children and got along well with them because, Joanne had often thought, *He is a child himself.*

After repeated invitations, Joanne had finally agreed to have dinner with Mitchell. She thought the encounter had been a complete disaster; he thought it had been great. Joanne realized quickly that they had little in common, while he kept insisting they could have a great future together. She saw him as a possessive man who, once he made up his mind, did not back off. He had decided Joanne should be his second wife regardless of whether she agreed with it or not.

Joanne cleared away the food and made her way upstairs, passing Jason who was still at the door, waiting for his ride. "Go get 'em, Jason," she said, lightly pinching his cheek in her motherly fashion.

"I'll try. I'm up to four goals this season."

"Keep it up. Next week I'll drive you and go watch the game."

"You will? Great! I need a break from Mr. Mitchell."

She smiled at her uncomplicated son, who had still not lost the innocence and openness of childhood. "Have a good time," she encouraged.

Once in her room, Joanne stretched her lanky body on the bed. Eating something had made her feel better. She decided to call Roger. His voice sounded sleepy.

"Am I disturbing you?" she asked.

"No. I guess I just fell asleep for a few minutes."

"The kids told me you called about a trip to Colorado. It's perfectly okay with me, Roger, as long as…" She hesitated, but she had to ask. "Well, are you taking someone with you?"

"No, Joanne, I'm not," he said defensively. "What kind of father do you think I am, anyway? This is a family trip."

There was an awkward silence. Finally, Joanne said, "Just make sure the kids get enough sleep."

"Don't worry, they'll be so tired from the slopes, it'll just come naturally." Taking her by surprise, he added, "You know, there's plenty of room if you want to come along."

"Funny. Terri asked me the same thing at dinner. Were you trying to get her to convince me to come along?"

"I never mentioned anything of the sort. It's just my idea. You don't seem to be skiing much these days, and I thought it might be a good chance for you to get away. Surely Peter could get along without you for a week. Besides, it would be good for the four of us to spend time together."

Yes. It definitely would be, Joanne thought. *We have not been a family for two years. Perhaps it is time to put aside my pride. Roger's efforts at a reconciliation are no longer merely subtle hints. I know he hopes a week together might make me forget the past, but I know I can't. Not yet anyway. However,* she thought, *this offer from Roger might be a blessing in disguise. Fresh air and exercise might be just what I need to get myself into shape for the surgery. But I have to wait for Dr. Calder's opinion before making any commitment.* "I'll have to let you know."

"I was planning to reserve the plane tickets tomorrow. What I can do is put in a reservation for you as well. It can always be canceled if you decide not to join us. What do you say? You'll have more than a week to make up your mind."

"Okay, Roger, go ahead. I'll let you know on Saturday when you pick up the kids."

"I'll be there early. We're going to White Mountain. It's such a long drive, we might stay over and come back on Sunday afternoon. Any objections?"

"They have to study at some point, Roger," she said, but, remembering her own youth, she added, "but if you promise to be back before four, I guess it'd be okay."

"Great! I'll see you Saturday."

She hung up, musing that she certainly had no complaints about Roger as a father. He spent as much time as he could with his children, which helped minimize the negative effects of their separation.

She dropped her head onto the pillow, and images of laughing children on clean, white hills of snow filled her mind as she dozed off. The soft ringing of the telephone on her night table woke her up a short while later.

"JoJo? Mary. I hope I'm not disturbing you."

"Of course not. How have you been?"

"Just fine, but what about you? Peter tells me you look tired. Is anything wrong?"

"Just generalized fatigue, I guess."

"I haven't seen you for a while now. How about dinner on Friday? We could talk the way we used to. I'll be making corned beef and cabbage, your favorite. Sevenish okay?"

"Perfect," Joanne said.

Joanne was certain that she had been the subject of discussion at the Malton household. They were worried and, sensing something was wrong, they wanted to help. Joanne contemplated that she was indeed blessed to have friends like Mary and Peter. Friday evening would be a perfect time to tell them about the needed surgery. She would get the results from Dr. Calder on Thursday morning and have time to make plans before breaking the news.

Things were working themselves out after all.

Chapter Four

John Calder took another sip of coffee, although he knew nothing would make him feel better. He had tossed and turned all night, finally getting up, careful not to wake his wife, before six o'clock to go for a walk that lasted nearly an hour. He normally exercised before his evening meal, but this particular morning he had wanted to kill time in order to free his mind from the awful task facing him.

Ever since he had taken his Hippocratic Oath more than three decades earlier, John Calder had had a humanistic approach to medicine. He strongly believed that physiology was not an autonomous vacuum, but rather only one component of the many-faceted human being. This philosophy had made him a compassionate physician who always took time to examine and take into consideration the feelings, perceptions, and attitudes of his patients before determining the origin of an ailment, and treating it. Through it all, however, he had avoided personal emotions. He cared deeply for his patients, but he was never their slave. He was a healing servant fully aware of his limitations and vulnerability, and he guarded his sensibilities from being ravaged by the distress, grief, and pain he witnessed almost daily.

Except where one patient was concerned.

He was remembering the child crying quietly at the kitchen table when he came downstairs after seeing his dying patient. The girl who was about to be orphaned had turned to him, pleading for him to stop the unseen, deadly enemy. He had promised he would, but the disease won because he was helpless to fight it. And, in his efforts to comfort and help the mother while attempting to lessen the child's first devastating blow of life, he had let himself become irrevocably entwined in their lives.

The child had become a well-adjusted woman now approaching middle age, but his deep concern for her had not lessened. Over the years, he had been there to explain the physical changes taking place in her teenage body, the sexual dilemma of youth, the wonder and confusion of pregnancy, and to guide her own children. She had had a normal share of physical problems over the years that had been easily corrected, but nevertheless where she was concerned, he worried.

He was contemplating that some of his colleagues who specialized in mental states and processes would have told him it was simply a case of his feeling guilty—*your first patient to die always does it, believe me, it usually doesn't last, except in your case, you've carried it with you your entire professional life*—when his nurse knocked softly before coming in.

"Ms. Blake's here, Doctor. Do you want me to show her in?"

The dreaded moment had arrived and there was no escape from scientific reality nor from his feelings. He wished someone else, maybe God, if he had believed in Him, could do the dirty deed. As his nurse waited, well aware of the painful duty awaiting him, he took a last sip of coffee and got up from his chair behind the bulky, dated desk. "Yes, ask her to come in."

A few seconds later, Joanne, a bright smile on her face, walked toward him and shook his hand. They always shook hands. It was a tradition that dated all the way back to the first time he had seen her as a patient in his office. Her father had waited outside, and she had gone in by herself, looking somewhat unsure, extending her hand. He had been touched by the gesture of the child trying to be grown-up and had responded. She had looked pleased, just as she did today.

"Good morning, Dr. Calder," she said and sat down in one of the relatively new beige leather chairs facing his desk. Joanne remembered commenting on the new chairs when he had first bought them three or four years back, glad that he had finally seen fit to get rid of the green padded monstrosities that had long ceased to be comfortable. No doubt, complaining patients had made him see the light.

"How are you feeling, JoJo?" he asked, sitting himself on the front corner of his desk, more for stability than comfort.

"As well as can be expected, I suppose. Some days are worse than others. This morning I feel just fine. So, what's the final verdict, Doc? How bad is my ulcer, and how soon will I need an operation?"

Poor child, if only it were that simple, he thought. He had rehearsed the words in his mind throughout the night, but now found he had forgotten them. After a moment he said, "Joanne, we'll need to operate very soon."

"How soon? You sound so terribly somber like…" *when mother was dying,* she wanted to say. Suddenly, the look on the doctor's face penetrated to her heart and she felt it was being squeezed by a vise.

He got up and reached for her hand. "Joanne, the news is not good. You'll never know how much I wish it could have been different." The blood had drained from her face, and her dark brown eyes showed overwhelming alarm amidst the pallidness. He had seen that look many times in his career. Now it was devastating his soul.

"What are you telling me, Doc? Say it," she was almost screaming.

He took a deep breath. "JoJo, we've discovered cancer, but," he continued quickly, "today there are many things we can do that were just not possible twenty years ago or even five years ago. We can operate and remove the malignancy, and with continued treatment, we can control it very well. Today, nearly fifty percent of cancer patients can be cured and lead a normal life. We didn't have those options when your mother was ill. We can help you, JoJo, but we need to act quickly."

Joanne felt nausea rising from deep inside and was convinced it was a reaction to the punch she had just been handed by Dr. Calder. *I simply can't be as sick as he said. It just can't be true. There has to be some mistake. After all, did my mother not suffer enough to expiate whatever sins needed to be absolved? Did my father not go through enough agony as he witnessed his wife's torment, helpless to help her, to change her destiny? Have I, Joanne, the child, not cried enough, not been plagued by enough nightmares?* Suddenly, the memories that could never truly die rose again. She saw her mother's frail body against the white sheets of the bed, her ashen face making a supreme effort to smile. *Am I, Joanne the adult, the mother, destined to waste away in front of my children, to make them suffer as I myself have suffered? History couldn't be repeating itself so cruelly. Yet, there it is.* In a short sentence, the physician had passed sentence.

She freed her hand from Dr. Calder's and went to stand by the window. The snow outside had turned into an ugly, mushy mess. *Just like me,* she thought. *I do not want anyone poking at my insides, making me suffer while hoping the long shot will win...while my children see me gradually becoming a skeleton, barely alive, barely able to communicate. I need time. Time for what? Time to think things over. But time is running out.*

The thought that there might be much more than a simple ulcer making her unwell had crossed her mind a few times in the last weeks, but she had dismissed it outright. She had simply refused to accept it as even a remote possibility; yet there it was, a reality. *Can I fight it?* she wondered.

John Calder broke the silence. "I've lined up a top specialist for the operation, JoJo," he said softly. "He's just waiting for my call. We'll all fight this thing together and we'll win. You're young, your chances are enormous."

Her dark brown eyes met his. "My mother was young and look what happened to her!"

"As I've said, JoJo, science has made tremendous strides since then, and I'm not just trying to give you false hope. From the extent of the disease, I know for a fact, we have more than a good chance."

"And if I don't have the operation and the treatments, how long have I got, Doc?"

He hesitated, and she continued. "Tell me the truth. I can take it. How long?"

"From my experience, I would say about eight months, a year, maybe longer." He was lying and hoped she would not see it in his eyes.

She sneered at him. "Eight months. How nice! Do you know, Doc, that in eight months I'll be, I should say I would have been, forty years old. Forty, that magic number no woman wants to reach. But let me tell you that now I want to be forty. I want to be fifty, seventy. I'd be a nice old woman, don't you think?"

He saw tears in the corners of her eyes and he wanted to hold her, but held back. He had to be as unemotional as possible if he was going to help her. "I promise you, you will be, but we have to get going right now. Do you want me to call Roger and break the news? He should be there for you now."

Her eyes shot him darts. "No, Doc, I don't want him to know."

"He's still your husband, even if you are living apart. He has a right to know."

"Doc, please. Let me handle it."

"Okay. If that's what you want."

"It is. I don't want anyone to know right now. I need time to think things over."

"There's no time to waste, Joanne. We have to get you in the hospital."

"I want time to think, Doc. A day. I promise I'll be back here tomorrow morning bright and early. I need to put everything into perspective. You understand that, don't you?"

At length, he said, "I suppose so. But you have to swear you won't do anything rash."

"Doc, you know me better than that." Now it was her turn to take his hand. "I'll be back tomorrow and then we'll talk. I'll be in better shape. You've got to admit this has been a mild, quote, unquote, shock."

Then he watched Joanne Blake turn and quickly leave his office without another word.

John Calder went to sit in his chair, feeling the fatigue of lost sleep. He knew Joanne was mentally strong, but he wondered if she could face such an ordeal alone. Experience had taught him that cancer patients who could share their feelings with someone close usually fared much better through surgery and treatment. He would have to convince her to lean on Roger in her time of need, although that would be no small task. Joanne Blake was a proud woman. She would not make any effort to welcome Roger back into her life—even though she still loved him dearly, Dr. Calder knew—because she could not forgive his affront to her self-respect. He had shattered a dream. To her who had worked hard for order and perfection in her life, his indiscretion had proven she was so much less than perfect. And now that he, the medical man, had delivered the ultimate blow, she would not risk having Roger watch her in a final defeat. John Calder understood his patient. He just did not know how to influence her.

We've discovered cancer. We've discovered cancer...the words rang out insistently in her mind as she made her way out of the medical building. Once outside, she held on to the cold concrete wall to keep from falling. *Surely I will wake up soon and find it is all a bad dream. I, after all, should not have to face such a devastating end now. It's supposed to happen only much later when my children have put me away and forgotten me in some crowded, impersonal nursing home. Then, and only then, should I have to face the inevitable. Surely not now. There has to be some sort of gross error. These things only happen to other people.*

She took a deep breath and fell in step with the crowd of morning shoppers. The cold air felt good on her face; it made her feel alive, well, and healthy. She had to continue feeling it. All day.

She had always been proud of her methodical mind. She had to make it work for her now. Now more than ever. She could not let despair take hold and strangle her. The fear had to be conquered with all the resources at her disposal; it had to be studied and compartmentalized to allow manageability.

What am I most afraid of right now? What will make me feel more comfortable? The death knell will ring whether or not I agree. What is important are my feelings and those of the people I love.

Dr. Calder was kind, offering me hope, but is there hope in his methods or are they simply undertaken to avoid the death of hope? To postpone the end of the dream? To illuminate the path to the inescapable end?

I need hope.

THERE IS NOTHING SO WELL KNOWN AS THAT WE SHOULD NOT EXPECT SOMETHING FOR NOTHING—BUT WE ALL DO AND CALL IT HOPE.

The words of Edgar Watson Howe came to mind, a remnant of her research before putting together copy for Scalls-Morton's newest painkiller. The lines had struck her as she read mountains of material, looking for a synonym for hope to express to chronic pain sufferers the ultimate relief the product would provide. *How true*, she now thought. *We all expect something for nothing. We all expect guarantees, guarantees that life is going to be as free from trouble as possible, as painless as possible, but most of all longer than what has been determined probably at the very first breath we take.*

We go through life, Joanne philosophized, *on a wave of hope. We plan, we dream, we fantasize as we move through each day, each year. Our minds desperately avoid the unthinkable—that our life span could be short, very short indeed. That we may not be given the time we eagerly covet. That we may not see our aspirations fulfilled.* Since her mother's death, Joanne had been painfully aware that hope can be very easily and decisively butchered and, no doubt because of that realization, she had relegated to the furthest recesses of her subconscious any thought that the same fate could be lurking in the dark shadows of her own life.

Her efforts to avoid even considering such a horrifying possibility had been in vain. Destiny was the final authority and the verdict was loud and clear. Joanne wished she could bargain. She could not let her own children travel the same Calvary she had been forced to follow years earlier. It simply was not an option.

Feeling suddenly cold, Joanne realized that she had walked more than a dozen blocks from the medical building and was now in the university area. She saw a sign announcing Coffee and Bagels, and decided to go in. She welcomed the warm air that struck her face as she entered the café, and chose a stool along the counter. She removed her wool-lined leather gloves and was instinctively rubbing her hands together, when a waitress in a blue uniform asked, "Coffee?"

"Yes, please."

"Still pretty darn cold out there," the woman commented as she put a cup on the counter and poured steaming coffee into it.

"Yes, it is."

"Well, that's what we get for living in this part of the world. I'm thinking of moving to Florida. I should have no problem getting a job there, and I wouldn't have to go through this nonsense every year!"

Joanne smiled faintly. "You should do what you want to do while you can. Life is short."

The woman looked quizzically at Joanne, thought for a moment, then said simply, "I might just do it," before shifting her attention to another customer at the end of the counter.

Joanne estimated the waitress to be a few years older than she, perhaps in her mid-forties. *A woman with a dream she is probably afraid to make come true,* Joanne thought, *yet always keeping it alive. People have dreams but fear change, afraid of taking chances. They should not be afraid of living,* she thought; *they should only be afraid of dying.*

Joanne sipped her coffee slowly and was warmed by each swallow as it reached her stomach. Taking in the surroundings, her eyes came to rest on a large clock on the far wall. Twenty minutes past eleven. Suddenly she remembered it was Thursday and that she had a luncheon appointment with Peter and the Japanese people. Peter would be furious if she didn't show up, yet she felt her job was over, that it had ended in John Calder's office. She would have to talk to Peter, but not before she had time to plan her life, such as it was going to be for the next few months.

She reached for her cell phone in her bag and dialed her office.

Peggy came on the line, "Ms. Blake's office, good morning."

"Peggy, it's me."

"Oh, thank God you called. Peter Malton has been bugging me for almost an hour, wanting to know where you are."

"I'll talk to him in a minute." Joanne hesitated for a second or two, then continued, "I won't be in the rest of the day nor tomorrow. Some urgent personal business has just come up. I'll be in on Monday morning."

"Is everything okay? Anything I can do?"

Only if you can work miracles, Joanne wanted to say, but answered simply, "Thank you. It's personal. Should anything important come up, pass it on to George. Can you transfer me to Peter, please?"

"Sure, just hang on," Peggy said, pushing numbers on her telephone console. In a few seconds Peter Malton was on the line.

"Well, at last. I thought you had disappeared from the face of the earth," he said. "Didn't you remember our lunch today?"

"I haven't forgotten, Peter, I just can't make it. I'm sorry."

"JoJo, what the hell's going on?"

"Something important's come up. Get George to go to lunch with you and the Japanese. He's pretty good and very eager. He should be given a chance to do more than write copy for our pill bottles and our promotional pamphlets."

"JoJo, I wanted you there from the beginning. George may have potential, but he doesn't have your experience. You're the one who's going to have to work with the Japanese throughout this project."

"I have a great deal of faith in George; he's proven himself as my assistant."

"JoJo, what's the matter? I think I have a right to know!"

"I can't discuss it with you now, Peter. Please..."

"Very well. We'll talk tomorrow night when you come over for dinner."

"Peter, I'm afraid I have to cancel that as well. Please tell Mary I'm very sorry."

"Is something wrong with Terri or Jason?"

"The kids are just fine. Don't worry, please. I'll explain everything on Monday morning when I come in."

"You mean, you won't be in before then?"

"Afraid not. I have something important to take care of tomorrow. Have a nice weekend and give my love to Mary. I'll see you on Monday." She pushed the button to disconnect before he could ask anything else, then turned off the unit before going back to her coffee, which the waitress refilled without any comment.

The diner was filling with a noisy noon-time crowd of students, when an idea started to take shape in Joanne Blake's mind. It was not yet fully outlined nor fully formulated, but it was rational and tenable and could offer, Joanne felt, the best solution under the circumstances. Although she was uncertain of all the details, a resolve had been born in her rational mind and she wanted to look at all its possibilities and ramifications, especially with regard to her children.

She decided to set it aside, as was her style with any major decision, and think of other things for a while—to give the idea time to mature and develop on its own in her subconscious. Later she would approach it again and face it squarely.

Feeling hungry, Joanne ordered a bowl of soup and a chicken sandwich. A young man, somewhere around twenty years old, seated himself on her right, and a girl, slightly older in Joanne's opinion, took possession of the stool on her left. Joanne looked at each in turn. Both were busy reading while waiting for their orders. *Exams on the way, no doubt,* Joanne reflected, *I wonder how my own Terri and Jason will look like at that age, what studies they will undertake after high school, how well they will succeed. Fate will not allow me to find out.*

Joanne's thoughts went back to Dr. Calder's remarks. She found it difficult to accept his optimistic opinion that surgery and radiation would eradicate her cancer. They would amount to a valiant effort but, she was afraid, little more, as they would be met with ultimate defeat, while her children stood at her hospital bedside, helpless and tormented. As she ate, she reflected that Roger would also be helpless and tormented, much like her own father had been almost thirty years earlier. Fortunately, she knew that Roger would guide his children well and help them make the best possible career decisions.

Despite her quarrel with Roger, Joanne recognized that he was a good and levelheaded man. *When the end comes for me, he will take Terri and Jason firmly under his wing and, perhaps if he remarries, they will be a family once again.* The thought jolted her. *Roger remarried. It was certainly very probable,* she had to concede. *He is only forty-one and surely does not intend to spend the rest of his days alone, although there seems to be no one in particular in his life at the moment. At least, no one I know of. But then again, I only know what he and the children tell me.*

After draining another cup of coffee, Joanne paid her bill. The cold air was welcome against her face. She was alive and well, for the moment at least. She took a different route back to her car, and walked slowly as an all-enveloping need to weep took hold. She did not try to control it, and soon tears were running down her cheeks faster than she could wipe them off with her heavy gloved hand. Passers-by looked at her, some wanting to stop and help, but she ignored them, barely aware of other pedestrians. Her world was crumbling and she was alone to face it. She had to face it alone.

As she continued to walk, the tears diminished and she found herself toying with the idea she had put aside earlier. She examined it again, weighed some of its facets, inwardly debated the options it offered. By the time she reached her car in the parking lot of the medical building, she was almost certain of the road that was to lay ahead. She warmed up her car, grateful for the heat it soon generated, and drove out to the lake on the outskirts of town. A few hearty fishermen had cut holes through the thick ice and were sitting on folding stools, waiting at the end of a line for a fish to get hungrily greedy.

Watching the action from inside her car, she continued her analysis of the idea, once more dissecting it into its various components. She studied these in relation to her feelings, but also attempted to step back and look at them through the eyes of those she loved. She saw Terri, Jason, and Roger, as well as Mary and Peter, living and reacting to various scenarios.

By the time dusk had started to settle in and the fishermen had left, the road she had to follow was clearly marked.

Chapter Five

Her decision made, she went home and found both Terri and Jason in their respective rooms, busy with homework. She went to Jason first, and he flashed her a bright smile.

"Hi, Mom. I called you at your office today. You weren't there."

"Was there something you wanted to talk to me about?"

"It's about my ski mitts. I'd like a new pair before we go away. Mine are shot. Can you get me some this week?"

Jason was seated at his desk, and Joanne went to stand beside him, caressing his straight, brown hair. "Sure," she replied. "What color did you have in mind?"

"I want exactly the kind I have now, and the same color, red."

"Okay. I'll get them on Saturday. How are you doing with your work?" There was no need to ask. She already knew the answer. Jason applied himself fully and eagerly to anything he did, schoolwork included. He was special, not because of his innate intelligence, but because of his determination. She knew he would succeed at whatever he chose to do in life, and it gave her a small but reassuring measure of peace in her tragedy.

"I was having a little trouble with math, but it's okay now."

"Good."

"Are you going to come away with us, Mom?"

There had been no place in her mind to consider Roger's invitation. Quickly she answered, "I don't know yet. I have to make arrangements at the office before I can decide."

"I hope you come. It would be so much fun if we could all be together."

His uncomplicated face was delightful, and yet soon she would have to say goodbye, never to see it again, never to see it mature over the years. A lump rose at the back of her throat but, true to the promise she had made to herself earlier, she flashed him a bright smile. "I'll see if I can work something out," she said, and kissed him on the forehead. "Dinner will be ready very soon." She left her son's room just as tears were gathering in her eyes.

She took a deep breath and swallowed hard. She had to be strong for her children, no matter how much she wanted to grieve and protest the hand that had been dealt her. She continued down the hall to her daughter's room, her head held high.

Terri was sprawled out on her stomach on the bed, reading a book. Her white sweater and blue jeans blended well with the light blue coverlet. She sat up when she saw Joanne.

"Hi, Mom."

"How're you doing," Joanne asked, sitting on bed beside her daughter.

"Okay, I guess. I just wish the exams were over already."

"You'll do fine. You always do. Sometimes I think you worry too much. You seem to be forever thinking you'll fail, yet you get mostly A's."

"I know. It's just the way I am, I guess."

Joanne had long realized her daughter lacked self-confidence. She not only doubted her own abilities in scholarly endeavors but, Joanne feared, socially as well. She seemed to avoid getting too friendly with boys on an individual basis, preferring to be part of a small group of friends, both male and female. Many mothers would have considered Joanne blessed that her daughter did not make boys her main preoccupation, yet Joanne could not help wonder if Terri was as confident as an attractive young girl should be. *Is it perhaps just a teenage phase?* She made a mental note to discuss this with Roger.

Joanne smiled at her daughter. "Nothing wrong with the way you are," she said while putting an arm around Terri's shoulders and kissing her curls.

"Mom, have you decided if you're going to come with us to Colorado?"

"No, not yet. I have to talk it over with your Uncle Peter."

"Oh, by the way, I almost forgot; he called around four o'clock. He wanted to talk to you. Is he okay?"

"Peter? Of course. Why?"

"I don't know, he just sounded strange. He was mad because your cell phone was turned off. He wanted you to call him as soon as you came in."

"I'll give him a buzz," Joanne said matter-of-factly, adding, "Well, I'd better get dinner on the table."

"How long before we eat? I'm really hungry."

"Just a few minutes, my love," Joanne said, leaving the room, proud of herself. Her children would have commented that she had been cool, very cool in fact.

As she prepared the vegetables that would go with the thick steaks she had taken out of the freezer that morning, Joanne thought of Peter Malton. She knew he sincerely wanted to help her, but she also knew she couldn't discuss her condition with him just yet. She still had too many details to work out, and she wanted to be totally ready with all the answers when she approached him. But if she did not call him, he would worry and call again. There was no way of avoiding it. Putting aside the meal preparation, Joanne picked up the white phone on the kitchen wall, pushing the numbers she had long memorized. Peter Malton answered after only one ring.

"Peter? JoJo. You called?"

"Yes. I know it's really none of my business, but we've been friends for too many years for me to just stand by and not try to help you. I know you're in some sort of trouble, and since Mary and I are both darn good listeners, we were wondering if we could come over to your house in a bit."

"Peter, I appreciate your concern, I really do. But there's nothing to worry about." *How can I get rid of him without offending?* She said quickly, "There's certainly no point you coming over. I'm going out. I have a date."

"Oh?"

"You mean I can't go out on a date if I want to?"

"That's not what I meant…"

"Really, there's nothing to worry about. I'll see you first thing Monday morning. Okay?"

"Okay, but if you should want to talk at any time between now and then, you know where we'll be."

"Thank you, Peter. Thank you for caring. Again, I'm sorry about having to cancel dinner tomorrow. Please tell Mary I'll make it up. Good night."

Joanne hung up quickly and noticed that her hands were shaking. It was the first time she had ever lied to Peter. It made her feel uncomfortable and nervous, but she consoled herself that it was for everyone's benefit.

At the dinner table with Terri and Jason, Joanne worked hard at being jovial. She laughed at her son's jokes, even if some were only a futile effort at humor, and listened to her daughter's plans for her spring wardrobe. She had felt pain in her insides only briefly earlier in the afternoon and was able to eat a decent meal. It did not go unnoticed.

"Well, you're finally eating," Terri said. "It's about time."

"I've just been feeling tired lately. It made me lose my appetite," Joanne said, noticing that lying was getting easier.

"Well, you should come to Colorado with us. It'd be a good chance for you to rest," Terri continued.

"I might just do that."

Both her children exclaimed, almost as if rehearsed, "Great!"

After dinner, the children resumed their studying and the house became very quiet. In the family room, Joanne turned on the television and scanned the offerings of the various channels until she found a sitcom she hoped would make her forget the despair churning her soul, choking her as if she were a non-swimmer in deep waters. She made an effort to get interested in the activities of the actors on the screen, but her mind constantly returned to the details of her plan. She was certain it was the best course of action, even though it would require an immense amount of discipline and courage. Life had required strength from her as a child; she would not leave life without it. Her thoughts were interrupted by the ringing of the telephone. Terri got to it first and called down to her mother.

"Hi, Joanne," the cheerful voice said. "Am I disturbing you?"

"Not at all, Carol. How have you been?"

"Just fine. And you? In love yet?"

"Do I want to be is the question," Joanne said lightly.

"Listen, kid, I'm a widow for the next few days. Gerry has to work on putting together a new program and he'll be busy all weekend. I thought it might give us a chance to get together, maybe tomorrow or Saturday. That is, unless you're going skiing with Roger and the kids this weekend."

Joanne sometimes thought that her long-time friend had been mobilized by Roger to help them reconcile their differences and resume married life. "No, I'm not going."

"Well, how about Saturday then? We could have lunch in town and go shopping."

"Carol, I'm not much in a shopping mood these days."

"You, not in a shopping mood? Have you been ill?"

"It's been a hard week." Joanne wanted to spend the weekend alone to finalize her plans without involving Carol. She planned to announce her departure only at the last minute. But, perhaps she could prepare the terrain. "Carol, how about you coming over here for lunch on Saturday?"

"Sounds good. About oneish?"

So many people to consider, Joanne thought sadly after she hanging up. In the quiet of her room after the children had gone to sleep, she spent some time scanning the out-of-town properties for rent in the classified section of the paper. A few listings were of interest and she settled on two, which she circled, then tore out and put into her wallet. She then turned off the light. Without taking off the skirt and sweater she was wearing, she adjusted the blind to let the soft light from the street lamp permeate the room, and settled herself in the lounge chair near the window. Time spent sleeping would be wasted. She wanted those few precious hours to complete her plans, to review any overlooked possibilities and analyze the script she intended to follow.

In the subdued lighting, the soft beige and yellows of her room felt very cozy, despite the outside temperature. In the last couple of years, the room had been a welcome refuge in times of pain and crisis, but it was also filled with happy memories of the years she had shared with Roger. Soon it would no longer belong to her. She would be just another statistic, her ski exploits of the past long forgotten. Tears slowly glistened on her cheeks and she didn't bother to wipe them away.

Dawn crept in the window of the bedroom, sheepishly at first, but as it gained confidence, infiltrated every corner and woke Joanne from a nightmare-filled sleep. Dried tears had glued her eyelashes together and she had to labor momentarily in order to open her eyes. The few hours of sleep had been a consoling escape.

After a hot shower, she felt marginally better than the previous day. With a very convincing outward cheerfulness, she woke up her children despite their complaints and grumbling and, after serving them a hot breakfast, sent them off to school.

As she had promised the previous day, it was nine o'clock on the dot when the nurse held the door open and Joanne walked into Dr. John Calder's office. She greeted him with a faint smile—and a handshake—and settled herself in one of the chairs facing his desk, while he sat wearily in his large leather chair.

Another mostly sleepless night had left him drained at a time when he would have wanted to be totally alert. Now the sight of Joanne added to his feeling of inadequacy, weighing him down with grief. Miracles did happen from time to time, physiological reversals that the medical profession could not explain. Now he was wishing for one, one that would somehow prevent the tragedy of thirty years earlier from repeating itself in the woman before him whom he still saw as the devastated, frightened child he had been, and was still, unable to help.

"How are you feeling, JoJo?"

"It's amazing, and I can't figure out why, but I've had little pain since your big surprise of yesterday. I guess the shock overwhelmed me."

"I've made arrangements for you to go into the hospital on Monday."

"Doc, I won't be going," she said. He started to open his mouth, but she went on firmly, clearly, "I want you to listen to what I have to say. I've made a decision about what I want to do with the little time I have left. I want to spend it alone, not in some antiseptic hospital where my family will see me deteriorate day after day…like I had to see my mother.

"I'm going away to be by myself. I'm renting a hideaway in the country, and that's where I'm going to spend my last days, away from the people I love. I would like you to ask your nurse to write a simple letter stating my condition; it's for my employer so I can get sick leave. I would also like you to give me a prescription for a strong painkiller, enough for a few months so that I can have something when things get really bad."

"JoJo, there's no way I'm going to let you do anything of the sort!" Dr. Calder told his patient, irritated. "We have so many means at our disposal now to treat and cure cancer…"

"Doc, I don't believe you can cure me. It's that simple. I know you want to try, that I certainly grant you, but you can't work miracles."

"JoJo, listen. Maybe I can't work miracles, but we can do marvelous things. I've seen too many people recover fully not to trust medical methods. As I told you yesterday, your chances of total remission are more than good. You're young and you've only had minor medical complaints over the years."

"But minor has now turned to major," she said in a biting tone, "and the rules have changed. You've handed me a death sentence. Don't you think I have the right to have some say in what I want for my last meal?"

"I can't let you do what you propose. It's insane! I'm a man of science, a physician dedicated to healing. I'm certainly not going to sit on the sidelines while one of my patients withers away alone without medical help, and certainly not you!" He paused and leaned closer to her across the desk. "You should not be facing such a burden alone. I'll call Roger in…"

"No way, Doc," she interrupted sharply. "Don't you understand? I don't want Roger to know. I don't want my children to know."

"JoJo, you're not being objective. The people who love you want to share your life, all of it, not just the good times. In a situation such as this, the family has to be right there with the patient. I'm convinced the support they provide is invaluable in arresting or delaying the progress of a disease. I have an obligation to help you, and I certainly won't let you do anything that is not in your best interest."

"You won't let me? You won't let me?" Joanne said more sharply this time. "How can you be certain that what I'm planning is not in my best interest?" In a gentler tone, she added, "Doc, I know you care for me, but I think you can't accept what I'm suggesting because to you it would mean another defeat as far as I'm concerned. You want to do all you can for me. I understand that very well. I've been very fortunate to have you as my physician over the years. You were never too busy to take time to listen to my problems and to offer advice. I'm simply asking you to do just that one more time. Please listen to me and try to understand how I feel."

Shifting her position and putting her hands on John Calder's desk, she added, "Being by myself is the only thing that's going to make me feel comfortable. I don't believe my children should have to see me die. It'd be much too hard for them. I've been there, remember? I know what it's like. When I was a teenager, my thoughts were full of death and dying instead of on boys, as they should have been. Why do you think I took up skiing? Because it gave me the opportunity to be away from the house, from seeing my mother's skeleton long after she was gone, from seeing my father so sad and lonely. It took me years to work it out. I don't want the same thing happening to my children."

"Dying is part of life, JoJo. You can't expect to shield your children from it. We all have to learn to cope with it. From tragedy comes strength. You yourself are a prime example. Your early experience has made you stronger than a lot of women I know. Maybe it's made you too strong…"

"You're right. If I wasn't so strong, I would never have devised such a plan, would I?" A weak smile appeared momentarily on her face. She was strong and she would not let John Calder deter her in any way from her objective. "Doc, if it will make you feel better, I promise to get in touch with you when the disease gets the better of me, and to come into the hospital then. The children and Roger should be able to handle seeing me die for a couple of weeks."

"JoJo, you're missing the whole point. Now is the time we can help you, not when the disease has progressed to the point of no return."

"Doc, please let me do this my way. As far as the children and Roger are concerned, I'll be away working on a special project overseas. That's what I'll tell them. I'm sure I can count on your discretion, Doc. You have taken an oath about that, haven't you?"

"JoJo, I have an obligation to do everything in my power to help you, and I'm going to take whatever means to do just that."

"What are you going to do? Force me to go to the hospital? Get a court order? I don't believe you could do that to me or to my family."

John Calder had to admire his patient. She was determined, and he was at a loss as to how to stop her. She wanted to protect those she loved. Did he really have a right to interfere? She didn't believe he could cure her, and he couldn't offer any guarantees, only a chance that the disease could be conquered. Suddenly, as he had done many times over the course of his career, John Calder wished he had gone into banking instead of medicine. Surely, no problems in the financial world could be as difficult to face as the one he now had to deal with. "I couldn't do that, JoJo."

"Can I have that letter and that prescription, then?"

"On one condition."

"Which is?"

"That you let me know where you are. I could look in on you from time to time."

"I'll be in the country."

"Not a problem. I can take a day off once in a while. How about it?"

"Very well. I'll be in touch before I leave town after all the arrangements have been made."

John Calder reached for the telephone on his desk, but before lifting the receiver, he told Joanne, "I want to go on record that I'm doing this under protest."

"Protest duly noted," she replied calmly.

After giving instructions to his nurse, Dr. Calder got out his pad and wrote two prescriptions. He tore off the two pieces of paper and told Joanne, "This one is the painkiller. I'm giving you enough for three months. This one is for the nausea, which will probably get progressively worse. Take it as needed, but, if you feel you need something stronger, let me know and I'll prescribe another drug."

She took the two notes on which were scrawled in almost indecipherable writing the names of two drugs she recognized immediately. Both had been developed by her company and were referred to by the production people as "death pills." *What an ironic turn life has taken!*

"Thank you, Doc, and thank you for understanding."

"Perhaps I understand," he said wearily, "but it doesn't mean I agree."

Dr. Calder's nurse walked in, placed a letter on his desk and retreated as quietly as she had entered. He read it, signed it and handed it to Joanne. It read simply:

> To Whom It May Concern
>
> It is with regret that we must confirm that exhaustive tests have shown that Mrs. Joanne Blake suffers from pylorus carcinoma. Prognosis is uncertain.

Seeing the words on paper for the first time made Joanne fully aware that her decision was the right one. *My life has been reduced to a few painful lines. There is no need for the pain to extend to anyone else.* She folded the letter neatly and put it in her purse.

Chapter Six

As she left the medical building, Joanne Blake experienced mild excitement. The first hurdle of her plan had been leaped, and she anticipated the others would follow just as naturally as birth follows conception and death follows life.

In her car, she fished her cell phone from her purse along with the ads torn from the newspaper the previous evening. She punched the number from one of the ads and waited just a moment before a female voice answered.

"I'm calling from the city about your ad. Can you tell me a little about the place?" Joanne asked.

"Sure," the woman replied amiably. "It's a good house, about twenty years old, just outside Penny Hill. Do you know where that is?"

"I think so."

"The place has almost a full acre of land. It's very nice in the spring and summer. Do you want to come up and see it?"

"First, tell me how far is it exactly from the village?"

"It's one of the last houses on the old road north."

"Then I can assume there are neighbors on either sides?"

"Sure, but it's a very quiet area. Not many cars take the old road now with the highway."

Joanne thanked the woman and ended the connection. It was definitely not what she was looking for. Perhaps the next call would be more fruitful. She instantly liked the deep voice of the older man who answered, and it lifted her spirits.

"It's a farm house, in good condition," the man was now saying. "My brother lived there until he passed away last year. My wife's been keeping it clean. You would have a couple of acres of land, which goes down all the way to the lake. The whole property has about sixty-five acres, and I farm most of it."

"How far are the neighbors?"

"My wife and I are the closest. Our farm is down the road a bit. There's nobody on the other side for over a mile, I'd guess."

"Sounds good. Can I come and look at it today?"

"Today? Sure."

"I need something right away."

He gave her directions which she jotted down. She was pleased. The description of the property seemed to be exactly what she had hoped to find. *The trip will take less than an hour*, she estimated, *which means I will be there just around noon. Perfect. I'll be back in plenty of time for dinner, and the ride up will give me time to work out the small details of my plan.*

When Joanne Blake reached the village of Triton, she liked what she saw as she traveled down the main street. The properties and commercial establishments, many of them reminiscent of building styles in a Swiss mountain village, appeared to be well maintained. She was delighted to see that there was a branch of the bank she dealt with in the city about halfway through the village. *Maybe by laying my plan I was simply carrying out a plan laid out for me*, she mused. *Everything is falling into place.* She easily found the food market where she had been told to turn off, and made her way along a well-plowed, snow-covered country road. The sun had appeared about a half hour earlier, but now only shone intermittently on the pristine snow.

She drove slowly, taking in the beauty around her, knowing the importance of always being on guard for hidden ice on the road at that time of year. The scenery brought her back to her skiing days. Suddenly she was a young woman, skis on the car roof, on her way to a day of thrills on the hills where pain, fears, and life's problems were forgotten for a few blissful hours. *I could experience it all again*, she thought. *Roger's offer of a week in Vail might be just the ticket to take my mind off the painful months that are inescapably facing me. It could be a short refuge for my troubled soul and my children would jump for joy. Why not one last hurrah*, she finally decided.

A short time later, she saw a well-kept wooden farmhouse and a relatively

40

new separate small barn a few dozen yards from the road on the right. A sign of large hand-painted red letters over a green background had been planted just over the snowbank and could not easily be ignored. "For Rent—Inquire Joe Wheeler next farm."

She drove the short distance until she saw the metal mailbox announcing Joe Wheeler's name. Turning in, she saw a roomy, sturdy-looking, brick house, a well-kept wooden barn and what appeared to be a henhouse. A man in his early sixties came out to greet her. He was dressed in a woolen jacket in a black-and-red checkered pattern with a matching cap. The untied earflaps reminded her of the ears of a basset hound as they moved up and down with each step he took. He had the weather-beaten face of someone who had spent most of his life outdoors.

"I'm Joe Wheeler. You the lady that called?"

She extended her hand. "Yes. I'm Joanne Blake. I assume the place you're renting is the one down the road with the sign."

"Yeah. That's the one. We'll go over so you can see for yourself."

"Fine. Let's take my car, it's warm."

Joe Wheeler agreed. "Nice car you've got," he said, as Joanne turned around and drove the short distance back down the road.

"Thanks."

"I thought you'd be comin' up with your husband maybe."

"Why?" she asked, briefly looking at him.

"Well, I don't think that's a good place for a lady alone. It could get pretty lonesome."

"I want to get away from it all, as they say."

They drove past the For Rent sign, and Wheeler said, "I plowed the driveway after you called, so you would have no problem getting in. And the heat's been turned on inside."

Joanne followed behind him along the path to the front door. "Take a look around," he invited.

On the right of the entrance hall, Joanne saw a large living room furnished with a Victorian sofa and matching chairs. She was surprised to see such elaborately detailed furnishings in the country. The Wheelers had either not heard of antiques or were keeping the pieces for posterity. There was a small bookcase on one wall with only a dozen or so books, and, on the inside wall, an old fieldstone fireplace she immediately fell in love with.

"Works well," Wheeler said, aware of her expression. "I can supply the wood. I've lots of it at my place."

As they moved on, Joanne saw a large porch around the living room and the south side of the house. An old dining room table with matching chairs, *probably priceless*, she thought, had been set up in the section of the porch that was enclosed with windows and screens. The kitchen had been modernized and appeared quite adequate with its large electric stove and refrigerator. There were a small table and two wooden chairs across from a black wood-burning stove and, beside it, an older model washing machine.

Wheeler opened one of the cupboards. "You've got all the plates and pots you need in here." He felt it necessary to add, "My brother wanted to keep the stove. It does come in handy. The house's heated with an oil furnace," he said, indicating the hot-air ducts, "but in the country, the delivery trucks are sometimes late in coming in to fill the tanks. When that happens, the stove and the fireplace keep the first floor warm."

Joanne had to admit she liked what she was seeing. Off the kitchen, there was a bathroom, which had been remodeled some years earlier, but remained quaint with its walls of narrow pine boards. The last room on the first floor was a good-size bedroom with antique mahogany dressers, matching bed and night stands. There was also a wardrobe, where linens had been neatly piled. The wallpaper was a delicate blue flower design. Wheeler invited her to see the second floor, where two additional bedrooms, with somewhat more functional and modern furniture, filled the space under the sloping roof.

Back in the living room, Wheeler said, "As I told ya on the phone, you'd have about two acres around the house." Indicating the snow-covered field that spread several hundred yards in front of them and to one side of the house, he added, "That field is very good soil for gardenin' and it goes all the way to the lake down there." All Joanne saw was what appeared to be part of a smooth field of snow. "You can't really see it at this time of year, but in the summer, the fishin's great. Do you fish?"

"Not yet," she told him with a momentary smile.

"What's great here is that the land's all zoned for farming. They won't let you sell off part of your property in lots for cottages for city folks. It's very quiet."

Looking out the window at the scenery, she noticed a house a few acres away. "I thought you said there were no neighbors. Who lives in that house?"

"No one really. There used to be a barn and the whole thing, a dairy farm, but the owner tore it down and moved to the city a few years ago. He still hangs on to the place. I guess he reckons he can come back some day. The place's empty most of the time. The old man rents it to a relative for a few weeks in the summer. This fella comes up for July and August. He's been comin' up for years now. Keeps pretty much to himself. We hardly ever see him. He told Agatha, that's my wife, that he's a writer."

Wheeler waited patiently as Joanne looked the room over one more time. There was no doubt in her mind. This place was ideal for her needs. She sat down on the antique sofa, weary from all the excitement, and told Wheeler, "I'll take it. For a year."

"But I haven't told ya the price yet," he protested.

"Then, I guess we'll negotiate."

Once she had agreed to his price, they went to the Wheeler house to sign the lease. Joanne immediately liked Agatha Wheeler, a warm, friendly, no-nonsense woman.

"Have you had lunch?" she asked Joanne.

"Not yet."

"Let me fix somethin'."

"Please don't bother yourself. I'll stop in the village on the way back."

"I won't hear of it. I've got some nice chicken. I'll make you a sandwich in a jiffy," Agatha said, getting busy without waiting for any more protest. "Go ahead, sit yourself."

"Thank you," Joanne replied, taking a seat at the table in the large kitchen.

"I bet you don't eat much. You're so skinny. I don't know why people in the city think they've got to starve. Ain't healthy, I say. Take my niece, Sarah. Nicer girl you couldn't meet, but she's like a pole. Says that's the way everyone is around city hall."

"City hall?"

"She works for Mayor Bristol in the city. Do you know him?"

"Afraid not," Joanne said, managing a smile.

Joe Wheeler came in with a piece of paper. "Look it over and see if everythin's okay."

She glanced quickly at the lease, feeling there was no need to read all the printed form. She simply verified the amount and signed the document, then wrote a check to cover the first month.

"I'll give you post-dated checks for the rest of the year when I've opened an account at the local bank."

"There's no need to pay in advance," Wheeler said.

"I prefer it that way," Joanne said. *Easier for my family*, she wanted to say. "The place's very nice, Mr. Wheeler. Why don't you sell it?"

"Well, it doesn't belong to me. Went to my nephews and nieces when my brother died. They want to keep it; think it's gonna go up in value quite a bit in the next few years, so they just want to rent it out for now."

Agatha Wheeler put a sandwich in front of Joanne, then poured her a cup of coffee from a pot on the stove as she spoke. "You really gonna stay there by yourself?"

"I want to get away."

"You married?"

"Mrs. Wheeler, if you don't mind," Joanne said quietly, "I'd really prefer it if you didn't ask me questions."

Chapter Seven

On her way back from the country, Joanne put any thoughts of the pain and loneliness she would have to face to one side, concentrating all her mental energy on finalizing her plan. It served her well, because even though there were a few sporadic episodes during the day when she felt poorly, she was able to fully enjoy dinner with her children.

A clean-cut young boy had come to the door to take Terri to a party, while Jason announced that he was going next door to watch a video with one of his classmates. Once alone, Joanne spent the rest of the evening doing and redoing lists and deciding on the type of clothes she would need for her stay in the country. All the while quiet music from the radio was her companion. It relaxed her and later sleep was easy.

She awoke the next morning to see the sun filtering through the blinds and felt refreshed.

Breakfast was underway when Roger rang the doorbell. His bulky red ski jacket set off his dark curly hair which showed only the slightest sign of thinning. To Joanne, he was still the most handsome man she knew, something other women surely noticed. No wonder he had strayed from their marriage.

He was in good spirits and exchanged jokes with his children as he drank the cup of coffee Joanne put in front of him.

"So, any decision yet on the trip to Vail?" Roger asked when the children had left the room to gather their gear.

"If the invitation still stands," she said, "I'd very much like to go. I need to get back in shape."

Roger's face showed slight surprise, which quickly turned to an unmistakable look of excitement. "Great. I'm glad, JoJo. It'll be good for the kids…and maybe for us."

She knew he was sincere, but now was certainly not the time to make any attempts at a reconciliation. "Roger, don't expect anything."

"I'm not asking for anything, JoJo, but I've got the right to hope, don't I?"

"We all do and we all need it," she said, suddenly very sad.

Terri returned to the kitchen to announce that she and her brother were ready for their weekend adventure. She was obviously struck by the glum expression on her mother's face. "I guess you're not coming to Colorado with us," she told her mother flatly.

"Of course she is," Roger quickly put in.

"All right!" Terri said, and went to hug Joanne.

"I've decided life is too short to pass up an opportunity like this. I think it's going to be fun," Joanne said. She would have to muster all her inner strength for the trip that, for her, would be bittersweet indeed, but she had firmly decided this final effort was important to her family and far outweighed the grief that would from now on be part of her life.

"Mom's coming to Vail," Terri told her brother as he came in the room.

"Super!"

Solemnly, Joanne said, "I'm going only on one condition." She enjoyed the questioning look on the three faces that were staring at her.

"What?" Jason asked.

"That someone takes care of having my skis checked and sharpened."

"Jason, old boy, do you think we could do what the queen asks some evening next week?" Roger asked his son.

"How much's in it for me?" Jason quipped.

"You'd better be careful. Queens have been known to be quite mean when dealing with mercenaries, you know," Roger replied, lovingly slapping his son's back.

They all laughed. They were a family again, and to Joanne it was a consolation, but only for a moment. She had to make a supreme effort to control the tears that were welling up without warning. She got up hurriedly.

"Better get a move on if you want to make the best of the day," she was able to say calmly.

When the skis, boots, and poles were all loaded up, Joanne kissed her children. "Be careful, now. Keep the showing off to a minimum."

There was a pat reply that they would.

Roger made a final check of the equipment as the children settled in the minivan. When he was ready to climb in himself, he stopped for a moment, started to say something, checked himself and finally said, "Take care, JoJo. You look tired. Take advantage of the weekend to rest."

"Thank you, Roger."

She waved good-bye and stayed at the curb for a time after the dark blue van had disappeared from sight. The unavoidable countdown had begun. There were few moments of closeness with her family left in the cards. *Oh God*, she prayed, *can't you work a miracle? Does anyone listen*, she wondered aloud as she went back into the house.

Joanne poured herself a fresh cup of coffee, and sat sadly at the table. Despair was suddenly taking hold and she did not like it at all. To carry out her plan efficiently, all thoughts of self-grief and hopelessness could not be allowed to undermine or weaken her resolve. But perhaps she had overestimated her inner strength. *I am, after all, only a human being facing the ultimate battle whose outcome has already been determined. Is my strategy doomed to defeat because I am venturing alone on a course where fear and loneliness can only be overcome with the help and love of those who are dear?*

She wondered if her plan had been conceived to protect herself rather than her family. *Is it simply a measure to alleviate my own future psychological suffering? No doubt at least partly*, she mused.

She needed to clear her mind, to step away from the problem for a while. Perhaps a little television would help. She moved to the family room and turned on the set, then frantically pushed the channel changer as cartoon after cartoon came on the screen until she found an old Rock Hudson-Doris Day movie on one of the cable channels. She forced herself to keep her mind on the story and soon was completely engrossed in the plot, enjoying the comedy. It was followed by another movie, this time a thriller by her favorite director, Alfred Hitchcock. She was grateful for the unexpected escape. The action was just ending when the doorbell rang.

She was momentarily surprised to see her friend, Carol Ferguson, through one of the small panels of glass at the top of the front door, then she remembered the date they had made earlier in the week. She had to concede that her mind was definitely not as orderly as it should be.

"Hi, kid," Carol said jovially as Joanne opened the door and invited her in. "I know I'm a little early, but I was out on an errand and I didn't think you'd mind. You don't, do you?"

"Don't be silly. Let me take your coat."

The two women settled in the family room, and Carol instantly began recounting the current events in her life. Her husband Gerry was overloaded with work, her oldest son was not doing too well in school, the dog needed to be clipped, the driveway was still not cleared of the snow to her satisfaction—in spite of Gerry's promises. The words flowed on and on.

Joanne half-listened as she made sandwiches and brewed fresh coffee. She had met Carol on the ski team more than twenty years earlier and they had remained friends. Carol had to give up competitive skiing a couple of years before Joanne, when she broke her left leg in a bad fall. She got back on skis, but only for pleasure. Because Carol worked part-time as a photographer for a large magazine, she could ski once or twice a week, while Joanne rarely skied these days.

As the two women were finishing their lunch, Carol inquired, "Are you okay?"

"Sure. Why do you ask?"

"I don't know exactly. You look tired, and it seems to me you're still losing weight."

Joanne was wearing black slacks, which emphasized how thin she was. *I wish people would stop reminding me*, she wanted to say. Now was as good a time as any to guide her friend into the plot that was unfolding. "I've got a big job. I suppose I'm a little tired. I've been wanting to get away and I'll be able to do just that."

"Where are you going?"

"Hawaii."

"Serious?"

"Why would I lie?" *Unless it was so terribly important!* "Here's what's happening. The company's been wanting to diversify for some time, and we've been looking at various projects, products, and so on. Anyway, now everyone seems to have agreed on the possibility of a joint venture with a Japanese firm that has been shopping for a foreign partner to produce and market a revolutionary new diagnostic machine. You won't breathe a word of this to anyone, will you?"

"You know me better than that. The Gestapo wouldn't get a word from me!"

Joanne smiled. "I'm not worried about you telling the Gestapo, but I am worried about you telling Gerry."

"Word of honor," Carol said, making a cross on her left breast with her finger.

"Good. Anyway, it's something that will replace the X-ray machine. Doctors will be able to photograph the human body just as they do with X-rays, but there won't be any radiation."

"You mean, like an MRI machine?"

"No, something totally different. I can't explain it because I don't understand it myself, but it's going to be big. If an agreement is reached, the Japanese will build some of the components, and we're going to put the machines together here and market them in North America to start. We'll go worldwide eventually. Big bucks for us."

"That sounds great, but I don't understand what it has to do with Hawaii," Carol commented.

"Well, management feels it's important that no one jeopardize the deal in any way, so I'm being sent to school."

"Say what?"

"There's a school in Honolulu where Westerners can learn the proper etiquette and so forth when dealing with Asians. I'm going to study there for a few months and then go on to Japan for a few more months. When I get back, I'll teach my co-workers what I've learned."

"Boy, I guess it pays to know the president personally!"

"Come on, Carol, it has nothing to do with that. I just happen to be the best candidate."

"When are you leaving?"

"In two weeks. Just after I get back from Colorado with Roger and the kids."

Carol's eyes widened. "You're going to Colorado with Roger?"

"It's not what you think. He's taking the kids during their break, week after next, and he's asked me to go along. I thought it would be a good opportunity to relax, rest, and spend time with Terri and Jason. Wipe that smile off your face, Carol. Roger got this large condo in Vail from one of his clients and there's four bedrooms. We'll each have our own space, as Terri puts it."

"Well, I don't care if there are four bedrooms. I think you and Roger are ready to patch things up. You wouldn't have accepted otherwise. Go for it, kid."

"Carol. Please."

"I know, stop pushing. But let me tell you, because you don't seem to know it, you still love Roger."

"Of course I do."

"I mean, you're still in love with him and he's still in love with you. I hate to see waste, and the way you two are living is a damn waste. Wake up, kid, before it's too late."

It's already too late, my dear Carol, Joanne thought, but quickly controlling herself, said, "We'll see. By the way, I haven't told Roger about Hawaii yet. I'll tell him some time next week, so not a word."

"Of course. Who's going to take care of Terri and Jason?"

"I'm going to ask Roger to move back into the house. I think he'll jump at the chance of being a full-time father. With Mrs. Lucas coming in during the week, there should be no problems. Besides, Mary and Peter will keep an eye on things, I'm sure."

"Don't forget me. I'd be glad to help; maybe have the three of them over for dinner once in a while."

"That would be very nice."

"My pleasure, kid. It'll give me a chance to play mother to Terri. Alone in a house of males, I occasionally wish I had a daughter."

"I'm a little worried about Terri. She seems so unsure of herself."

"That's a cause for worry? Come on, kid. You mean, you don't remember when you were that age? All teenage girls are unsure of themselves. It goes with the territory. She's growing up and trying to fit in. If it'll make you feel better, I'll take her shopping one weekend soon and I'll talk to her. I have a lot of experience with teenage girls. Remember my four sisters, when you and I were skiing?"

Joanne smiled. She had not forgotten Carol's younger sisters, each going through one crisis after another, while Carol kept wishing her parents would have had sense enough to beget sons. Joanne was convinced that during her two pregnancies, her friend had willed herself into having boys.

"One week, they felt ugly, the next they were *grandes dames* worthy of the highest admiration. One week boys were a nuisance, the next they were delightful, cute, charming, sweet, etcetera, etcetera. We were the same, I'm sure. It's just that memory has a way of being selective."

"I suppose you're right," Joanne said

Carol looked at her watch. "You're sure you're not up to shopping? I absolutely have to get a new pair of boots today. Mine are shot. Why don't you come with me?"

"Jason needs new mitts before we go to Vail. Might as well get it over with."

On their way out, Carol put an arm around Joanne's shoulders. "Hawaii! You've got it made, kid. I certainly wouldn't miss a chance like that."

"Yeah," Joanne replied evenly, wishing she could tell her friend the truth. But she had decided on her course of action and would stick to it.

When Carol had finally decided on a pair of black leather boots and Joanne had found the mitts Jason wanted, Carol invited, "How about some dinner at Pascale?"

Joanne felt tired and would have preferred to go home, but she let Carol drive them to the little Italian restaurant they often frequented.

Studying the menu, Carol said, "I think I'm going to have the linguini. Who cares if I put on another pound. Gerry doesn't like skinny women anyway. You, though, can definitely afford to put on a pound or two."

"Okay, I'll join you. Two linguinis," Joanne told the waiter who had just brought them a basket of warm bread.

Carol immediately helped herself. "I just love their bread."

"I noticed," Joanne said. "Tell me something, Carol."

"Sure. What?"

"What would you do if you had cancer?"

"What?"

"I said, what would you do if…"

"I heard you the first time. What kind of question is that? Are you okay?"

"Of course. It's just a question."

"I'd fight like hell, let me tell you. Wouldn't you?"

"I suppose. This fellow at work, one of the researchers, just found out he has cancer." Joanne consoled herself that it wasn't a complete lie. "I want to call him, but I don't know what to say."

"Tell him to fight it. D'you know how many people are completely cured of cancer today? I don't know the exact figures, but a lot. I think it's the ones who fight, the ones who don't let it get the best of them."

"I don't think it's that simple," Joanne commented.

"Maybe not, but I believe attitude has a lot to do with any disease. I'm an optimist, and will be till my dying day. My mother and her sisters are always depressed about something or the other and, as you well know, always complaining about some illness or the other. I promised myself a long time ago that I wouldn't be like them. I try to look at the bright side of life, and I'm never sick. I don't mean that it's the perfect answer, I'm just saying that I think attitude helps a lot. If doctors gave me just a few months to live, I would certainly try to prove them wrong. That's what you should tell your friend."

"But that's false hope."

"Without hope, kid, false or otherwise, none of us has a chance. Some people say cancer happens because of the stress we live under; others say it's the food we eat; some say it's psychological. My philosophy is that probably all those things put together get us into trouble, whether we get cancer, heart disease, or other problems. Of course, when it comes to eating habits, I could improve, but since it's my only vice, I don't worry too much about it.

"In twenty or thirty years from now, I think cancer will have become an oddity, something that happens only once in a while. There probably won't be a cure as such, just that a combination of things will work in fighting it."

"So, I'll tell my friend to live a quiet life, eat well, and he'll get all better. Come on, if it were that simple, everyone would get cured."

"Why not try it? I'm convinced that with a positive attitude, we could all live to a ripe old age. I intend to. I don't take myself too seriously and I expect to be around sixty years from now. Never mind counting on your fingers how old I'll be!"

Joanne smiled. "Do you really want to live to be that old?"

"My dear, I intend to tell my great-grandchildren about the first man on the moon. By then, of course, they'll probably be going to the moon for their vacation! I intend to be around for a good part of the twenty-first century. It's going to be great to see all the innovations, technological or otherwise, that we'll have in fifty years."

"I suppose it would be interesting."

"You mean you're not going to be around with me? That's not fair. I had visions of both of us coming in here to celebrate our one hundredth birthdays."

Joanne laughed genuinely.

"Can you see me at one hundred?" Carol continued. "It goes without saying that I'm hoping that by then we'll have progressed enough so that I can look and feel just the way I do now! Wouldn't it be great to be ninety and still be able to flirt with forty-year-old guys? Now, that's false hope, kid!"

Chapter Eight

On Sunday morning, as if tired from its efforts of the last two days, the sun was unable to fight the gathering gray clouds. From experience, Joanne knew that more snow would be falling in the next few hours. She hoped Roger would decide to return early from White Mountain. The thought of her family traveling in a snowstorm did not appeal to her.

She had had a restless night. In the hours of darkness, she heard Carol's voice over and over again, urging her to fight, while at the same time, a large tiger kept coming toward her, never quite catching her. She awakened with a steady pain in the pit of her stomach. Groping her way to the bathroom, she swallowed two painkillers and went back to bed. Mercifully, she fell asleep again only to see herself crying at her mother's grave. She woke up when she saw her rise from the ground, calling to her.

As a teenager, dreams of her mother were a regular, sad occurrence. She hoped they were not coming back now, night after night, bringing with them the distress of the past. The present had enough sorrow of its own.

After breakfast, Joanne enjoyed a leisurely bubble bath, an exotic scent filling the room. She remained nearly submerged as the water gradually cooled, reviewing her plans for the day. She needed to get an early start, if she wanted to be home before Roger and the children returned from their skiing. From her closet she chose a flowing green wool skirt and a white sweater, which, when she looked at herself in the full-length mirror behind the bathroom door, hid how thin she had become. She carefully applied makeup, but found it impossible to hide new lines around her eyes. The weary look that testified to her inner turmoil could not be tricked into disappearing.

Once downstairs, she decided to wear the mink coat Roger had given her on their thirteenth wedding anniversary. She usually only wore it on special occasions, but now considered this was a special occasion. After all, special did not mean only happy; it also meant degree of importance, and if her plan worked as she wanted, today could become the most important day of her remaining short life.

Thirty minutes later, Joanne was ringing the doorbell of an elegant brick house with large white pillars that reached to the roof above the second story. Mary Malton opened the door, a bright smile on her face at the sight of the visitor.

"Well, at last," Mary said, hugging Joanne. "I'm glad you came."

"I'm not disturbing, am I?" Joanne asked as Mary took her coat.

"Don't be silly. We were just reading while babysitting." In a louder voice, Mary called to her husband. "Peter, look who I found at the door."

Peter Malton appeared in the hall, his gray hair tousled. "Hello, JoJo. I was hoping you'd change your mind." A boy of about three came running in and hung on to Peter's pant leg, a thumb in his mouth. "You remember Byron, don't you?"

"Of course," Joanne said, bending down. "How are you, Byron?"

"Fine," the small voice replied.

"You've certainly grown, haven't you. The last time I saw you, you were just a little baby."

"They grow fast, don't they?" Mary said. "It seems only yesterday that Mark was that age." Taking her grandson's hand, Mary told him, "Byron, why don't you play in the kitchen with your blocks for a while? Grandma and Grandpa have a visitor."

"Okay," the child said amiably, disappearing through a swinging door.

Joanne was seated comfortably in a high-back leather chair in the elegant Malton living room, sipping a cup of freshly brewed coffee. The moment had arrived and she wanted to leap this wall as quickly as possible. "You were right, Peter. Something has been bothering me."

"I knew it. How can we help?"

"You can help a great deal, but it might be more than you bargained for."

"We'll do everything we can to help you, JoJo," Mary said.

Joanne knew the offer from the woman who had taken her under her wing when she needed it most was sincere. In her mid-fifties, Mary Malton looked younger. Suddenly Joanne was envious; she wanted to reach that age and be as happy as her friend seemed to be. She took a deep breath and forged straight ahead. "Peter, I have been away from the office quite a bit lately, but there was a good reason. I was undergoing some tests and now I have the results."

The Maltons looked at each other without saying a word.

"The results are definitely not what I had hoped for. I have cancer."

"Oh, my God," Mary exclaimed, her hands going to her face, while Peter remained quiet, his face frozen.

"I guess it runs in my family and there's nothing I can do about it. But," Joanne continued, "I have a choice on how I'm going to spend the rest of my life. I don't want my children suffering the way I did when my mother was dying. It takes too much out of you." Pausing for a moment, she tried to understand the look in the eyes in front of her. Both Mary and Peter appeared too dumfounded to react. "I've rented a hideaway in the country where I'm going to live until the end. I don't want Terri, Jason, or Roger to know. That's where I've got to ask an immense favor of you: That you keep this a secret."

"But," Peter put in, "you can't just disappear. I mean, they'll want to know where you are."

"So I'm going to lie. Peter, in Hawaii there's a school that teaches Western executives how to deal with Asian customs and traditions."

"I've heard of it."

"I'm going to tell my family that you've sent me there. It's far enough away that I don't think they'll question it. Now, as far as work is concerned, I'm going to be leaving at the end of the week. George can take over. He's eager and I think he'll do very well. I can give him a few pointers before I go. I'll tell people at the office that I'm taking a sabbatical to study. They don't need to know anything else." Retrieving her purse, Joanne extracted a letter which she handed to Peter. "This letter from Dr. Calder explains my condition. I would like you to make arrangements for my long-term disability payments. Tomorrow, at the office, I'll give you the account number and the bank where the checks are to be deposited. I ask that you to swear to secrecy the personnel officer who makes the arrangements."

"It's pretty cold-blooded the way you've figured everything out," Peter said. "Don't do this, JoJo. Let us help you."

"And what exactly are you going to do? Work a miracle?" Joanne snapped. "I'm sorry. I'm a little edgy, but I'm sure you understand why."

Mary got up and went to put an arm around Joanne's shoulders.

Joanne continued. "I've always appreciated what both of you have done for me over the years, but especially at the time my mother died. I was very fortunate that you both cared so much. I know I told you before, but I want to repeat it. Thank you for everything."

Joanne felt tears welling in her eyes as Mary embraced her.

"You were always so easy to love," the older woman said. "It wasn't a burden, it was a great joy, believe me." Straightening herself, she added, "JoJo, things are so different now. A lot of progress has been made since your mother died. Chances are that you can get through this with treatment. We'll get the best specialists around."

"I know you want to help, but please understand that I don't want to go into the hospital and submit my body to all sorts of radiation or whatever it is they do. Besides, I only have a few months left, so it probably wouldn't be of any use anyway."

"JoJo, you're giving up before you even start," Peter said. "That's not like you."

"I guess a death sentence can change a person," Joanne said matter-of-factly.

"Your family loves you very much. It's going to be much harder on them not knowing what's happening to you," Mary commented.

"Mary, please try to understand. I'm doing this because I love my family. After I've been away for a while, they'll get used to living without me. It'll make things a lot easier on everyone when the end comes. I'm not going to change my mind. I feel very strongly that I have the right to choose what I do with the little time I have left."

Joanne swallowed hard and continued. "I'm sorry I had to tell you. Had there been any other way, I would not have said a word, but arrangements had to be made at the office."

"Where exactly are you going?" Mary asked.

"I don't want either of you to know where I'm going to be. However, I'll give you a phone number where you can reach me, but only on the condition that you promise, both of you, that you won't use it unless it's a real emergency about the family. Otherwise, I want to go through this alone."

"We can't let you do this," Peter said, standing up and starting to pace. "There has to be another way."

"My way is not only the best but the only way."

"Perhaps I could send you overseas, Paris for example, and you could get treatment there. No one would have to know, and you'd be getting the help you need."

"That's very kind, but I just don't want doctors poking me and making me feel worse than I already do. Please, Peter!"

Little Byron came running into the room. "Grandpa, Grandma, I made this big castle with my blocks. Come see it." He was pulling at Mary's skirt.

"Why don't we all go and see it?" Joanne said.

When Joanne left the Malton house several hours later, snow was beginning to fall. None of the arguments presented by her friends had influenced her plan of action and, finally, both promised, on her mother's grave, to keep her secret.

The parting embraces had been more difficult than Joanne had anticipated, and on her way home she felt desperate and confused. Mary and Peter had finally gone along with her scheme because she wanted it, because she begged, but she had been hard on them. She asked them to agree to the plot she wanted and to let her go completely without looking back. Did she have the right to do so? She knew that they probably broke down and cried after she left. It broke her heart.

Today the grandchild would be a bright light in the otherwise gloomy day of the Maltons, but what about tomorrow when they were once more alone? What about all the tomorrows to come? Suddenly tears began running down Joanne's cheeks, not letting up until she reached home.

Chapter Nine

Joanne got to her office early on Monday morning, feeling reasonably well, even though she had awakened early and had not been able to go back to sleep because of discomfort. The pain had lessened for the time being and she was eager to continue on her chosen road. Reinforcing herself with a cup of hot coffee from the shop around the corner from the office, she tackled some final details. By the time Peggy arrived, Joanne had already made the necessary arrangements for a telephone to be installed at her soon-to-be hideaway near Triton.

Joanne barely had time to exchange a few words with Peggy, when Peter Malton appeared in her doorway. Peggy left quietly, closing the door behind her

"JoJo," Peter began, seating himself in one of the chairs facing her desk. "Mary and I talked things over last night and we feel strongly that we must help you get medical attention." She was about to talk but he continued quickly. "We understand how you feel, believe me we do, but we promised your mother to take care of you and we intend to do just that."

"That's very noble, Peter, but you know damn well that your promise to my mother was satisfied a long time ago. I'm now a middle-aged adult and quite capable of making my own decisions. You may feel you owe me or my mother something, but that's due entirely to the situation, quote, unquote, that has presented itself. You've already done much more for me than was ever required."

"Even if that were the case, we want to stand by you now at a time when you need friends more than ever."

Joanne saw fatigue in Peter's roundish face. He and Mary had probably spent part of the night reviewing and revising possible options, finally getting little, if any, sleep. She had tossed an overwhelming crisis into their laps, all the while asking them to ignore it. *Is that fair? Couldn't I have simply told them I wanted to take time off? No. Not if I want financial independence as well as keep my situation and my whereabouts secret from Roger.*

However, by trying to save her family from pain, she had forced it head-on toward her best friends. The decision had been a difficult one in her hours of self-resolution, and she wondered now if it had been the right one. *Is genuine concern or simple hardheadedness the real criterion in any of my decisions involving Roger?*

"Perhaps I have not been fair to you and Mary," she said at length, "by asking you to simply walk away from me, but it's the last favor I'll ever ask of you both. Please, Peter, don't make this situation more distressing than it already is. Didn't you understand what took me so long to explain yesterday?"

"We understood, JoJo. The problem is that we don't agree with your decision. We certainly couldn't be called friends if we simply stood idly by while you make no effort to live. We feel you have given up, and we have an obligation to restore your will to fight the illness."

"You are wrong, Peter. I haven't lost my will to live. I intend to fight vigorously, but in my own way. No one can live my life or make decisions for me, no matter how well intentioned. I realize only too well that both you and Mary care very much for me, and believe me, that's a great consolation. But you have to put our friendship in the right perspective and respect what I want."

"We want to respect your wishes, but it's utterly difficult because we see so many options for you."

"I regret putting you in such an impossible situation, but you must let me follow the road that I feel is right for me." Her last words had been spoken softly, almost tearfully.

Peter stood up slowly. JoJo was strong and he knew that at this point in time no argument would stop her from carrying out her plan. She was a brick wall of determination, and he realized the futility of continuing the painful discussion. He would try another approach at another time.

"Very well," Peter said, bending down to embrace her. When he left her office, he knew she was crying softly.

Joanne composed herself and buzzed her secretary. "Peggy, would you please call my husband and see if he's free for lunch? I'll meet him at his office whenever convenient."

"Yes, of course," Peggy said, standing at the door a few more seconds than necessary and departing when her boss offered no explanation.

Joanne had just started on a list of the work in progress she intended to present to George the next day when Peggy told her Roger was free and had suggested twelve-thirty.

"Peggy, please sit down for a moment," Joanne invited. "I want to tell you something, and I guess the best way to do it is to come right out and say it. Peggy, I've decided to take some time off, probably a year."

"A year?" Peggy said louder than she would have wanted to.

"I want to travel, study, get myself back into shape."

"This is a shock, but I'm glad for you," Peggy said sincerely. "You look pretty tired these days."

"So everyone keeps telling me!"

"Will someone be replacing you?"

"George will be taking over. I hope you won't mind working with him."

"He's okay, but I'm going to miss you."

"Same here, Peggy. We work well together."

"When are you leaving?"

"On Friday."

"This Friday?" Peggy's dark eyes widened.

"Yes, but we'll have enough time to get organized, don't worry," Joanne said, smiling reassuringly.

"Everybody'll be surprised. I mean, a decision on such short notice. Will you be staying in town?"

"My plans are not finalized as yet," Joanne said, knowing that Peggy could barely wait for the lunch hour to spread the news. *Tongues will certainly wag, exploring a variety of reasons for the sudden departure, finally settling on the most unlikely, but no doubt the most colorful.*

It was a few minutes past noon when Joanne left her office. She decided to walk and give herself time to rehearse the words she would use to inform Roger of her decision. The cold air refreshed her, and although the sun was absent, the clouds did not appear threatening. They seemed to be simply assessing how the city was coping with the heavy snow that had fallen the previous day.

Joanne stopped at her bank and spoke with the manager. All the arrangements were complete in just a few minutes. A bank account would be opened for her in Triton and every month an authorized amount would be transferred from her account in the city.

Pleased with the unfolding of her plan, she briskly walked the few blocks to Roger's office building. She rode the elevator to the tenth floor and faced the huge oak door with its brass letters announcing: McBride, Porteous, Riverside and Blake, Attorneys. Roger's career had progressed well and faster than he had expected. Joanne was momentarily taken back to the day he had been offered a partnership in the firm. It had come unexpectedly for Roger, who had been too busy to realize that the two senior partners and founders had judged his work well above average. Exhilarated, he had come home with a magnum of French champagne, which they shared late into the night as they reached new heights of passion.

Joanne stopped for a moment, took a small mirror from her purse and checked her makeup. Thankfully, the walk in the cold air had given her cheeks a healthy glow. She stepped inside and the walls in the reception area again did not fail to impress her. The dark cherry wood suggested luxury while at the same time imparting a feeling of warmth. After the receptionist announced her arrival, she said, "Mr. Blake's waiting. Please go in."

Joanne followed the corridor until she came to the familiar door. She knocked and the door was promptly opened by Roger, who smiled warmly. "Come in, please. Let me take your coat."

She was wearing her gorgeous dark mink, having decided that morning that there was no longer any need to enshrine it, protect it from wear and tear. "Roger, why don't we just go out right away? There's something I want to talk to you about."

"Okay." He crossed the room to the closet in the paneled wall. She remained silent as she watched him put on black boots and a heavy navy coat. A distressing twinge could not be ignored. *Soon he will no longer be part of my life.* She took a deep breath to quell the emotion. When he was ready and motioned the door with a sweeping motion, she smiled at him.

"Where do you want to go?" Roger asked as they waited for the elevator.

"I would very much like somewhere really quiet."

"Most spots around here are pretty jammed at this time of day, except for my club."

"That stuffy place? No, thank you."

They were silent as they rode the crowded elevator. In the lobby, Joanne said, "If it were warmer, we could get something at the deli and eat in the park."

Over the years they had often shared lunch in the park when there was a particular problem to solve or decision to reach, or when they simply needed to be close to each other. She would always remember those meetings fondly.

"We can still do that," he said, "but instead of the park, we could go to my apartment. It's not far."

She agreed. It would afford the relaxed atmosphere necessary for their discussion. Instead of deli, they opted for Chinese, which Roger picked up at the restaurant a few doors from his building.

"You'll have to excuse the mess. I'm not as neat as you, I'm afraid," Roger said as he unlocked the door, but Joanne was pleasantly surprised. The place was in better order than the only other time she had been in Roger's apartment. A newspaper and a couple of magazines were strewn over the beige sofa and a half-empty mug on the coffee table waited to be cleaned. Everything else in the combination living and dining room was orderly.

"Let me take your coat," Roger said after depositing the food on the round table near the window. She saw that he hung her mink with care.

"The kids tell me the conditions were good at White Mountain," Joanne said.

"Super. Just super. They had a ball. Sit down. I'll get some dishes." From the cubicle that served as a kitchen, Roger added in a louder voice, "I hope you haven't changed your mind about coming to Colorado with us."

"No, I haven't. I'm looking forward to it."

"When Peggy called, I was afraid you wanted to cancel out," Roger said as he came back with dishes and cutlery.

"That's not why I wanted to talk to you." Joanne opened the bag and handed one of the containers to Roger.

"Go ahead. Ladies first."

They both filled their plates. All the while, Joanne was aware that Roger was eyeing her furtively, but she waited until they had both eaten some of the food before making her case.

"Roger, I'll get straight to the point. I have the opportunity of going to Hawaii and then on to Asia for about a year and I've decided to accept."

"What?" Roger said in disbelief.

"So, I want to know how you'd feel about coming back to live in the house and taking care of Terri and Jason while I'm gone. Mrs. Lucas will stay on, of course. She can come in an extra day if you need her."

"Is this some sort of vacation?"

"No, I'm going to study Asian customs and ways. We're involved in a joint venture with a Japanese firm and the company wants to make sure we don't make any blunders that could threaten the deal."

"I see. When are you leaving?"

"As soon as we come back from Colorado. This is my last week at work."

"Boy, you didn't leave me much lead time, did you?"

She could see disappointment in his eyes. "I had to make a decision quickly and I decided to go for it because it's a chance that'll probably never present itself again." She realized that she was becoming an expert at lying.

"And you never thought of consulting me about it?"

"I was sure you'd enjoy being with the kids again."

"Of course, I will. It's just that I can't just pack up on a moment's notice. I've just renewed my lease on this place for another year. You remember, don't you, that you threw me out in the middle of winter!"

"Don't try to make me feel guilty; it won't work. You deserved it," she said, surprised at the snap in her voice.

"JoJo, it didn't mean anything. It seems to me you could have made an effort to understand, to save our marriage after almost fifteen years."

"You mean, you had the right to cheat and I was supposed to just forget it had happened?"

"Of course, you, Miss Perfect, had nothing to reproach yourself! Everything had to be planned and organized. There was never any room for spontaneity. Our vacations had be planned at least six months in advance, just like our lovemaking. Did you ever think that maybe I was tired of perfection and momentarily looked for imperfection?" He smiled faintly, ironically. "If you had been fair enough to accept some of the guilt, I think we could have worked things out."

"I don't know, Roger," she said simply. She didn't want the argument to continue because it was preventing her from finalizing her plan and it was fruitless in her time frame. "How about it?" she asked.

"How about what?" he replied sharply.

"You coming over to live in the house," she said slowly. "Can you arrange something for the apartment?"

"I suppose. One of our lawyers, who is single, is looking for a new place. I'll talk to him and maybe sublet."

"Good. Thank you."

"I must say I'm quite surprised. It's not like you to decide things at the last minute, going to Colorado, moving halfway around the world. What next?" Roger asked, a hint of sarcasm in his voice.

"I'm simply taking advantage of opportunities, that's all."

Roger began gathering the food containers.

"Let me help you," Joanne said. Coming across two fortune cookies at the bottom of the bag, she said, "Let's see what it says." She handed Roger one of the curved confections and pulled out a small piece of paper from the one she had kept. "Take the bull by horns." She was certainly taking that advise literally, she thought. "How about yours, Roger?"

"Love is a sickness full of woes," he read. "How true!" He crushed the piece of paper, tossed it into the bag and continued clearing.

Joanne went to sit on the sofa. She felt tired, pain suddenly making itself known. She closed her eyes. *Is Roger correct in his assessment of our relationship? Did I drive him into an affair? Was I too harsh in judging? Would it have been better to forgive than to live without closeness?* She felt confused and frustrated. *Yet, with death waiting straight down the road, doesn't life owe me some measure of peace?*

"Are you okay?" Roger's words startled her. He was standing over her, his face full of concern. "You look pretty beat."

"Just getting older, I guess."

"Getting away'll be good for you."

"Does that mean you understand?"

"Of course I do. I was just a little miffed that you didn't consult me, that's all."

"Because I'm not giving you much of a choice as far as the children are concerned?"

He sat down beside her. "No, that's not the reason. I'm going to enjoy being with the kids, but since I'm going to have to change my life to suit your plans, I think it would have been nice to have more of a notice."

"You're right, of course, but as I said, it came up rather suddenly."

"Don't worry; it's okay," he said, putting a hand on one of her knees. His touch felt good. Suddenly, she wanted to have his arms around her, consoling her aching spirit, pushing away the despair and the hopelessness, erasing the loneliness. Quiet tears reached her downcast eyes and she lost the battle to control them.

"What is it, JoJo?" Roger asked, putting a comforting arm around her shoulders.

She didn't answer, letting her head find its way to his broad shoulder. He held her close, as if afraid that if he loosened his grip she would fly away, until the sobbing became a soft weeping. Then, he gently pulled himself away, and taking a handkerchief from his pocket, wiped her face. "Let me help you, JoJo." His voice was compassionate.

She put both her arms around his neck as an unexpected desire to be his wife again took hold. She wanted to forget the past and the future. She yearned only for the moment. Roger heard her tender beckoning, "Make love to me."

Chapter Ten

Careful not to disturb Joanne whose head was resting on his shoulder, Roger lifted the telephone receiver on the bedside table. She awoke from a short but deep sleep as he spoke to his secretary. "Evelyn, I've been delayed. When Mr. Raskin gets there, please offer my apologies. I'll be in as soon as I can...Thank you."

"You're late for an appointment?" Joanne asked.

"Not yet, but I'll be in fifteen minutes. If I hurried, I could make it, however," he added, letting his body fall back on the bed, "I don't feel like hurrying." He looked at her and gently let his fingers contour her face. "You're sure you want to go away?"

"I have to."

"No, you don't. You could quit your job and I could support you and we could all be a family again."

"Roger, don't..."

"Don't what? Look at the truth? I mean what just happened was probably the closest we've been in a long time. Thank you," he added, kissing her cheek.

"Roger, don't read more into this than there really was."

"Oh," he said. "You mean you just wanted to fill a physical need and I was an appropriate pawn? I must be losing it because I read a lot more into it."

"Roger, please. I never stopped caring for you, but I don't think there's any possibility of a future between us." That lie hurt her more than he would ever know, but she had to be strong after the wonderful middle-of-the-day self-indulgence.

He sat up, his eyes fixed on hers, full of fire. "It was just a one-night, or rather a one-day, stand. How nice!"

"Roger, stop it. You know that's not true. I needed you and you needed me…it just happened. Let it go at that."

"But we just shared something very special, or at least I thought we did."

"Yes, we did, but now we have to go on with our lives."

"Why, JoJo? Why did you trap me?"

"I didn't trap you. I didn't exactly have to force you, did I?"

"So now that I've served your purpose, I'm supposed to forget the whole thing?"

"Please try to understand."

"Well, I don't," he said sharply.

Quietly, she got out from under the sheets and gathered her clothes from the chair where Roger had piled them neatly as he had undressed her, both relishing the anticipatory moment. Her thin body was exposed to his scrutiny, her breasts sagging from the lost weight. She rushed into the bathroom and locked the door.

When she reappeared, he was fully dressed. He gently put his hands on her shoulders. "I'm sorry, but don't you see that I meant what I said? It was not just the heat of passion, I really do love you."

"And I you," she said softly. "We'd better go or Mr. Rascal may be annoyed."

He chuckled. "It's Raskin."

"I know," she said, planting a kiss firmly on his lips.

They walked back together, gloved hand in gloved hand, and Joanne felt a new vigor. Neither spoke until they reached his building. "You're still coming to Vail?"

"Of course," she said, and continued her walk without looking back.

Joanne had barely time to remove her coat and boots when Harvey Mack, the red-haired production manager, charged into her office.

"So, where is it?" he asked bluntly.

"Where is what, Harv?"

"The positive statement you were supposed to issue about the company, what else? This company has had enough bad publicity for one year, yet nothing is being done, and I hear you're leaving."

"Good news for you, isn't it, Harv?"

"I can't say I'm going to cry. At last we're going to have a man in this job. George's not in his office; I thought he might be here. I want to make sure he understands what we agreed on before you leave."

"Harv, whatever you want you can discuss with George and Peter Malton. I don't have to put up with you anymore and I won't." Feeling stronger than she had in many weeks, Joanne said quietly, "Frankly, Harv, as far as I'm concerned, you can go to hell."

He was taken aback for a moment, but he soon saw a long-craved opportunity to express his opinion. "You think you're better than anyone else, but I know what's going on. You're taking off because Peter Malton has probably found himself a new, younger whore, and he won't be protecting you anymore. You broads are all the same, taking advantage, and then complaining we don't give you your rights. Ha!"

"Are you quite finished?"

"It'll be nice working with a man for a change."

"So I understand," she said, her voice low and cutting. "I must remember to warn George about you. I don't believe he knows you're a closet queen."

Harvey Mack's ruddy face rapidly turned a darker shade of red. Joanne had long suspected that the man in front of her was gay; now she was certain. She felt suddenly sorry for him because he belonged to a generation that never admitted publicly or even to itself the inner torment it had to face. Harvey Mack led an outwardly normal life—he was married and had a child—but Joanne considered that he would one day be irreparably crushed when the wall of his private hell came crashing down.

She suddenly felt remorse and wanted to take back her last remark. "Why don't we just forget our differences and part on good terms," she said, extending her hand.

For a long moment, his eyes pierced hers with the hostile glance of an enemy fully aware of his defeat, then, abruptly, he turned on his heel and left.

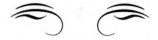

Joanne went home early after transferring the work in progress to her successor. She had no desire to hang on to the past. The script had been written without her approval and she was simply saying her lines. The company had been good to her, and, in turn, she had given it her best, but she was amazed at her ability to dissociate herself emotionally from the work that took up such a great part of her life over so many years.

Terri and Jason were making themselves milkshakes when Joanne walked into the kitchen. "You're home early," Terri said.

"If that's a reproach, I can always go back to the office."

"It's just nice," Terri said honestly.

"Why don't you both sit down? I've got something to tell you," Joanne said, making an effort to keep her voice even.

Jason took the straw out of his mouth long enough to say, "What is it?"

"My company has offered me a great opportunity and I've decided to accept it." The children looked at each other. "Unfortunately, I'll have to go away for a while."

"Where are you going?" Terri asked.

"I'm going to Hawaii for a few months and then on to Japan because of a deal the company is working on."

"How long will you be gone?" Jason asked timidly.

"About a year." The sudden look on her children's faces made her want to cry.

"What?" Terri cried. "You can't be serious?"

"You mean, until next winter?" Jason asked in shock.

"What's going to happen to us? You can't just take off and leave us?" Terri said, her unbelief turning to anger.

"Your father's going to come and stay with you here. It'll be good all around, you'll see. You'll both have a chance to accept more responsibility and to be more independent."

Joanne could see that they were both trying to assess how their lives would be affected.

"Come on, guys, things will work out. Aunt Mary and Uncle Peter will be around too. Think of it in terms of a new adventure, of an exciting experience."

Certain that Roger would be more lenient when it came to curfews, rules and regulations, she said, "It'll give you a chance to prove that all I've been trying to teach you hasn't been lost."

Both children still appeared in a daze and were staring at her.

"I realize this is a bit of a shock, but I had to make up my mind very quickly. Think about it and we'll talk again. Okay?" she said, kissing them each in turn. "We'll talk about it a lot next week when we're in Colorado. You can tell us whatever is bothering you about my decision, and your father and I will try to work it all out. Okay?"

During the meal she answered the questions thrown at her, being careful that lies told earlier did not conflict with any present statements. She even surprised herself by sounding excited about the new episode of her life.

After dinner, when Jason was getting ready for his hockey game, he reminded Joanne that she had promised to attend. She had not forgotten about seeing her son on the ice for the last time, and she was determined to not let the future interfere with her enjoyment of the game.

As she was putting on warm fleece-lined boots at the kitchen table, the doorbell rang. Afraid that it might be Gordon Mitchell coming to pick up Jason out of habit, she let her daughter answer.

"Mom, it's Dad," Terri called from the entrance hall.

Joanne could not deny surprise. "Hello, Roger. I didn't expect to see you."

"A promise is a promise," he said, entering the kitchen, smiling. "I came for your skis. You still want them looked over, don't you?"

"Of course."

"Are you going out? You look dressed for a blizzard."

She was wearing blue ski overalls over a heavy wool sweater. "I'm taking Jason to his hockey game." Without really thinking about it, she added, "Want to come along?"

"I'd love to," he replied, his voice not hiding his excitement.

"Can I come too?" Terri asked from the stairs where she had been standing, listening to her parents' conversation.

"Don't you have some studying to do?" Joanne asked, surprised that her daughter wouldn't find it imperative to review material the night before a test.

"Tomorrow's algebra. I think I know it pretty well."

Terri was out of character, and Joanne realized how important, at this point in time, a family outing was. It even warranted risking getting an A instead of an A+.

"Well, what are you waiting for? Go and get ready?" Joanne urged.

"I'll just be a minute," Terri said, running up the stairs.

"I hope you weren't too late for your appointment," Joanne told Roger.

"No. Mr. Raskin was late himself. He's usually very difficult to deal with, but somehow today he readily agreed to all my suggestions."

"It must have been your delivery."

"I was unusually charming," he said, a mischievous grin on his face. "Must have been the lunch! Wish I could have more of these lunches. I wouldn't mind at all."

"I did enjoy it myself," Joanne said.

They were smiling at each other, when Jason appeared from the basement with his hockey gear. His delighted expression reminded Joanne of his uncomplicated joy when he opened gifts on Christmas morning.

The star at the local arena that evening was undisputedly Jason Blake. Joanne, who had not seen her son on the ice for several weeks, was as impressed as everyone else watching the game. He led many of his team's offensive plays and scored no less than three goals, two of them totally unassisted. On Joanne's left, Terri's piercing voice of encouragement and jubilation at her brother's exploits drowned out the cheers and yells of the crowd while, on her right, Roger kept repeating to anyone around who would listen, "That's my boy," while exhilarated by the congratulatory praise.

When Jason scored his third goal, Joanne joined in the intoxicating ambience all around her, jumping up and down. After a few jumps of his own, Roger embraced her tightly in spite of the heavy garments, releasing her, reluctantly, Joanne thought, as the other parents around began praising Jason's superb form. When one of the fathers told Roger, "You should consider getting him a good coach; he's superstar material," Joanne half expected the zipper on her husband's jacket to give way from the pressure of the pride-inflated chest.

"I didn't realize he had gotten so much better since last season," Roger told Joanne. "You should have told me."

She didn't reply. She was delighted that Jason devoted himself to hockey with the same determination he applied to everything else in his life, but she knew that he was far from being a superstar. Jason was an average player at best, very pleased with himself if he scored the occasional goal. She was a bit shocked by his untypical performance. *Was his family cheering him on the impetus that spurred him on?*

"Maybe we'll have a great hockey star in the family, " Terri told her parents as they made their way out after the game. "That'd be cool."

"You shouldn't expect too much," Joanne said. "Very few players make it to the big leagues."

"Well, I think Jason's got what it takes," Roger said proudly. "I'm going to speak to the coach."

"Roger, this was the first time you saw Jason play this season. Why don't you wait until you see him a few more times before getting too excited?"

"Why are you putting him down? You saw it for yourself. Three goals in one game. I'd say that's exceptional."

"I'm not putting him down, not one bit. I just think that pride has made you jump to a conclusion that may not be fair to Jason…or to you, for that matter."

"Mom, why are you doing this?" Terri asked.

"Doing what?"

"Spoiling it for Dad. Like you don't want Dad to be proud of Jason."

"Terri, we're all proud of your brother. I just don't think his performance this evening should go to our heads."

"When we're all together, you always ruin things. Anyway, what do you care? You're going away and, who knows, you may not come back," Terri said, rushing away from her parents.

"I'll go and talk to her," Roger offered.

He moved through the crowd, catching up to Terri at the refreshment stand.

The deed was done. Joanne was certain that Terri was bleeding inside at the thought of losing her mother. She had probably daydreamed about her parents getting back together, but was suddenly faced with the harsh reality that it was not to be. Joanne sat wearily on a bench against one of the walls. *My plan is progressing well, as well as any plan laid out by a mortal could, but at what price to those I love?*

Joanne could see Roger talking to Terri, making her smile and nod her head. A father and a daughter sharing an exclusive bond no one else could penetrate. The father would help the daughter face the next few months, while the daughter would, by her presence, nourish paternal capabilities. Roger kissed Terri's forehead and they made their way back to Joanne, Roger carrying two cups of hot coffee.

Joanne gratefully accepted one, and soon heard congratulatory remarks of "Well done," "Way to go," from the people crowded in the lobby of the arena.

Jason squeezed out from the horde to join his family, the sweat from the exertion of the game still glistening his forehead. His hair remained unbrushed, while the dampness emphasized auburn streaks. Roger rubbed his son's head, congratulating him enthusiastically, and Terri joined in.

Joanne praised her son guardedly. "Good game, Jason."

"Things went well tonight. I wish I had more games like that. It would be fun!"

"All your games can be like tonight if you try," Roger put in.

"Ha, Dad, I'm not that good a hockey player. Tonight was a fluke. Can we stop for a hamburger on the way home? I'm starved."

Roger's face showed disappointment. With a few words Jason had assessed his talent realistically and, in the process, his father's balloon of pride and vanity had burst. Joanne felt for her husband who, totally innocently, had let himself be seduced by the rapture of his son's eagerness to please. She briefly put her hand on Roger's shoulder as they left the arena.

The following day Joanne came home during her lunch hour to speak with her part-time housekeeper, Mrs. Lucas. The woman who was at ease in her organized world was taken aback by the news of Joanne's impending departure.

"A whole year?" she asked, unbelieving.

"I'm afraid so, but you'll be getting a raise," Joanne said, pleased at the smile that appeared on the other woman's face. "There might be a little more work for you."

"I don't mind," Mrs. Lucas said agreeably.

"Then you'll stay?"

"Of course; I like it here."

Joanne was pleased. The uncomplicated woman would continue to be happy, unpressured by strict schedules, arranging her daily work to fit her disposition. "Here's your pay for next week while we're away," Joanne said, handing her an envelope. "I'm sure you can use a little vacation yourself."

"Thank you, Mrs. B. I can come in to check things and bring in the mail if you want."

"That would be very nice. Thank you."

Joanne's world was unfolding very satisfactorily indeed. On her way back to work, she took a detour to visit the largest bookstore in the city. She spent nearly an hour looking, reading, searching, inquiring. When she was done, she purchased a dozen books dealing with various aspects of healing—from nutritional and exercise guides to spiritual and metaphysical approaches. She knew some of the books were probably a waste of money, but she hypothesized that the smallest new insight would foster her determination to fight the devil inside her body.

Mary and Peter are wrong. I will fight. I will give it my best. I will confront the enemy dead-on until my dying day.

I will fight like hell.

Chapter Eleven

John Calder hung up the phone and turned his attention back to the patient sitting across the desk.

"I'm sorry for the interruption," he said to the fleshy woman. Picking up a small, clear plastic container filled with bluish caplets, he added, "As I was telling you, Mrs. Norris, I got these for you. They're brand-new. Doctors are amazed at the results. Try them for two weeks, then I want to see you again. You should start feeling a marked difference in a week, maybe less. Can you keep a record so that I'll know exactly when things improved?"

"Of course, Doctor," the woman said, delighted.

"Good. That'll give me a chance to adjust the dosage next time." He stood up, indicating that the visit was over.

His patient gone, John Calder sat down again, pleased with himself. He was certain Mrs. Norris would report great improvement in the intensity—if not the complete disappearance—of her headaches on her next visit. She would expound on the almost magical power of the new pills, unaware that they were merely placebos. He knew some of his colleagues might consider his methods risky, if not harmful, because he was treating symptoms without getting at the cause. *I know the cause*, John Calder thought. *I simply can't cure loneliness.*

Softly, his nurse opened the door. "Do you want me to send in the next patient."

"Not yet. Please get Joanne Blake on the phone for me."

At the buzz of the telephone, Joanne turned from the boring report she was reading, welcoming the interruption. She instantly recognized John Calder's voice.

"JoJo, I have some exciting news. I was just talking to a doctor in New York who has been getting amazing results treating cancer patients with a new light-sensitive drug combined with laser therapy. Together they prove lethal to cancer cells, and the response rate is nearly 100 percent."

Joanne could hear the emotion in Dr. Calder's voice.

"It took a bit of bargaining, but the doctor can get you into his program right away. You'll have to go to New York, but that's not a problem, I'm sure."

Joanne was grateful. Her old friend would not rest until he had tried all possible avenues, had explored all possible terrains. "Doc, I thought I had made myself clear about my plans."

"I know. I know," he said, dismissing her wishes as irrelevant in the light of the information he had just given her. "But this is a completely new approach. Everyone in the medical profession feels that we've come one step closer to a full answer."

"Doc, I…"

He interrupted her boldly. "JoJo, this is the answer I've been praying for. I spent most of the weekend talking with several doctors who specialize in cancer treatment. There's a hospital in New York that's been getting results that are much too exciting to be ignored! You wouldn't even have to stay in New York all the time. A suitable schedule could be set up after your evaluation. I'll go with you because I want to look at this treatment more closely myself. What do you say we leave tomorrow?"

Joanne sighed. *How can I make the man of science understand my lack of faith in a profession that is still so fallible?* "I'm sorry you went to all this trouble for me, Doc, but I won't go."

"JoJo, listen to yourself. You're giving up before you even start!"

"I've not given up, Doc. I just don't want to undergo treatment."

"This treatment is not the regular radiation therapy. It's something new that might just be the answer everyone's has been looking for."

"Might be. That's the problem, Doc. You can't guarantee anything."

"I never could. There are unforeseen factors in any treatment. I've seen young, healthy people die on the operating table during a routine procedure,

76

while old men, generally in poor health, survived open-heart surgery. Some people have been known to recover fully from serious ailments without any medical intervention. We doctors don't have all the answers. We don't pretend to. Medicine is a science that's forever changing, evolving, expanding, and will always be as new ailments surface. But, my dear, we have made unbelievable strides in our quest to ease the suffering of mankind.

"Perhaps we cannot guarantee a cure in all cases, but we can accurately diagnose and follow a charted road of treatment. That road's immeasurably brighter today than it was just two years ago, and before the end of the year, it will be even brighter than it is right now. We have an obligation to attempt all that is attemptable, and in your case, JoJo, I feel my obligation is quite clear."

"Doc, your sole obligation is to give me the facts. You've done that. Now it's up to me. I'm the one with cancer, and unless laws were changed in the last five minutes, I, and I alone, get to decide what I want to do with my body."

Joanne could picture the look of grief on Dr. Calder's face, but she had to make him understand. "I am well aware that medicine has changed since my mother died. I know you can do a lot more for a patient now than you could thirty years ago. I appreciate all that. I also appreciate your concern for me. But face it, Doc, I won't change my mind. I don't want my body poked and filled with pills so that my life can be extended a few more days or a few more weeks. I just won't do it. I'm sorry."

John Calder suddenly realized that his patient's decision had not been determined solely by concern for her family. Joanne Blake was panic-stricken at the thought of medical intervention and her fear, no doubt dormant but alive and well somewhere in her subconscious since childhood, made her unable to see clearly the curative road it could open for her. He had lied, "*After the operation your mom's going to be okay, you'll see*," and she did not trust him.

"So am I, JoJo," he said, and he was indeed sorry.

His discussions with colleagues far and wide in the last few days had convinced him that her form of carcinoma would be especially powerless to fight the laser treatment. These were odds a doctor could not ignore. "I'm offering you a chance to live until old age and you won't take it. It shows me that I have failed you miserably."

"You haven't and you know it. I'm just stubborn," she said, laughing awkwardly.

"I failed you a long time ago in the kitchen of your parents' house. In wanting to give a little child some hope, I made an adult lose faith. I'm sorry, JoJo."

The lie of the young, caring doctor, uttered so many years ago for the sole intention of lessening her anguish, was destined to cause her more grief today.

"Come on, Doc. Don't do this, blame yourself. You've done all you could. Much more, in fact. Let me do this my way, please."

John Calder was suddenly annoyed. If any other patient opted for the road Joanne intended to take, he would simply admit defeat and go on with only an occasional sense of frustration at his inability to provide care that had a good chance of ending in total victory. Now, with Joanne Blake on the other end of the line, he felt hurt and ineffective. But he couldn't give up. He would think of another approach to challenge her. "You promised to give me your telephone number so we could keep in touch, remember?"

"Of course, Doc. I just don't have it right now, but I should be able to give it to you when I return from Colorado."

"Why are you going to Colorado?"

"I'm going skiing for a week with Roger and the kids. I thought it would be good if we were all together for a while before I left."

"I'm glad to hear that, but are you feeling well enough?"

"I feel a bit tired, but the fresh air'll do me good. Don't worry, I'll be fine. If I have any problems, I'll call you. Okay?"

"Any time, day or night."

"Thank you, Doc, for everything. I'll think about what you said while I'm skiing and I'll be in touch when I get back."

"D'you promise?"

"I promise."

"Good. I hope you all have a good time."

Hanging up John Calder felt marginally better. There was hope, albeit limited, but hope nevertheless that his patient would reconsider her options in light of the new information he had provided.

"Excuse me, Doctor," his nurse, who had come noiselessly, said. "Roger Blake's on the phone. Do you want to talk to him?"

"Roger Blake?" he asked, surprised. "Of course." Lifting up the receiver, the doctor's voice was casual, "Roger. How are you?"

"Just fine. Thank you. I really didn't want to disturb you; I was calling for an appointment to get professional advice. I have a potential witness who claims he can't testify in court because he suffers from colitis. Basically I want information on this disorder. I would like to see you when convenient. No great rush."

"I'm not going to have to testify in court, am I?"

"No. I simply want an informed opinion."

"No problem, Roger. My nurse will call you to give you an appointment. How's the family? JoJo?" He had managed to keep his voice professional.

"Just fine. She's coming to Vail with the children and me for some skiing next week. She looks a bit tired, but I think she's okay."

"Glad to hear it, Roger." A potent force was making it very difficult for the doctor to keep his promise to Joanne, but he did manage to remain strong.

The rest of the week sped by so quickly that Joanne lost all sense of time. Yet, to her surprise, when Friday afternoon sneaked up on her, wily, like a child with the upper hand in a game of tag, she was able to cross out the last items on her To Do lists. Each day, as she completed a task on either her personal or her professional list, she methodically checked it off. One by one, each objective had been reached.

As per her personal list, at midweek she took a long lunch hour to shop for birthday presents for her children. Both Terri and Jason were born in May, just a week apart. At the time of the second arrival, Roger had joked that surely there had to be some hidden purport to having both children born in the same month. Joanne's organized mind interpreted it simply as a blessing—combined birthday parties in childhood and double-duty birthday-gift shopping trips later on.

After deciding on a new ski jacket for Jason and a knit top for Terri, Joanne went looking for more extravagant things. It would be their last birthdays during her lifetime and it was important that they be memorable. For Terri, she chose a pair of small diamonds for her pierced ears, and for Jason, she settled on a gold watch.

Roger will find the gifts totally unacceptable, which they probably are, she thought, but she went ahead nevertheless. *What will I do with the money I have saved over the years?* At that point in time, spoiling her children seemed a most reasonable decision. Leaving the jewelry store, a display of leather briefcases caught her eye. She remembered giving one to Roger a few years earlier and, reasoning that it surely was worn out, chose one that gleamed under the store's lights, unashamed of its price tag. She had it gift-wrapped for his birthday in late August. *Why not?* she thought. *We'd had some very good years together and he deserves a token of my appreciation.*

Later, after the children had gone to sleep, she wrote a note to each of them on birthday cards she had spent a long time choosing. She expressed her disappointment at not being able to celebrate with them, indicated that she expected them to continue to be conscientious, and closed with an optimistic annotation that they would soon be together again.

As she reread the words, her eyes misted with tears. It took a few minutes before she could bring her emotions under control and pile the gifts in the closet of the spare room, which served as a studio whenever the urge to paint overtook her. She affixed the cards, each name clearly marked, to the two most expensive presents at the top of each pile, and made a mental note to call Mrs. Lucas in the morning so the presents could be put in the appropriate room on each birthday.

Roger's present she put in her own closet. She had trouble finding the right words and would ponder the problem a few more days. Whatever she wrote had to be an honest expression of her feelings. That presented a problem because of the dichotomy of emotions. Part of her surely loved him and always would, yet part of her could not forgive the indiscretion, the affront to her integrity and dignity. Perhaps in the days to come she would be able to express herself in a coherent manner.

On her last day at the office, Joanne accepted an invitation to lunch from the people with whom she worked most closely. Peter Malton made it a point to join the group. The emotional stress of the last few days had taken its toll and, once seated in the little Italian restaurant, Joanne felt drained. She hoped some white wine, her first drink since it had become obvious she had serious stomach problems, would energize her. It did.

She faced an endless barrage of questions about her plans, yet was able to keep her answers somewhat vague, smiling as much as she could. By the time dessert was served, she wanted to escape. The false pretense was becoming too hard to handle. She had tried to avoid Peter Malton's eyes with little success, since he was seated almost directly across from her. He was quiet throughout the meal, and whenever she glanced at him, his eyes pierced back.

When, on several occasions during the week, she had seen him, he had not mentioned her illness, and she wondered if he was mapping some new plan to attack her defenses.

After coffee was served, Peter Malton stood up and called for silence. His speech was short. "Dear friends, I always feel sad when an employee leaves our family because it is almost always a final decision. Today, however, the atmosphere's different. We're not saying adieu to Joanne but rather so long. We know that she'll be back with us, and that makes her departure easier. Joanne, we hope your hiatus will be rewarding and we look forward to having you return with a new vitality. Good luck."

The applause was strong as the company president sat down. Joanne's effort to appear casual demanded superhuman control and she surprised herself at being able to carry it off after briefly making eye contact with the personnel manager seated at the far end of the table. His glance was full of compassion.

On her return to her office for the last time, she was able to finalize the few remaining details with George and Peggy, although she was interrupted countless times by co-workers who stopped in to wish her well.

The last visitor of the day was the personnel manager who embraced her warmly. After giving her a last pay check, he said, "Arrangements have been made as you requested. I've put a few insurance claim forms in your pay envelope. Send them to me directly when filled out and I'll take care of everything personally. If you need help of any kind, please call. I mean that."

After he left, she went to stand at the window and made no attempt to stop the tears that were cascading down her cheeks. Her departure was to be tearful after all, but as Peggy, herself crying, told Joanne, "After so many years, it would not be normal not to cry."

When everyone had gone home, Joanne remained seated at her desk for a time, hoping that Peter Malton would come out of his office, where he had barricaded himself with the accountants, long enough to see her off. He did not. It was nearly six o'clock by the time she got up, gave a last look at her office and left without looking back.

Later, the activity around her house afforded little time for thoughts of self-pity. There was a sort of festive mood as the children got ready for their week in Colorado. Terri's friend, Susan, dropped by to help select the right wardrobe, the visitor just as excited as the traveler. Jason, himself elated, enlisted his mother's help for the final packing. Joanne had to veto extras by making it clear that there was to be only one piece of luggage per person. When he eventually closed his bag, Joanne fully expected that the zipper wouldn't hold, but somehow it did.

"You better make sure you lock this thing," she told him. "I would hate to see your stuff all over the airport in Denver." He laughed the laugh of a child nurtured in a good balance of love and discipline. Joanne rubbed his head gently and kissed him good-night after he promised to go to sleep early.

When Joanne inspected her daughter's packing, she was confronted with pleadings that a small extra tote was needed since her bag was smaller than Jason's. Joanne had to agree, and Terri hugged her mother in appreciation.

When the children had settled down and she had completed a last inspection of the house, Joanne went about her own packing. She was busy folding a sweater when the phone rang.

"Kid, I want you to promise me one thing."

"And, what's that, Carol?"

"That we'll be able to get together when you get back from Vail before you leave for Hawaii. You'll make time, won't you?"

"Of course. I'm not leaving until a week Tuesday. How about Monday?"

"That'd be great."

"Let me guess. You want to be the first to know how things went in Colorado between Roger and me."

"Absolutely. Kid, no one deserves to know more than me. I've been wishing for a reconciliation for two years now. It's about time you worked things out."

"Don't hold your breath."

"I'm an optimist and I say you'll get back together. Anyway, have a good trip. You're lucky. I wish my husband would take me on a trip like that. Sometimes I wonder why I married a guy who doesn't ski!"

A moment after Joanne hung up, the telephone rang again.

"Remember the lawyer I told you was looking for another apartment?" Roger said after salutations were exchanged. "Well, he came to look at it again this evening and has agreed to sublet."

"Great!"

"I was lucky to find someone so quickly, even though I'll be losing a month's rent since he'll be taking it only at the end of next month."

"I'll split the cost with you, if you want."

"JoJo, don't be silly. All set for tomorrow? I mean…you haven't changed your mind, have you?"

"Why would I want to do that?"

"Because it's the first time you've accepted one of my invitations in the last two years. I suppose I keep thinking that you'll have second thoughts."

"Roger, I'm not playing a game. I want to spend time with the kids before I go away. And besides, I love Vail."

"Good. If it's okay with you, I'll be over around eight and we can all have breakfast at the airport."

Joanne finished her packing, then made her way downstairs where she poured herself a good measure of gin. She sat in the living room, with only the soft light of the street lamp shining through the sheer curtains, and slowly sipped the liquor. She was certain the next seven days would be the hardest of her life. She wondered how she would find the strength to put up a cheerful and composed outward comportment, knowing that this was to be their last moments of closeness as a family; that soon she would be separated from those she loved most.

After a while, she reasoned, *Since I have managed my life very well since Dr. Calder's shocking announcement, there is no reason for me to falter in this, my last hurdle. I will keep my objective clearly demarcated should thoughts of the future spring up like rain on a bridal procession.*

The gin relaxed her. She closed her eyes and her life paraded in front of her. Moment by moment she analyzed it—from the most painful and agonizing to the most happy and ecstatic. On balance she had to concede that fate had been good to her. She had experienced forty years when so many—like her mother—had been given a more meager tally, and in those forty years she had been able to follow a course that had for the most part been enjoyable. Even now, with the death knell a short distance away, she was afforded the opportunity of managing what was left of her life the way she wanted. Many women did not have that option.

The persistent ringing of the telephone woke her up. Feeling somewhat groggy, she went to answer, surprised that it was daylight and that she had slept on the sofa all night.

"Good morning," Roger said. "Just wanted to make sure you were awake. Are you?"

"Just getting up now," she replied. She did not remember falling asleep; she only knew she felt rested.

Chapter Twelve

The day was still bright when Joanne pointed to the village that came into view. From the back seat, Terri and Jason cheered at having finally reached their destination. Roger had easily driven the family out of Denver in their rented car directed by Joanne's instructions as she read the map whose spiderweb of roads she could only vaguely recollect. The trip had taken longer than Roger had anticipated; however, the sight of the village of Vail with the high peak as a backdrop had a soothing effect on everyone.

Roger took a folded piece of paper from his pocket, and Joanne read the directions from the owner of the condo. A few minutes later, Roger was parking the car near a four-story modern building. As she got out of the car and stretched, Joanne saw the many chimneys protruding above the roof of the building and guessed that each apartment had its own fireplace. The air was full of the rich smell of burning dry wood and it transported Joanne to many years earlier, the first time she had been in Vail.

She could almost hear the laughter emanating from the inexpensive hotel where the group of young skiers had lodged. It had been a happy time, a time of free abandon, when enjoyment of life had preeminence over everything else. For young Joanne, it had also been a time of discovery. It amazed her that now she remembered only vaguely the young man who had made love to her, awkwardly, ineptly, but with the dedication of the young. She had been only briefly captivated by the young man, but she still recalled this milestone experience as sincere and tender.

"You must see quite a change since the last time you were here," Roger said, taking her out of her reverie.

With a soft smile, she replied, "Yeah, but it's still charming."

"Just like you," Roger said, while the children brought in the ski equipment to the door. Joanne looked at him for a short moment and knew that he was sincere. They smiled at each other, and got busy with the luggage.

From the raves, it was obvious everyone was delighted with the accommodations, their home for the next few days. A spiral staircase separated the two levels of the apartment, which was furnished in Colonial style. Terri and Jason quickly claimed two bedrooms on the second floor, leaving Roger in the third one with its own fireplace. Joanne settled in the small room on the first floor, next to the large combination living-dining room with its imposing fireplace. A bathroom, a large hot tub, and a compact kitchen made up the rest of the first floor.

With the children complaining that they were hungry, the Blakes went out to explore the village and find a restaurant. Terri and Jason marveled at the holiday atmosphere of the shops with their glittering Christmas lights, and seemed to momentarily forget their hunger. Each store was an exciting revelation.

Stomach distress was Joanne's companion as they walked around. The excitement and the trip had drained her. They finally ate a light meal at a fast food restaurant, and Joanne was grateful for the opportunity to swallow a painkiller in the restroom. After coaxing her children into helping with grocery shopping, while Roger went to buy lift tickets for the week ahead, she began feeling better. She was dreaming of a long soak in the hot tub back at the condo while the butcher was cutting her meat order, when she heard a somewhat familiar voice. "Joanne? Can it possibly be you?"

Joanne stared with her mouth half open at a mature version of a face she had known years earlier. The man, who was about her age, was just under six feet with a markedly receding hairline of dark blond hair. Despite his ski suit, she could appreciate the taut shape of someone for whom physical activity was still very important. "Dennis? God, this is a small world!"

"I've been looking at you for a few minutes. I just couldn't believe it. You've hardly changed."

"You still lie very well, Dennis."

"It's the truth. How many years has it been?"

"Too many to count! I kept up with your career for a while. You did well. A silver medal, nothing to sneeze at! I felt very proud to have skied with you when I watched you on TV."

"Unfortunately, it's ancient history. What are you doing in Vail?"

"Skiing vacation with my husband and our two kids. They're in one of those aisles, no doubt filling the cart with all sorts of junk," Joanne said moving about, looking for signs of their whereabouts. Dennis Mercer was still standing in the same spot, staring at her, when she returned. "What about you, Dennis? What are you doing here?"

"Me? I live here. Been in Vail for over five years now. I invested in a hotel, but I still manage to coach skiers who come here to train."

"That's sounds great."

"It is." Changing the subject abruptly, he added, "I'm surprised to hear you're here with your husband. Someone from the old gang who was up here last year—Bill Walker, you must remember him? Sure you do. You two went together for a while, if I'm not mistaken. He told me you were separated from your husband."

Bill Walker. Of course, Joanne thought suddenly. *That's the name of the young man responsible for my fond memories of Vail. He still manages to keep abreast of the happenings in my life.* She felt touched. To Dennis Mercer she said, "We decided to take a family vacation for the sake of the children. That's all. We're quite civilized about it all. What about you? Married? Children?"

"None of the above, although I was married for a while. It just didn't work out and I guess I've been sort of scared about trying again."

Terri and Jason rejoined their mother and the proper introductions were made. Before leaving, Joanne explained to Dennis where the family was lodging and invited him for after-dinner drinks. He quickly accepted.

As she had promised herself, Joanne soaked in the hot tub while the dinner roast was cooking. She had been enjoying the relaxing effect of the water on her thin body for some ten minutes when Roger asked to join her. Technically she was his guest. He, more than anyone else, had the right to enjoy all the amenities at their disposal.

At her affirmative response, he sat on the side of the tub, dangling a foot in the water. "I hear you've invited an old boyfriend over."

Joanne was taken aback by the sprinkle of sarcasm in his tone, but answered matter-of-factly. "He was on the ski team. You know him: Dennis Mercer. He was at White Mountain the day we met. I hadn't seen him in years and I thought it might be nice to reminisce a little."

"I think you should have asked me before inviting anyone over," Roger said, now unmistakably irritated.

Technically she was his guest, but she was also an adult. "Well, I'm sorry!" Joanne replied, her voice mocking. "Perhaps you should have set down on paper the conditions for this trip before we left, Roger—all in concise legalese. Then we would not be facing this problem, because I'd have known that I'm to be governed at all times by the decisions and the policies that you and you alone choose."

"Give me a break, JoJo. All I'm saying is that you could have mentioned it to me when we got back here instead of my having to hear it from the children."

"It just skipped my mind. Terri and Jason were so excited about everything they saw that I..."

"Forget it," Roger said sharply, then added in a softer voice. "For the sake of the children, please let's not argue."

Roger, you're the one who started it, Joanne wanted to say, but checked herself. *It will not solve whatever is bothering Roger.* The pain in her stomach came back suddenly, sharply, and she closed her eyes as she took a deep breath. *Is Roger afraid there might be competition at a time when he wants me exclusively to himself?* The next week could turn out to be more difficult than she had envisaged for reasons not at all related to those she had contemplated. She could feel him staring at her, and opened her eyes.

Abruptly, he shifted his glance.

"I had no intention of upsetting you, Roger, believe me."

"Let's have a good week, JoJo."

Joanne and Roger were enjoying after-dinner coffee by the roaring fire in the living room when Dennis Mercer appeared at the door. Under his jacket he was wearing a blue turtleneck that showed off his tan to advantage. Although he was not what most people would consider handsome, Joanne thought that his overt exuberance for life, which put Roger at ease, made him attractive.

The adults sipped cognac and the visitor produced an old album of photos taken when he and Joanne were on the ski team. As each picture was examined and explained, Joanne was once more young and full of life. She laughed loudly at the children's remarks about the vintage ski equipment and dress code. The evening made her forget the script fate had written for her, and she found herself wishing it would go on a while longer. Before leaving, Dennis extracted a promise from Roger and Joanne to be his guests for dinner at his hotel before leaving Vail.

With the laughter and the shared memories of the past few hours still dancing in her head, Joanne fell asleep easily. She never heard Roger's knock on her bedroom door after he had changed into new blue pajamas.

Unrestrained, the Blakes displayed a great deal of style and skill as they skied in single file down the majestic slopes, the adults exhibiting the indisputable aplomb of years of practice and the children showing the promise of the devoutly trained young. All week the sun warmed and colored the skiers' faces with the surging energy of its approaching spring axis. Joanne began to believe that the previous ten days or so had somehow been just a bad dream. She was again feeling as she had many years earlier, when skiing was the sole aim of her existence and life was effortless in its unfolding. To presume that it should suddenly end without regard for her innermost aspirations was surely the fantasy of an incubus!

With each day's skiing over, invigorated by the zest of physical activity in the fresh air, the Blakes welcomed the warm haven of their living quarters. Terri and Jason rushed to their upstairs rooms to change into their bathing suits and race each other into the hot tub, while Joanne and Roger enjoyed a cup of hot coffee before joining their children. As she watched the affectionate exchanges between Roger and his children, Joanne contemplated that her husband was happier than he had been in a long time. Now that the children were getting older, he seemed more at ease, more eager to enjoy their company as much as he could for as long as he could.

Everyone helped with dinner, after which they sat by the fire Roger kept stoking, telling stories and playing games until the children, exhausted from the wholesome fatigue of the day, sauntered off to their rooms.

Joanne and Roger could then enjoy discussing the children's exploits on the slopes or the beauty and serenity of their surroundings, unashamed of the silence that sometimes fell between them. It was totally savored as if the years of quiet affection and understanding they had written together had never been interrupted.

Soon, warmed by the fire, Joanne's head nodded involuntarily. In the first few days, she had simply let her body fall on the sofa to welcome sleep, but Roger had awakened her, as much as he could, and helped her to her bed. Her body and spirit had welcomed the hours of restful sleep that obliterated the turmoil of her future.

By midweek, Roger was disappointed and it nagged at him. When, in the kitchen of their once-shared home, JoJo had finally accepted his invitation to Vail, he had wanted to shout in jubilation. A few days later, he became certain that a new closeness would naturally flow from the love they shared as eagerly as young, unfulfilled lovers in that delightful midday episode in his apartment.

Each night his hunger for her had to be suppressed as fatigue caught up with her early, and he began thinking that perhaps JoJo was skillfully playing a game of avoidance. Perhaps she regretted the sexual, loving encounter they had shared at her invitation. He had to find out.

In the first few days, whenever they used the double chair lift, Joanne went up with one of her children, leaving the other to share the next chair with Roger. On several occasions he suggested that the children go up by themselves, but Joanne had simply ignored his remarks. By midweek, he was determined to get his way. As the family skied to the chair lift departure point, Roger kept at Joanne's side, and as they were getting ready to line up on the double set of tracks furrowed in the snow by the constant traffic, Roger jabbed one of his poles directly in front of his wife, stopping her abruptly. He motioned to Terri and Jason, "You two go ahead. Your mom and I will follow."

Joanne did not miss the smile that quickly appeared on her daughter's face as she and Roger followed their offsprings in silence.

"I was tired of you ignoring me," Roger said when the chair had settled after the jerky start.

"How can you say that? We've been together constantly since we've been here."

"Yes, we have, but always with the children."

"Wasn't that the whole idea of this vacation, that it'd be a family affair?"

"Of course, and I'm enjoying being with them immensely. But I also want to spend time alone with you."

"Roger, we've been spending time together every evening after the children go to bed."

"Oh, yeah. Of course. The five minutes before you fall asleep in my face!"

Joanne chuckled at her husband's choice of words. "Roger, believe me, it hasn't been my fault. It's just that after eating, I feel completely wiped out from all this fresh air and exercise."

It was partially true. She had fallen asleep early the first couple of nights. The previous evening she had not been quite as tired and had playacted the overwhelming fatigue. When Roger had come to sit close to her on the long sofa after stirring the logs in the fireplace, she had closed her eyes, her head on one of the cushions. She was now wondering if he had seen through her facade.

"JoJo, how about you and I having dinner in town together tonight? Terri and Jason might enjoy going out by themselves and meeting other kids. What do you say?"

"Sure. We could hold Dennis Mercer to his invitation."

"No, JoJo. I mean just the two of us."

Joanne looked down at the gorge below their ski-fitted feet and was suddenly frightened. She knew height had nothing to do with it. She was afraid because Roger was pushing her against a wall. She needed his strong arms around her frail body and she longed for shared intimacy more than at any other time since they had been together. Yet she had to refuse. Her acceptance would propel Roger into a new round of efforts to try and convince her not to go away. She could no more change her plans than she could tell him the reason behind her decision. "Roger, it might not be a good idea."

"What are you afraid of, JoJo? That there'll be a repeat of what happened in my apartment last week?"

"Maybe."

"What of it? We're still married."

"I'm not going to change my mind about going away, Roger."

"I know. You're strong-willed and you're going to do what you want, no matter what I think—perhaps to get even with me. Maybe I deserve it. However, I still don't see why we shouldn't try to grab the precious moments that could be ours this week. Memories are very important, don't you think?"

"Last week you felt that I had used you. What would be different now?"

"I was way out of line, JoJo. I was hurting at the thought of you going away, especially since I was just about to make a supreme effort to win you back. To make amends."

She did not reply.

"I'd like to start now and continue when you come back. What do you say?"

He was looking at her, his cheeks beginning to redden in the cold air. She knew him well and she saw that the tender look in his eyes was sincere. *How can I tell him that I won't be back. He is right on one point. Memories are important, more so now than ever. Memories are all that will soon be left for me to hold on to. Why not be indulgent and write memories? On the other hand, will we not merely bask in each other's passion, leaving unresolved the distress that led to our separation? Clearly, an attempt at a resolution at this point is useless.*

Joanne was remembering how tired she had been. After someone in New York had taken their best-selling over-the-counter pain reliever to task for causing strokes, Scalls-Morton's star had become a bomb that threatened to destroy the entire organization. However, company reaction had been wise and swift, but not without a human cost of personal sacrifice and exhaustion.

It had happened at a time when Roger was himself involved in a sensational case, defending a high-profile female banker accused of fraud. There had been little time for family life as both were forced to commit themselves fully to their work. For a while, they hardly saw Terri and Jason, who were left in the care of Mrs. Lucas and Mary Malton, the latter fully aware that the turmoil at Scalls-Morton was no small task for the director of public relations.

After it became clear that the lunatic who had launched the lawsuit wanted to make a quick buck by settling out of court, Scalls-Morton had retaliated with its own legal stand. It had been a long day for Joanne, and it was nine o'clock by the time she had finally been able to leave her office. Roger was himself working late, so she drove by his building, hoping that they might have a nightcap in town before going home. She did not have to take the elevator up to his office. As she was about to park her car, Roger had come out of the building arm-in-arm with a tall blonde, kissing her before helping her into a sports car and himself taking the passenger seat. Joanne had recognized the woman as the banker he was defending and had followed them to the woman's house.

Joanne waited in her own car a few houses away, feeling cold and miserable, until midnight, when a cab picked up Roger, who kissed the woman lingeringly before leaving.

That night, Joanne's world had collapsed. Roger had repeated that he did not love the woman and that he had simply been mesmerized into confusing feelings. At times she believed him. Today, on the chair lift, she saw no reason not to. She smiled faintly at him. "Let's see how good you are at making amends."

Roger's gloved hand went up around the back of her neck. She felt the soothing, affectionate touch through the thickness of her scarf. After a moment, warmth spread down touching every cell of her body.

It was well past noon when Joanne, racing against herself with perfect weight shift and body rotations, interrupted her adroit descent to glide her skis, the two tips so close as to be one, to an easy stop on the side of the steep slope. Roger and the children, not too far behind.

"What's up, Mom?" Jason asked.

"I think we should stop for lunch."

"Great," Terri said. "Let's go to the restaurant just there," she added, pointing with one of her poles. "It's just down a ways."

"I'm all for it," Roger said. "Race you down," he challenged, turning quickly and pointing his skis downward. Soon he was a high-speeding silhouette, showing off perfectly controlled movements and skillfully adapting to the surface of the snow. Terri and Jason followed their father, their turns and twists a little less refined, but nevertheless worthy of notice. Joanne felt proud as she watched their descent.

"They're good," a voice said, as if reading her mind. She turned to see Dennis Mercer stopped a few feet above her, his skis parallel to hers. "I can see your influence in their style."

"Come on, Dennis. You haven't seen me ski in almost two decades."

"Wrong. I've been skiing behind you and your gang all morning. You certainly haven't lost your form."

"Thanks. That's terribly nice coming from an Olympic medalist. Do you ski every day?"

"Not every day, but I do try to put in a couple of mornings a week."

"You lucky dog."

"I'm not complaining, believe me. Are you free for lunch or are you meeting your family?"

"My gang's waiting. Why don't you join us?"

"I think I will."

The children stood at the cafeteria counter, trying to decide what to eat, while Roger found an empty table near the large glass wall of the restaurant overlooking the slope they had just tackled. He loosened his boots and was gently rubbing his ankles when he saw Joanne and Dennis Mercer racing down and coming to a sharp and precise stop near the ski rack. They exchanged humorous remarks as they kicked off their skis, and Roger felt a pang of jealousy. Dennis belonged to a wedge of Joanne's life that he, Roger, had not shared. It made him feel like an outsider. Dennis picked up Joanne's equipment and secured it with his own on the rack while they talked and laughed. Soon he put his arm into hers as they came into the restaurant. The sight made Roger glower, but he managed a faint smile as their bulky boots clicked in unison on the hard floor.

The two men shook hands, and Dennis praised the family's great form on the hills. Roger sensed that the compliments were directed at his wife and felt uncomfortable, out of place. In the two years since their separation, Roger had often wondered with whom JoJo had made love. The thought of a strange face on the pillow, which had been his for so many years, raised an anger in him that he found hard to control. He had often questioned his children, discreetly, only to learn that they had never seen any of their mother's dates. But on the weekends when he took the children on short trips, he imagined JoJo sharing intimate, candlelight dinners with a slew of different men, who eventually carried her upstairs to the bedroom in *his* house.

He had wondered if she ever thought of him when she caressed the strangers with the firm, yet delicate movement of her hands he so desperately craved. He prayed that during such encounters his face had haunted her mind just as her face had flashed in front of him during his liaisons with the few women he took to bed. He had tried desperately to shut her off, but she always returned. These women, whose names he would have been at a loss to remember, had been quite frank. "Get rid of that monstrous torch before you call me again." He never called back.

Seeing Dennis chatting away with JoJo, making her laugh, making her happy, frustrated Roger. During their marriage, he and JoJo had seldom laughed. *Our relationship was one of deep passion and soft smiles. Is that not the sort of marriage that should have gone on forever?*

"Well, are you going to eat or just pout?" Roger heard Joanne ask him.

"Of course. What do you want? I'll get it."

The two men went to the counter together. "You're lucky to have kids. I wish I did," Dennis said.

"It's not too late," Roger commented, glad that the server behind the counter interrupted the conversation.

At the table, Dennis impressed the children with his account of the history of the various Colorado ski areas while Roger ate in silence, his mind wondering if Joanne would have been tempted into Dennis' arms, had she been here alone. He concluded it would be a natural.

"So, when are you going to take me up on my offer of a gourmet dinner at my hotel?" Dennis asked, his eyes on Joanne.

"How about Friday evening," JoJo replied, looking momentarily at Roger, who did not protest.

"That'd be great. I'll reserve a nice table for five. At the risk of sounding pretentious, I must tell you that my food is the best you can get in these parts."

Well, buddy, we'll be the judge of that, Roger thought, exasperated.

That evening, while Joanne and the children were getting ready for their night out, Roger had lingered in the hot tub. He was well aware that his feelings of jealousy were a total waste of energy. Just as he had, his estranged wife had been free to befriend whomever she had wanted. *It is irrational for me to be bothered by what might or might not have happened in her life,* he thought, his eyes closed. *The past has been lived; the only thing that matters now is the present. And if I play the right cards, that present might alter the future. After all, the secure intimacy and the comforting, easy contentment are still here and can possibly bolster my plea for a continued relationship*

"Are you standing me up?" JoJo asked, stopping his thoughts in their track. She was wearing a winter white sweater, which brought out the gleam of red in her shiny brown hair. Her face, colored in the last few days by the sun and the wind, had a healthy, wholesome glow, and, for a moment, he saw a mischievous spark in her dark eyes.

"Of course not," he replied, smiling.

"Terri and Jason have gone already," she said, watching him step out of the water and dry himself. "They were glad to be going out on their own."

"I'll be ready in a flash," Roger said, running past her and up the stairs.

Joanne went to sit by the living room window, pushing aside a brief pang of despair. She was happy and would concentrate solely on prolonging as long as possible the stimulating force the last few days had provided.

She soon heard Roger coming down the steps. He wore a beige sweater, and a rebel curl, which danced effortlessly on his forehead as he moved, made Joanne smile. In maturing, he had somehow managed to retain a certain boyish allure.

They shared an exquisite dinner in a small restaurant, while watching window-shoppers leisurely inspecting the displays in the colorfully lit shops. The conversation centered on the children, with Joanne making a point of alerting Roger to their daughter's seeming lack of confidence.

"You're worrying needlessly, JoJo. All girls that age are like that. I saw enough of them around the house when I was growing up to know. Somehow, by the time they turn eighteen, they miraculously outgrow that stage. You'll see."

No, I won't, Roger, Joanne thought, but, with great effort, concentrated on pushing aside the impending reality. "Perhaps you're right," she said.

"If it'll make you feel better, I'll talk to her." Reaching for her hand across the table he added, "Look, JoJo, we have two great kids, and I think that's mostly due to your giving them so much of your time when I was busy building my career. I've always appreciated it, although I might not have said so. Now, it's my turn and I feel good about the chance to be a full-time dad. Of course, it would be better if you were there as well."

"Roger…" she began.

He squeezed her hand more firmly. "JoJo, you can't blame me for wishing, can you?"

She simply nodded and met his glance. The reflection of the lights against the snow outside made his eyes shimmer, and kept her mesmerized until their server came to offer coffee.

"Would you like to go dancing?"

Roger's question caught her by surprise. "Well, I don't know. Are there any decent places around here? Without the loud music, I mean," she said, indicating other diners in the restaurant with her hand, "everyone seems to be so young."

"Well, in that case, 'old lady,' can I take you home?"

Chapter Thirteen

In the entrance hall of their condo, Roger drew JoJo to him after closing the door noiselessly. His arms circled her and her head nestled on his shoulder for a long embrace.

"I'd better check on the kids," she said softly in his ear.

"Let me do it." He took a few steps toward the stairs, then doubled back to firmly kiss her warm lips. "Don't go anywhere."

He took the steps two at a time and checked the rooms of his two sleeping children in succession. *The gods are being kind. Please make JoJo change her mind,* he prayed.

He went to his own room to change into his new pajamas and was quickly on his way back downstairs. He found JoJo standing by the window of the living room, studying the mountains in the distance. He gently slipped his arms around her waist. "They're both sound asleep. Would you like a drink?" he asked.

"No, thank you." She covered his hands with hers and soon felt warm and gentle kisses spreading from the side of her neck to the back under her shoulder-length hair. No reason in the world would justify her asking him to stop. His lips reached her earlobe, and as his teeth gently bit in, she purred with delight. *How many times, alone in bed in the dark of night, have I yearned for this simple yet wonderfully erotic gesture!* Shortly, he was nibbling at her other ear. *How can I ever have let him go!*

Effortlessly, he led her to turn around and, holding her face in his strong hands, repeatedly kissed her open mouth. Her hands went around his neck, as they had so often done, caressing his hair as she accepted him with feverish desire.

When he released her, he whispered softly, "What precious time we've wasted!"

She smiled softly and thought of her friend Carol's remark. *Our living apart has, indeed, been a damn waste. Perhaps Roger is right. I may not have been completely blameless in the collapse of our marriage, but that is no reason to waste time now.* She searched for his hand and he followed her into her bedroom.

A silvery beam from the full moon high in the clear sky penetrated into the room, weaving a glittery cloak on everything it touched. Joanne was seated on the bed, and slowly kneeling in front of her Roger was unbuttoning her jacket. He slipped off the vest, and his mouth tenderly kissed the white skin of her shoulders, making its way down to her partially exposed breasts. He slipped his hands behind her, but found it difficult to unhook her brassiere.

"Why don't you let me do it?" she said softly, easily undoing it and tossing it on the chair.

"You realize, of course, that this embarrassing moment is entirely due to my lack of practice!"

With me, you no doubt mean, she thought, but quickly dismissed the disturbing reflection. *Why torture myself now that he is all mine.* He was caressing her breasts and she felt her passion rising quickly inside.

"How I've missed you, JoJo," he said before torridly kissing her craving mouth.

After he had removed her remaining garments, she guided him on his back and began to kiss him. Starting on his forehead, her mouth traveled to his mouth and to his ears. He heard the words he was longing for her to say, "Roger, I've never stopped loving you." His arms went around her and she was fully aware of his strong arousal as he clutched her small frame so strongly that she gasped, unable to breathe for a moment.

He released her, and she let her body fall back beside him.

"Something wrong?" he asked.

His vigorous embrace, or perhaps the wine she had sipped at dinner, brought on a twinge of pain in her stomach, which made her mouth twitch.

"Of course not." She smiled, forcibly at first, but her determination, now more than ever, to fight yearnings of self-pity won out. "You should be careful. That hug of yours was almost lethal," she told him with a mischievous grin.

"I'm sorry, hon."

"The only way I'm going to forgive you is if you make it up to me!"

"If you say so!"

His soft kisses quickly became inflamed with mutual arousal as their hands stroked and fondled with a comfortable and enthusiastic reciprocity until neither could restrain the intoxication.

Joanne had totally forgotten the turmoil in her stomach, and welcomed him inside her as enraptured as someone deeply underfed would accept an exquisite feast. His potent thrusts brought their shared unrestrained excitement to a breathless level of ecstasy that she considered would never be repeated.

But repeated it was. Each night until they returned home on Sunday they found in each other total gratification and reconciliation. The past two years were erased and forgotten as the present became an aphrodisiac and the future nonexistent.

"I suppose I understand," Terri said, her eyes downcast, "but a year is such a long time!"

"It seems a long time now," Joanne replied, caressing the black curls of the girl sitting on the floor, "but it'll be over before you know it, believe me." Together in the living room of the condo, the Blakes were enjoying a couple of monstrously large pizzas while discussing Joanne's impending trip. On their last night in Vail, Joanne would have preferred to forget reality for a few more hours, but the subject had to be dealt with for everyone's peace of mind.

"There's nothing preventing us from visiting Mom in Hawaii during summer vacation," Roger put in, flashing a grin.

"Cool!" the children exclaimed, almost in unison.

For a moment, Joanne panicked at the possibility she had not considered, but she was able to remain calm and think quickly without giving herself away. "I'll be living with other students, so I probably won't be able to put you up. It would be terribly expensive, Roger."

"Probably, but it would be well worth it for all of us," he replied, winking at her.

Damn, Joanne thought. *What now? Relax. Better not make a fuss. Let it ride.*

"Boy, that would be neat," Jason exclaimed. "I could learn to surf!"

"I don't know anyone who's gone to Hawaii," Terri said, suddenly realizing that her mother's departure might have some advantages after all.

Calmly, Joanne said, "I'll write to you and let you know all about it and then your father can decide." Her laboriously calculated plan had flaws after all. The thought depressed her. She would have to work hard at finding a way to dissuade Roger from going to Hawaii. She had to.

"You don't seem too keen on us going to Hawaii," Roger said as he lay close to her. They had once more shared a totally satisfying rapture.

"That's not the problem, Roger. I have absolutely no idea at this point what my schedule's going to be like. What if I can't spend much time with you? The children might feel cheated."

"My God, you're certainly going to have a few hours off each day. That would be enough. The rest of the time we could go to the beach and visit around."

Double damn, Joanne thought angrily. She knew Roger would start planning a trip as soon as they returned home, and she couldn't think of any argument to stop him. She said, "I'll get in touch as soon as I can and we'll go from there. When would you want to make the trip?"

"It would have to be in August. As you know, old man McBride always takes off in July for his annual golf binge, and Porteous spends the month at his cottage. They want the rest of us around while they're gone. I could probably get away the second week of August."

Perhaps she wouldn't have to do anything after all. By that time, she would be very near the end. Dr. Calder would be more than happy to break the news to Roger. "I'll keep that date in mind. Who knows, perhaps I could make arrangements for time off in August."

Joanne turned on her side, away from Roger. He covered her naked body and put a firm hand around her waist. "Try to put on some weight while you're in Hawaii. You're wasting away."

"I'll try," she said.

"Good night, JoJo. Happy?"

"Very."

In response, Roger kissed the back of her neck.

In the dismal scenario she had to follow, Roger was playing a delightful role, and she was grateful for having been granted a gust of blissful escape. She had not lied to him. She was very happy, and she decided to concentrate on savoring the feeling a little longer instead of attempting to solve future problems that would come soon enough. A moment later, she fell into a renewing sleep.

Chapter Fourteen

Joanne was carrying two large bags containing enough personal-care items to last her, she hoped, a few months. Satisfied that she had everything she needed, she was making her way to one of the mall's exit doors when she froze dead in her tracts. Her friend Carol had entered the mall and was headed in her direction, at least a half hour early for their lunch date. Luckily, store windows had her attention.

Joanne quickly turned and headed toward another exit. She had to get rid of her purchases before Carol started to ask a thousand questions. Someone traveling by plane to Hawaii would not bother with all she had in the bags. She took a last long look down the large expanse sparsely dotted with Monday morning shoppers, and sighed with relief. Carol was now nowhere to be seen.

High in sky, the sun was in the first inning of its struggle to melt winter into submission, and the thought that spring was approaching lifted Joanne's spirit. Her self-imposed exile would be easier to bear in a setting concerned solely with new life, new beginnings. *Dare I think it might even postpone the inevitable!* She dropped her packages in the trunk of her car and walked back to the mall, forcing herself to concentrate on the light of the day, rather than on the darkness of night that would be hers soon enough.

She smiled her brightest smile when she saw Carol.

"Hi, kid. How was Vail? What a stupid question. You look like a million bucks. I don't know if it's the tan, but you look rejuvenated."

"Thanks. I had a great time. We all did."

Putting a hand through JoJo's arm, Carol lowered her voice. "So, how did it go?"

"I told you. It was great."

"Come on. You know what I mean. How did you and Roger get along?"

"We always get along, Carol. Let's go and find a place to eat," Joanne said, gently pulling the other woman in the direction of a delicatessen.

"Don't do this to me. I won't see you for a year. I think I have the right to know. I demand to know," Carol said, stopping abruptly.

When Joanne went on without comment, she reluctantly caught up to her friend.

"At least tell me if there's a chance things will work out when you come back?" Carol asked after they had chosen a table.

"I don't know about a year from now," Joanne said finally, "but right now we could make a go of it. I think I understand why Roger did what he did."

"In that case, kid, don't go to Hawaii. Grab him now."

"I have to go, Carol."

"You don't *have* to. Just say no to Peter Malton. He'd be the first one to understand. As you say, who knows about a year from now. It might be too late. Do you really want to risk it, kid?"

No, I don't, but I have no choice. Again, the supreme effort to smile. "That trip is important to me, Carol. I'm going."

"Important enough to, maybe, have to give up Roger a second time? In case you've forgotten, I remember how you felt when you two separated. You were so lost, for a while I was afraid you'd go off the deep end. I don't want to see you go through the same thing again."

"It's a chance I'll have to take."

"JoJo, I don't understand you. No job is worth risking a marriage over."

"Perhaps not, but I can't change my plans."

"You won't, you mean."

"Carol, please. My mind's made up. Let's talk about something else."

"I think you're a fool, kid. Unless…"

"Unless what?"

"Unless you're meeting someone in Hawaii. Of course, that's your business."

Joanne laughed fleetingly. "Your imagination's running wild."

"Is it? It's the only plausible reason for your determination."

"I only wish it were true," Joanne said, meaning it. She was tired of the conversation, and decided to end the discussion abruptly. "By the way, Carol, do you know who we ran into in Vail? Dennis Mercer."

"Really!"

"I'd forgotten. He was your boyfriend for a while, wasn't he?"

"For a while. We had a great time, if you know what I mean," Carol said, with an impish smile, "but he wasn't my type. What's he doing now?"

Joanne answered Carol's many questions about Dennis, and the two women ended their meal reliving the life they had shared on the ski team.

"I hope you'll be in touch," Carol said as they headed for the parking lot.

"I'm sure I'm going to be busy, but I'll certainly try."

"I hope you do more than try!" Carol said as she warmly embraced her friend.

Tears swelled up in Joanne's eyes, and she was unable to control her voice. "Goodbye, Carol. Thanks for everything."

"Come on, kid. I know it's hard to leave," Carol said, a gloved index finger wiping a tear from Joanne's cheek. "I only wish I knew why you're doing it...and why you didn't trust me enough to tell me!"

Joanne saw hurt in her friend's eyes. For a fraction of a second, she contemplated telling Carol the truth, but the idea was quickly dismissed. The hurt of the parting would be brief, so much briefer than the pain the truth would generate.

"Carol, one day you'll understand," Joanne said, quickly getting in behind the wheel of her car and turning the key.

The words she wrote inside the white card were simple, but they said it all. After returning home, Joanne thought for a long time before finally writing the note to Roger. She tried to imagine his expression as he read it, but to no avail. She supposed that she simply couldn't let herself see him overwhelmed by pain.

She reread her words before putting the card inside its envelope and passing it through the white satin ribbon decorating the large box wrapped in blue paper.

She had finally found the right words for her husband's birthday card, and Mrs. Lucas had promised to deposit the gift in plain view when Roger's birthday arrived in August. Joanne could only wish that by then the reasons for her lack of communication would be clear. At least he would know she had spared him.

Joanne put the box in the closet of the spare room next to the gifts for her children, and quickly closed the door, pushing back tears. *The parting will not be easy but*, she consoled herself, *I am at least giving my family a few extra memories that, had I not been so strong, would have been denied.* The thought was meager consolation.

In her room, she zipped up one of the suitcases on her bed. Since it contained mostly winter clothing, she wanted to put it in the trunk of her car before her children came home from school. She was pushing the trunk closed when she saw the luxury sedan stop in front of the house, and Peter and Mary Malton getting out. Joanne felt suddenly very sad.

"Can we talk, JoJo?" Peter asked.

"Of course. Come in," she invited.

When they were all seated comfortably in the living room, Peter spoke. "Still going ahead with your plan, JoJo?"

"Yes," she answered with firmness.

"We understand your not wanting to tell your family," Mary said. "We have accepted it because we know you won't change your mind, but we want to keep in touch. It's not too much to ask, is it? We can't let you down in your hour of pain and grief. We want to be there to help you, do whatever we can for you."

"JoJo, we can't stand the thought of you all alone in the country. We want to visit you, help you through this." The familiar kindness was unmistakable in Peter's eyes.

Joanne looked at each of her friends in turn. They had always been there for her and she would never be able to repay them. She had to let them down easy. "I'm going to be comfortable only if you don't know where I'm going to be living. I will, however, give you my telephone number as I had promised."

"JoJo, you know damn well that I could easily find out the location of that telephone, even if it's unlisted, so why don't you spare me the trouble?" Peter asked in a sad voice.

Joanne got up and went to stand by the large window. *Peter is right, of course. He could easily find me.* Her plan was full of holes and it made her angry, yet she had no right to be angry at the two people who respected her decision, and whose only concern was providing support. "If I tell you where I'm going to be, do you promise you won't tell Roger?"

"Of course," Mary said. "We agreed to that last week and we'll keep our promise." After a pause, she added, "Don't you see that the only reason we want to know where you're going to be is that we want to keep an eye, a distant eye, on you, to help you if…"

"If I change my mind?"

"Yes. We think you will. When that time comes, we want to be there for you."

"What if I never change my mind?"

"We'll have helped you a little. We're not asking for more," Mary said softly.

"Very well," Joanne said, aware it would be a loss of time and energy to discuss the matter further. As she wrote down her Triton address and phone number for them on a piece of paper, deep inside she was grateful that a line of communication with the outside world would remain open.

The Maltons left just before Terri and Jason came home from school.

Chapter Fifteen

"When are you going to write to us?" Terri asked, melancholy showing on her face.

"Just as soon as I can," Joanne promised, making a sublime effort to keep her voice normal despite the pain that was nearly suffocating her. She was sitting on Terri's bed, an arm around the girl's shoulders.

"I guess this is the last time you come to my room to tell me good night for a while," Terri said sadly.

"In life, things happen that you just can't change."

"You mean, you don't really want to go on that trip?" Terri asked.

"It's not a question of whether I want to or not. I simply have to."

"I still don't understand why. Daddy makes enough money for all of us to live on. You could quit your job and stay here with us. You just don' t want to do that, do you?"

"Terri," Joanne said, "please don't make it any harder than it already is. When you're older, you'll understand."

"When I'm older, when I'm older! That's what you always say when you don't want to explain things. That's what you said when you and Dad split up: 'When you're older, you'll understand.' Well, maybe I understand. You just don't want to make the effort to patch things up with Dad, although he's been trying. So you're running away. That's not fair to Jason and me." Terri's voice had reached a crescendo that took Joanne by surprise.

I am running away, Joanne wanted to tell her daughter, *but not from your father. I'm running away because I love you so very much.* Out loud, she said, "There's nothing I'd want more than for your father and me to be together again. I never stopped loving him, Terri. We had problems to work out, that was all. When I get back, I think we'll be able to go back to the way it used to be."

"But a year, Mom. That's a long time."

"It might be less. Why don't we just wait and see what happens?" Joanne kissed her daughter's cheek as her eyes filled with tears.

Terri warmly embraced her mother. "I just wish you'd stay."

"I know, Terri, I know." Joanne held her daughter to her breast a long time. When she finally let go, she was more determined than ever to fight the hand she had been dealt. She would see her children again.

Jason was already in bed, pouring over a ski equipment catalog, when Joanne came into his room. "I would really like to have new skis," he said, casually. "Mine are not very good anymore. Do you think that for my birthday…"

"Well," Joanne said, wondering how he would react to the array of expensive gifts she had already chosen for him, "why don't you drop a hint to your dad?"

"I will," he said, amiably. "I keep forgetting you won't be here then."

"I certainly will be in thought."

"I wish you were staying, Mom."

Not wanting a confrontation similar to the one she'd just had with her daughter, Joanne said quickly, "I know, but time goes by fast and, who knows, I might be back sooner than you expect."

"Really! That'd be great." He lifted himself up and let his mother's arms encircle his body. "I'll miss you, Mom."

"Not as much as I'll miss you!" Joanne said frankly, now better able to control herself, her new purpose giving her courage.

Joanne sat alone in the dark living room and wept. The tears and sobbing were left uncontrolled to take their natural course. Nearly a half hour passed before the tears were spent. She went to the kitchen to pour herself a stiff drink of gin and tonic, and was returning to the living room when she heard a soft knock on the front door. Through the glass panels, she saw Roger's smiling face.

"Hi. I know it's late, but I had to finish a brief," he explained, coming in, a garment bag in one hand. "That's all I brought tonight. I'll get the rest of my things tomorrow or the day after."

Joanne was taken aback. "I didn't expect you to come over tonight."

"I thought that was understood when we came back last night. I mean, this is going to be our last chance to be together for a long time." He spoke casually as he removed his coat and his boots.

She had half-expected him to come over to say good-bye, but when ten o'clock had come and gone, she figured he had decided to show up in the morning.

"Roger…"

Before she could continue, he took her face into his hands. "You've been crying. I guess I don't blame you. I feel like doing a little bit of that myself." He kissed her lips squarely and Joanne felt unable to move away. "If this trip upsets you so much, why don't you just cancel it?"

"It's too late to cancel."

"Why? You probably just think it is." Seeing the pain in her eyes, he added quickly, "I'm sorry. I promised myself not to bring it up. Can I have one of those, too?" he said, pointing to her glass.

"Of course. There's some Scotch if you want."

"That'd be good. Thanks."

He followed her into the kitchen. "So, at what time is your plane tomorrow? Since I worked late tonight, I'll be free to take a couple of hours off to drive you."

More hitches. The plan, which she thought was perfect, had been devised hurriedly and had failed to take so many factors into consideration. She certainly had not anticipated their new closeness. She watched him pour himself a drink and reminded herself not to panic. Calmly she said, "You don't have to drive me. I've already made arrangements."

"Oh."

"I'm selling my car tomorrow." Another explanation, another lie. "The buyer will drive me to the airport after we finalize the transfer."

"You're selling your car? That's not very wise, JoJo. It's hardly got any mileage. Why don't you just leave it in the garage while you're gone? At least you'd have transportation when you get back."

"I prefer to sell it, Roger," she said sharply.

"Okay. Okay. I don't want to upset you. I'm just trying to be practical." He took a long sip from his glass. At length, he said, "You've changed, JoJo, and I'm afraid I'm finding it difficult to understand you now. There's something bothering you and I think it has to do with the trip somehow. I only wish I knew what it was!"

Joanne sipped her own drink. She had dismissed too quickly the fact that Roger knew her well and could probably see through the lies. "I don't feel like discussing any of this now. I'm very tired, Roger. I just want to go to bed," she said, and made her way up the stairs.

It was definitely not the kind of reception Roger had expected, but he couldn't blame her. *I pushed too hard and she is protecting herself. From what,* he wondered.

Joanne was in bed, the sheets over her head, when he came upstairs. The sight of the room he had not seen in so long made him feel like an intruder. He sat on the side of the bed that used to be his, hoping Joanne would give him a signal that he was welcome. She did not.

"Do you want me to sleep in the spare room?" he asked softly.

There was a long silence before she said, "Of course not." At that moment, the ring of the telephone on her bedside table made her jump.

"Hello, JoJo. How are you? I hope I'm not calling too late."

She wished Dr. Calder would have chosen another moment to call. "Not at all."

"Good. How was the skiing?"

"Just great."

"Good. Now," he said a little abruptly, "let's stop this nonsense. You had promised to call me to let me know where you're going to be. Since you didn't, I was afraid I'd miss you."

"I just didn't have a chance. Can I call you in the morning?"

"D'you swear?"

"I do."

"Very well. I'll talk to you tomorrow then. Good night."

Roger wondered who the late caller was and decided to get right to the point: "JoJo, do you have a boyfriend? Someone you're running away with?"

"What..."

"Don't be afraid. I won't get upset. You're an attractive woman and your husband made a huge mistake. I wouldn't fault you."

"Roger, that call was from the fellow who's buying my car. That's all. Don't read things where there's nothing to read."

"I didn't want to pry. I just want to know where I stand."

"Roger, there is a man in my life...you."

His arms reached for her, pulling her close to his chest. "Thank you, JoJo. I needed to hear it."

She felt warm and satisfied when she fell asleep in his arms some time later.

Chapter Sixteen

Like a frightened child, the sun was hiding behind large gray clouds as Joanne drove to her new home. *I wonder how much Roger's intuition told him, what he suspects. He is a lawyer. He never relies entirely on surface information; he searches for the truth behind the truth. Will he begin to investigate what I did or did not leave behind?*

If he does, he will see that I did not take any of my business clothes. In fact, since I packed only casual slacks, tees, and sweaters, along with a few warmer-weather things, most of my clothes were left behind in my closet, inviting his inspection. Should he decide to look closely, will his inquisitive mind notice that I took two ski jackets?

And if his search were to be at all thorough, will he notice that my laptop is on the floor of my closet, that the painting of the children I have been attempting to finish is no longer around? Nor my brushes and tubes of paint? Hopefully, he will think I gave up painting. Even if he does not, it is too late to look back. I left my past behind. I will force myself to concentrate on the present and only the present. Nothing else matters. I have a purpose that requires all my attention.

She had said her last tearful farewells to her children and her husband many hours earlier, resolute that she would see them again. She kept telling herself, *You just wait and see. I am going to fight. Fight like hell. I'm not going to give my cancer a chance to take a firmer hold on my body. It's my body. My will will win out. It has to win out.*

Reaching the village of Triton, Joanne parked in front of what she judged to be the main grocery store and went in. There were a half-dozen people inside, and she couldn't help notice the curious glances in her direction. She could almost hear the questions, *Wonder who she is? Does she live around here?* It was a strange feeling for Joanne, who was used to the impersonal I-don't-care-about-you-one-bit city. To those who continued to steal glances she responded with a faint smile.

After she transferred her purchases from the cart to the black moving apron at the checkout counter, the cashier began scanning her purchases with what Joanne thought was a robotized hand. "New around here?" she asked.

"Yes, I am."

"I see you have a small family," she said punching in three oranges. "You can tell a lot about people by the food they buy, you know. For example, you got smoked oysters. That tells me you're inclined to want the good things in life."

Joanne suddenly realized that she was listening to the overweight woman with her mouth open. It was definitely going to be difficult to remain anonymous in these parts. She was sure that, within an hour, the whole village would know about the dark-haired woman who likes oysters. "Interesting," Joanne managed to say.

"Where do you live?" the woman pursued, her fingers continuing their agile movements.

"About five miles that way," Joanne replied, pointing to the front of the store.

"Oh, I see," the woman said simply. Joanne was to learn only much later that "five miles that way" was a major employer of the region—a maximum-security correctional institution.

The cashier continued working without another word.

The groceries in her car, Joanne noticed that the clouds had darkened and that the smell of snow was in the air. Spring was definitely not ready to come out of hibernation just yet. She walked to the local bank and was pleased that the money transfer from the city had been completed as she had requested. Like the people in the grocery store, the bank employees did not hide their interest in the new customer. She had landed in Snoopsville!

Under normal circumstances, she might have welcomed the attention, but these were far from normal circumstances. It made her feel uncomfortable as she traveled the country road to her hideaway. When her new home came into view, her mood improved quickly. She drove on to the Wheeler farm to inform

Joe and Agatha that she had arrived and to pick up the key. They both welcomed her warmly.

"If ya need anything, let us know. Don't be shy," Agatha said. "We go to the village for groceries at least once a week. It'd be no trouble to pick up whatever you need."

"Thank you. I may take you up on that," Joanne replied.

"The furnace's been turned on. If ya have problems with it, just yell."

Joanne was cheered by their amiability, and once inside the rented house, the lingering smell of furniture polish and the half-dozen house plants arranged in the living room and kitchen made her appreciate them more.

She had dreaded moving in by herself after being part of a family for so long, but now found a certain pleasure in settling in. Putting her clothes away in the first-floor bedroom, she felt gratified that her course of action had, so far, been successful. She had managed to shield her family. Even if she did not manage to smother the progress of her disease, each day she was away would be one less day of grief for those she loved so very much.

So very much.

By the time darkness fell, she saw through the living room window that snowflakes were lazily adding to the white blanket outside. The only indication of life around her was a faint light sparkling through the curtain of falling snow from across the lake. Momentarily, loneliness engulfed her. She quickly forced herself to focus on the enemy she had to face.

She started a fire in the hearth and soon the flames were steady and bright. The heat warmed her as she sat on the floor, sipping a cup of instant coffee. She knew she should make an effort to eat, but the pain in her stomach made her decide against it. She would wait until she felt better.

The emotional cost of surrendering her orchestrated life had elevated her stress and she contemplated that it was feeding the demon inside her body. *A bad start indeed for the fight I intend to undertake!* She was tempted to take one of the painkillers prescribed by Dr. Calder, but quickly dismissed the idea. Before accepting the conventional, she had to try to contend with the enemy by herself, do battle on her own terms.

The box of books she had brought along stood in a corner. She took them out one by one, examining each, and soon began reading. The words she read fascinated and absorbed her for many hours until sleep became a necessity.

For the next several days, she interrupted her reading only to take a daily walk or when hunger could not be ignored. As she progressed in her search for the specific knowledge that interested her, she took notes. By the time she had devoured all the books, she had filled two dozen pages of a notebook.

She spent the better part of a day scrutinizing and organizing her notes, finally mapping her plan of attack by selecting plausible actions, which could, if not heal, at least ameliorate her physical and emotional condition, as well as her spiritual side. When she was finished, she was sure the list she had devised to guide her new life was a sensible one. She felt that the chances of bringing her disorder to its knees were as legitimate as the therapies proposed by Dr. Calder. And so much easier to face. The fear was now manageable. Deep down, she knew that fear had been and would have been her greatest enemy in accepted therapies, subconsciously parading in front of her the futility and pain of her mother's dark fight.

Her own fight would be full of light and promise.

Secured and pleased by her decision, Joanne was lazily watching the playful flames in the fireplace when her mind wandered to Terri, Jason, and Roger playing out a happy scenario. They were exchanging witty remarks and laughing freely when the telephone on the mahogany table in the corner of the living room surprised her with its intermittent ring.

Only the Maltons and Dr. Calder know the number. Why would they be calling so soon, not giving me a chance to properly adjust to my new milieu? She got up and went to the ancient black instrument, stopping before picking up the receiver. She was not ready to talk to anyone, and decided to let the caller assume she was not in, but the insistent ringing won out.

"Edith?" the male voice said. "Jack won't be able to go help ya saw that wood tomorrow, he's..."

"Sir," Joanne interrupted. "You have the wrong number."

"Oh. Who am I talking to?"

"You have the wrong number," she repeated and put down the receiver.

She had not left the world behind. It was right at her door.

Chapter Seventeen

Despite last minute maneuvers, the tired winter quickly lost ground to the sun-armed attacking spring and hastily withdrew without a trace. The soil overthrew its white blanket to cover itself with new life and color. Around Joanne Blake's country hideaway, yellow and red tulips raised their silky bell-shaped blossoms to watch the maples burgeon into new leaves and the apple trees prepare to show off their pink and white flowers.

Joanne was leisurely looking over a catalogue of seeds left for the former owner by the mail carrier when she saw Agatha Wheeler coming up the drive.

"Good morning. Come in," Joanne invited.

"Don't want to disturb ya," Agatha said, taking the time for a long look around the living room as she sat down on the Victorian sofa.

"You're not disturbing me. I was just trying to figure out what sort of vegetable seeds I should buy. I want to have a large garden."

"That's a good idea. The soil's good. Ya can grow anythin' ya want. Joe can plow the field for ya."

"You're sure he wouldn't mind?"

"Of course not. He'd come in here with his tractor and have the whole field done in a jiffy."

"That would be very nice, Mrs. Wheeler."

"No trouble, my dear. And please call me Agatha. We don't stand on formalities in the country, ya know." Without pausing for more than a second, the visitor continued, "We see ya runnin' every mornin'. D'ya do it in the city?"

Joanne smiled. She was not to be unnoticed in these parts where any unusual behavior was probably welcomed to relieve boredom and loneliness. "No, I didn't run in the city. I only started when I got here." *And I'm getting a little better each day if you noticed*, she wanted to add. "At first, I was out of breath in a few seconds; now I can jog a few minutes before I have to slow down."

"Ya paint?" Agatha wanted to know now, pointing to the easel on which the back of a canvas was visible from where she sat. This was the first time Agatha had been inside the house since Joanne's arrival. She had stopped by a few times with an offer to shop for Joanne in the village, but had never before come in to talk. She was obviously determined to find out more about her neighbor, and Joanne could hear the conversation in the Triton grocery store: *Agatha Wheeler, ya mean to tell me that she's been livin' next door for months and ya still don't know nothin' about her?*

"It's just a hobby. I've just started on this one. I'll show it to you when I'm finished."

"I'd like that," Agatha said frankly, adding, "I'm goin' to the village. Get ya anythin'?"

"I'd like a few things if it's not too much trouble."

"No trouble at all."

"Thank you very much. I've made a list," Joanne said, handing Agatha a piece of paper from the coffee table. Then she went to the bookcase where she took out a couple of bills from the money stashed between the pages of a large book. She knew her visitor was watching with curious eyes, and it made her smile.

"I think a book is a good place to hide money in case someone comes in when I'm out walking or jogging, don't you think?"

The older woman said, rather indignantly Joanne thought, "No robbers around here!"

"Probably not. Force of habit, I guess," Joanne said and handed the money to Agatha, who folded it neatly while apparently searching for the right words to express a question or a remark. Much to Joanne's frustration, she finally said simply, "It's nice to see spring again," and engaged in an insipid conversation.

Once Agatha was gone, Joanne stretched out on the sofa and breathed deeply in an effort to subdue the pain that had assailed her while Agatha chatted. Her attacks were becoming more frequent and harder to handle, but she was determined to continue to fight with her self-ordained regimen.

She closed her eyes and, in the absolute quietness that was now her world, she willed herself to a degree of concentration where any and all thoughts were deleted from her conscious mind. Reinforced by hours upon hours of practice, she reached the level of serenity she had been seeking in record time, and quickly focused on the aim of the exercise: a visualized battle against the diseased cells in her body.

The imagery she had been practicing animated a mission in her mind. A large, self-powered pistol, traveling the maze she had plotted for it, rushed through her body until it reached her stomach. There it went to work. Aiming at malformed cells, it shot white-beamed bullet after white-beamed bullet, each one exploding as multicolored flashes against the imaginary protruding ugly heads of the invaders of her body.

Tenacious, many of them laughed at the attack being mounted against them, but Joanne repeated the mental exercise until the battling weapon had disintegrated one of the miserable intruders. When she opened her eyes, she felt totally relaxed, and noticed that the pain in her stomach was not as fierce as it had been before she began the mental drill. Her efforts had paid off and she savored a great sense of satisfaction at her ability to instruct her mind into such deep concentration.

Two of the books she had read offered countless testimonies of once fatally ill people who had managed to conquer their diseases by using imagery. She saw nothing wrong in trying the same thing. *It could be just as effective,* she reasoned, *as lying inside a long metal capsule while radioactive rays penetrate my body and I die the thousand deaths of intense fear. My choice is so much better.*

Looking out at the lake from the living room window now, she contemplated, *With the warming air, the day when I can swim to my heart's content is not too far off. In the meantime, there is nothing preventing me from fishing.* Her new lifestyle included a strict diet gleaned from the information extracted from the books she had brought with her. Reading and rereading the various data and claims, she had compared, analyzed, and selected. From her selection, she had compiled a long list of foods and vitamin supplements, which she had judged would be most beneficial.

While she tried to feed her family an adequate diet over the years, she had not made an effort to reduce or eliminate what the authors she read claimed were the culprits in the ill-health of Western people. Now, however, every morsel she consumed was as fresh and as natural as possible. She had eliminated meat, but still ate fish.

No reason that fish could not be fresh from the lake in front of her.

Dressed in jeans, now markedly loose around her hips, a bulky off-white sweater, and wearing a pair of work gloves, Joanne made her way to the barn a couple of hundred yards from the house. On her early exploratory inspection, she saw that the barn, no doubt once used by Joe Wheeler's brother to store the harvest of the land, was now mostly empty. Neatly hung on large nails along one wall was an array of implements, including shovels, a mattock, a hoe, large forks, an ax, and saws, while another wall served as storage for more pleasurable items. There was an old pair of cross-country skis that she promised herself to put to the test the following winter when—not if—her health was restored. Also, on that wall were a couple of fishing rods. Having no knowledge of which to use, she picked up the one on which the dark yellow line appeared in good order.

She was trying to determine what sort of bait she could use when a movement across the straw covering the concrete floor gave her a start. She turned around, fully expecting to see a rat or some such unfamiliar animal, and was contemplating making a run for it, when she saw a dog. She smiled because the animal was not totally unknown to her.

"Boy, you startled me," she told the animal as he lazily approached, stopping for a moment to stretch his slender, muscular body and yawn shamelessly. She patted the reddish-brown coat of the mongrel when he stopped at her feet. "What are you doing here, anyway? Is this where you sleep? No wonder you're always around to walk with me in the morning! I'm going fishing. Want to come along?"

The animal followed her into the bright daylight through the small door that was an opening cut from the larger door sitting on a strong steel rail. Joanne smiled when she noticed that the hook that would have kept the small door closed was missing.

"So that's how you've been getting in, is it? Pushing it open with your nose and letting it close by itself. You're a sly one, aren't you?"

Like a team that had been together for a long time, the dog followed her down to the water. Ahead of them, the surface of the lake rippled lightly in the mild breeze, and Joanne took a deep breath. It was indeed good to be alive.

A few days earlier, Joe Wheeler had told her she could use the boat housed in the shed near the lake. "There's oars in the shed, but if you want to use the motor, it's in your basement. I'd be glad to bring it to the lake when you're ready." She told him she had no intention of using the boat, especially one with a motor, since it was all foreign to her. "This motor's a piece of cake. You turn it on and go," he said, but she was not convinced. Today, although she had changed her mind about using the boat, she certainly was not ready for the motor.

Joe said his brother had built the small protective shed for his boat a few years earlier because he was tired of hauling it from the lake to the barn in the fall and back again in the spring. When she opened the door, however, Joanne questioned his strength. The boat was, in fact, a small rowboat that almost anyone, it seemed to her—until she tried to move it—could easily displace.

Her attempts at removing the boat from its support of large wooden beams were frustrating at first; she did not even manage to budge it. "Damn," she said, resting momentarily against the wall of the shed. "How am I going to move this thing?" she asked the dog whose dark, moist eyes looked at her, questioning. "If only you could help. By the way, what's your name? You must have a name. I'll tell you what. I'll call you Red. Do you like it?"

The animal tilted his head to one side in reply to the sounds she was making as if recognizing them.

"Well? What do you think, Red?"

The dog barked, and Joanne chuckled. "I bet I'm right-on, Red?" He barked again then came to Joanne to be petted. "I must say it's nice having you around, Red."

Using the wall as leverage, Joanne put one foot against the boat and pushed as hard as she could. After a few tries, it finally budged slightly and a cracking sound disturbed the quietness. "All right, Red. We'll get it yet. It was just stuck. It probably hasn't been taken out in years." Inch by inch, she finally succeeded in pushing it out of the shed onto the moist soil. From there, she had no trouble pulling it to the water's edge.

"Well, are you coming with me?" Joanne asked Red as she came back from the shed with the oars and the fishing rod. The dog watched her position the oars and, after a moment, jumped into the boat. "All set, except I haven't got any bait. Don't leave without me," she exhorted the animal.

A few yards away, she dug lightly into the wet ground with one of her heavy shoes and immediately saw a blueish-gray worm wriggling in an attempt to find its way back to the darkness of the soil. "No, you don't," she said, bending down and picking it up in her gloved hand.

Back at the edge of the lake, she told Red, "If people at the office could see me now, tongues would be wagging!"

She put the hook of the fishing line through the body of the still fighting worm and, suddenly, felt quite ill. She let the rod fall into the boat and rushed a few feet away, near a tree. There several spasms in the muscles of her stomach came in succession. She could not control the vomit.

When she returned to the boat many minutes later, she was still slightly dizzy and wondered if the culprit had been the worm or the diseased stomach. "No point worrying about it now," she told the dog.

She filled her lungs with fresh air and began to feel better. Relying on the memory of seeing people put crafts in the water, she pushed the boat fully into the water and jumped in, managing to stay dry.

She rowed from her sitting position on the center plank with Red facing her. Her arms soon grew tired, and although she had gone no more than a few hundred yards, she decided that it was far enough for her first try. She took the rod with both hands, swung it out over the water in a feeble attempt at casting, and the hooked worm remained suspended in midair.

"There's obviously something I'm not doing right," she told Red, who was eyeing her. She unwound some of the line and the hook disappeared into the water. She waited for a hungry fish, contemplating the water.

Triton Lake just like the village, Joe Wheeler had told her, had been named for one of the early settlers of the region. As she looked up and down, Joanne was thankful for the unspoiled shore. Fields and pastures, a few with milking cows enjoying the spring weather, circled the lake, while the houses had been built farther away along the road. There were no cottages to spoil the tranquillity.

About a mile long but not as wide, the lake offered a fresh oasis of peace. She was the only one out on the water. There was nothing to spoil her world, the one to which she had easily acclimated. One of space, beauty, and clean air. If only she could share it with Roger and her children.

Although her family was constantly on her mind, only on rare occasions did she allow herself to ruminate on what her life should have been as she briefly did now. Mirrored with her own face on the water were the faces she loved most, dancing as a family again and sharing a new closeness. *Why could that scene not be real? What crime did I commit to warrant the tears and bruises that are now stamped on the fabric of my being? Did I not always attempt to do my utmost best in all circumstances as I faced life's problems head-on? Is this my reward for being a devoted mother? For staying up half the night with my son when he had a bad case of the flu, although I had to be at work the next morning? For sacrificing a long-awaited concert to help Terri learn her lines for the Christmas play at school?*

She was aware that she was not perfect, and wondered, *Am I being punished for being too organized, too disciplined. In planning and ordering the family's life, am I to blame for driving Roger away as he claimed? Was I condemned for refusing to continue living as his wife after I saw him brazenly covet another woman? Should my duty have been to examine the reasons behind his action? But have not the last two years of self-recrimination, tears, and loneliness been payment enough for my brutal, hardheaded decision to send Roger packing, if it had indeed been brutal and hardheaded?*

Or have I been judged much less than the dedicated employee I presumed to be? Had the merit of my positive efforts to help the company weather potentially stigmatizing situations been totally erased by my lack of kindness and understanding for Harvey Mack? Or had the turmoil and anger he unleashed in me eaten away, like a vile poison, at my immunity until it had to accept defeat?

What unforgettable offense have I perpetrated?

She closed her eyes, and using all the mental capacities she could muster, pushed away the thoughts of self-pity. They served no useful purpose. They only drained her of much-needed physical and emotional strength. She had to look at the present and only the present. Thankfully, at that moment, something pulled on her fishing line.

"Red, I think we've got something," she said, excited.

She held on to the rod as tightly as she could to counteract the movements at the end of the line. "Think about it, my very first fish!"

Slowly, she reeled the line in and soon saw a gray-skinned fish desperately disagreeing at being pulled out of its habitat. She disliked seeing the fish putting up such a fight, but managed to hold on to the line over the water until it no longer moved. She then put the end of the rod at the bottom of the rowboat and, putting her foot on it to prevent it from slipping, she let the fish dangle over the edge. Red barked, wanting to know what creature she had found in the water.

"Just a fish," she told the animal. "Don't worry. It's dead." She grabbed the oars and rowed back the short distance to the shore.

With the boat pulled partially on ground and solidly tied to a metal rod positioned a few feet from the water's edge, she made her way back to the house, the fish still dangling at the end of the line, Red in tow. "How in the world am I going to clean this thing?" she said aloud, more to herself than to the dog.

At that moment she turned the corner of the house and saw Agatha driving in.

"Ya went fishin'?" the older woman commented in disbelief, getting out of the car, a bag of grocery in her hand.

"Your husband told me I could use the boat."

"I know, but I'm surprised. Ya don't look the type that would like fishin'."

"I don't. I mean, I've never done it before. I wanted to try it, but now I don't know how to clean this thing."

"It's a trout and a good-size one by the looks of it. I'll fix it for ya."

"I don't want to impose, Agatha."

"I've offered, haven't I? My Joe's very good at catchin' them but no good at preparin' them, let me tell ya. I'm used to it." Giving the grocery bag to Joanne, Agatha said, "Fetch me a towel so I don't dirty my dress, will ya."

In a few minutes, the older woman was expertly cutting the trout on the kitchen counter, removing the insides with her bare hands. Joanne quickly turned her head away. The last thing she wanted to do was regurgitate again, especially in Agatha's presence.

"Want me to prepare it?" Agatha asked as her agile hands removed the scales. Hearing no answer, she added, "Fillet it? Remove the bones?"

"You can do that?" Joanne asked, amazed.

"Of course. Do it all the time. Easier to cook."

"That'd be great." Joanne had always considered herself reasonably sophisticated and knowledgeable, yet today it was clear there was much to learn.

"Ya got a few meals here. I'd say this thing is about five pounds."

"Is that good?"

"For Triton Lake, I'd say it's mighty good," Agatha said, washing her hands at the sink. She put her jacket back on. "I see Red has decided to come back."

"You know this dog?"

"Sure. When Henry, that's Joe's brother who used to live here, bless his soul, got sick, Red practically moved in. Was good for Henry. A presence in the house, ya know."

"Who does it belong to?"

"Never could find out. He's a vagrant. Seems to just roam 'round and hang on to different people for a while. If ya don't send him away, he might take a likin' to ya."

"I don't mind. I like him," Joanne said, patting the reddish coat.

"Suit yourself."

Watching Agatha getting back into her car, Joanne smiled. Unwittingly, she had given the country woman interesting fodder with which to gossip in the village. "I tell ya, couldn't have cleaned the fish herself if I hadn't come along. And that dog is back, ya know!"

For her lunch, Joanne broiled a nice-sized fillet of trout. Her very own trout. Watching it cook, she wished she could share it with her family instead of Red, who was quietly watching from his half-sitting position in the corner

A few days after her arrival, she had removed her watch. There was no longer any need to monitor time; it would end soon enough. Yet she always seemed to know the approximate time of day. As she slowly ate the fish and some carrots, she calculated it was around one o'clock. *Roger wouldn't be eating alone. He is probably in a nice restaurant with a colleague or an important client, perhaps a female. Is he thinking of me? Will the memories we wrote in Vail be strong enough to keep me in mind till the end?*

The nights were the hardest. Half-asleep or half-awake, she often turned in her bed, calling him, expecting him to be there to hold her and erase the harsh reality. She wondered if his love was as strong, if her absence was as noticeable to him as he lay in their bed.

She would never know.

Try as she might, although the trout was excellent, she could not eat all the food in front of her. Her stomach still felt a little queasy from its earlier experience near the lake.

"Red, how would you like some fresh trout?"

At the sound of her voice, the animal tilted his head and came to her, devouring the offering.

"Good, isn't it?" Suddenly, the stomach rebelled again. "Excuse me," she told the dog and ran for the bathroom.

Lying on her bed some time later, Red curled up at her feet, Joanne felt depressed. *Things are not working as I wanted. How can I fight my disease if I can't keep food down? My efforts at a cure through dietary improvements will not, cannot, bear fruit in these conditions.*

I need to reexamine my options.

Since her arrival in her hideaway, she had been exhilarated by her improved ability at managing both her physical and mental activities. *Why is my stomach giving up at this early stage?* She didn't have the answer, but one thing was certain, she needed nutrition to fight the invisible enemy within her with all her might.

If she were in the hospital, a tube would be attached to her arm to feed her body by bypassing her stomach. Here, alone in the country, she did not have that option. Her only choice was to try to eat again.

Slowly, she sat up on the side the bed and opened the small drawer of the night table, taking out two plastic containers filled with the pills John Calder had prescribed for her. She put the painkillers back in the drawer, and examined the other pills. One capsule as needed, the instructions read. She had filled the prescriptions solely to serve as a crutch after coming to the conclusion that even though she was ready to fight, she might not be able to do it without chemical help. *But do I dare use the anti-nausea medication now? Or should I continue on my self-tutored and self-determined road without the assistance the pills could provide?*

At length, she decided on the latter. Perhaps her stomach would be less irritable in the morning.

She let her body fall back on the bed. Soon the imagery of the inner visualized battle was clear, tenacious and purposeful for many minutes, until one more ugly head had been shattered.

She spent the rest of the day working on the painting of the pastoral scene visible through the living room window, forcing herself to hum. Many songs of love lodged themselves in her mind as she painted. She let her subconscious guide her hand while the conscious thought of Roger. She contemplated that she had never been attracted by any other man, and that he had indeed always been the half that made her better.

When she began to feel tired, she put down the paintbrush and poured herself a glass of apple juice, which she drank slowly. Sitting at the kitchen table, she could not erase the picture that kept popping into her mind. Although she could only guess at the time, she assumed it was around dinner time. Roger, Terri, and Jason would be sharing a meal, recounting their day. She ached to be with them. She could be. They were, after all, only a set of numbers away.

She went to the telephone in the living room. Her right hand picked up the old receiver and brought it to her ear. The dial tone was clear. *What will I say? How can I explain? I am in Hawaii. That's all I need to say. But there will be so many questions: Where do I live? What is my e-mail address? My telephone number? Why haven't I been in touch?*

With the receiver still in her hand, Joanne realized the avalanche of things she had failed to take into account when formulating her plan. For one thing, she could have tried to find someone to forward mail for her from Hawaii, giving the return address of the sender as her own. It would have been a good way to correspond. And if she had brought her laptop computer, she could be keeping in touch with her family, with Carol, with people in the office.

But, Joanne thought, *if that were the case, I would still be entangled in my old life at a time when I need all my energies for myself and only myself. If I dial the number I know so well now and talked to my husband and my children, it would tear me apart, it would consume me, drain me. My first and only priority at this time is myself.*

She replaced the receiver. *I cannot lose sight of my goal. Surely, occasionally, my family misses me, but if I phone, it would only aggravate their feeling of separation. As it is, they are now no doubt fully involved in a new routine that, if not perfect, is at least free of the painful reality.*

Besides, she wondered, *would I have enough courage to sound happy and well? What if I falter and give it all away? What then? I cannot risk it.*

She took a deep breath. Her family would survive without her. She had to let go. She went to the bathroom to fill the bathtub. Soon her thin body was soaking in the warm water while her mind went to work battling the enemy in her stomach for almost an hour.

Chapter Eighteen

Red's barking woke Joanne from a deep sleep which had come only after a long struggle to will away the exhausting distress in her stomach. The pain had finally disappeared, and she was wondering now if her mental efforts were indeed getting stronger or if the pain simply ran its course. There was no sure answer.

"Okay, Red." He was still barking at the front door. "I'm coming."

Her hair disheveled, she wrapped her housecoat around her as she went to investigate the reason for Red's impatience. Her eyes widened when she saw the familiar late-model sedan parked near her own car in the driveway. She was totally amazed that she had not heard any sounds, especially since there was no one in the car. She rushed into the living room and saw Mary and Peter Malton standing a few feet from the balcony, absorbing the scenery.

"Talk about a surprise visit," Joanne muttered and disappeared into the bathroom. She had little time to do much more than comb her hair and pinch her cheeks so they would have a little color before she heard the knock at the door.

Both Mary and Peter Malton embraced JoJo warmly.

"You mean that I look better than you expected," Joanne said, smiling, after warm greetings were exchanged.

"Definitely. You look relaxed and rested. Obviously, this life is agreeing with you," Mary said happily.

"I'm doing well both physically and emotionally, I assure you. I like my hideaway. More than I expected, in fact."

"It's so lovely, so peaceful," Mary said, pointing at the lake. "You couldn't have chosen a nicer spot."

"I admit I was lucky to find this place."

"How are you feeling, really?" Peter asked.

"Overall, well. I exercise, I eat right, I rest when I'm tired, I have no stress. I can already feel a change in me."

Mary and Peter exchanged looks.

"I know you think I'm a little kooky for doing this, but I tell you honestly that I am certain I'm controlling the cancer. I'm using imagery and I know it's working. I am going to get better," she emphasized. "Don't worry, I'm far from having given up."

"What do you mean you use imagery?" Mary asked.

"I simply imagine my body is fighting the disease. There are many documented cases where victims of serious diseases have cured themselves by using this type of therapy. The mind can have a tremendous impact on the workings of the body; much more than the average person is willing to acknowledge or believe.

"I'm convinced that the various pressures I've been under in the last few years, coupled with a less-than-perfect diet and lack of proper exercise, have contributed to my disease. So I don't see why I can't reverse the process and cure myself by changing my lifestyle and using the great capacities of the mind positively. Many of us let our minds make our lives hell; I'm using mine to make my life harmonious again."

"At the risk of offending you, JoJo," Peter said, "you sound like some arrogant preacher you hear on television on Sunday morning. I can't believe you're convinced this is going to work!"

Joanne saw his face redden as he spoke.

He continued. "You have a serious disease that has to be treated medically. Wishing it away won't make it go away! What you're saying is so unlike you, it's frightening."

"Now, dear," Mary put in, "there's no point in getting upset."

"Yes, there is. She's wasting precious time. JoJo, I grant you that being away from the responsibilities of your family and your job might have helped you to relax and rest, but it doesn't mean that you're cured."

"Peter, I don't think I am cured. Not yet. But I will be, in due course. It will take time but I'll get there. I'm sure of it."

"Rubbish!" Peter said, this time noticeably annoyed.

"JoJo, I think what Pete is trying to say is that if perhaps you combined your method of…imagery, is it? with more conventional methods, it might be the right answer."

"Still haven't given up, have you?"

"We never will," Mary said. "We thought that by now you might be ready to see the error of your ways and come back with us. I see that's not the case."

"It's not," Joanne said firmly. "Let's change the subject here. How about some coffee? No, on second thought, I can't offer you any because I don't have any."

Peter Malton was amazed. "You've stopped drinking coffee? You who drank as many as three cups in a two-hour meeting?"

"Yes, I have. It's amazing the things you can do once you set your mind to it. I have some fruit juices and I can make you a chicken sandwich."

"I'm okay," Mary said.

"Nothing for me, thanks," Peter said. "We stopped in the village for some lunch on the way in."

Joanne was amazed. She had obviously slept well past noon. She could not remember having done that since she was a teenager. *Sleep is a regenerating agent, is it not?*

"Who's your friend?" Peter inquired as she returned from the kitchen with a glass of water for herself.

"That's Red. He sort of adopted me, but I'm not sure if it's because he knows I'm sick or if it's because he's sort of used to the place. In any event, it's nice having him around. We went fishing together the other day."

"You went fishing?" Mary asked, disbelieving.

"Caught my first trout. And a big one at that."

"You have changed," Peter put in.

"We had Roger and the children over for dinner last night," Mary said. "They seem to be doing very well, although the children miss you, especially Terri. They're anxious to hear from you."

When she had first seen them at the door, Joanne had hoped the Maltons would give her some news of her family. Now that they had, it made her desperately lonesome.

Mary continued. "It seems Terri is seeing a boy. Roger doesn't approve, but I think Roger wouldn't approve of anyone interested in Terri, so I wouldn't worry too much. Roger wants to send Jason to a camp for part of the summer, that is…until they go to visit you in Hawaii."

"What are you going to do about that one, JoJo?" Peter asked. "Roger keeps asking me if I've heard from you. I'm tired of having to face his questions: 'What's the name of that school again?' 'You mean to tell me that she has not contacted you or anyone else at Scalls-Morton in all these weeks?' And so forth, and so forth. I'm running out of excuses."

Joanne rested her head in her hands. Her dear friends were burdened because she had indulged in welcoming back the man she loved. If she had remained separated from Roger, physically and emotionally, he would not be so intent on getting answers to what were, after all, very reasonable questions from a concerned husband.

"I'll find a way to get in touch very soon," Joanne finally said, knowing that her children's birthdays were approaching and that they would be getting her gifts.

"What are you going to say?" Mary asked.

"I'll keep it very general, but they'll know I haven't forgotten them."

"I hope you do it soon! While you're at it, drop a line to someone at the office. I'm constantly being asked if I've heard from you," Peter said.

"I wouldn't worry too much about people in the office, Peter. I'm sure everyone will keep right on believing his or her own theory, whether or not they hear from me. The ladies' washroom has always been a pretty prolific rumor factory!"

"I guess you can't avoid that in a large organization," he replied. "A couple of weeks ago, my secretary told me, or I should say I got it out of her, that some people were saying you left because I had broken off our affair. I was totally shocked. I thought our employees were above such nonsense!"

"People are the same all over. They love to gossip. But I'm sure that particular rumor was started by Harvey Mack."

"JoJo, I know you have no great love for Harv, that he's been hard on you over the years, but I don't think he'd…"

Joanne interrupted. "Why don't you just ask him? If you're firm enough, you might be surprised at what you find out!"

"Now is probably not a good time to get on Harv's back. He seems to have health problems of his own."

"I'm sorry to hear it," Joanne said frankly.

Peter looked at her, not convinced.

"Even if I don't especially like him, I do sympathize with him." Changing the subject abruptly, she added, "What else is going on at Scalls-Morton?"

Peter was happy to oblige her.

After the Maltons had left a couple of hours later, Joanne sat at the kitchen table for a while, sipping a glass of well water. She was grateful for the visit. *Trying to live without contacts to my former life is absurd on so many levels*, she thought. She needed to have her mind put at ease about her family from time to time. She needed to know Roger was worried about her. *And, the visit was also good for my friends*, she decided. *They saw for themselves that I am not going downhill as they expected. It was a good day all around.*

Feeling hungry, Joanne went to the refrigerator and brought out a head of broccoli and a bag of carrots. As she had done in the last few days in the hope of absorbing a little nutrition, she very slowly ate a small flowerlet of broccoli and a little piece off a carrot. She waited a while and then repeated the process. She would do so again later on as she busied herself painting.

By the time she went to bed, she happily noted that, for the third day in a row, she had been able to keep food down. She was improving and she would continue to do so.

It was imperative.

Chapter Nineteen

John Calder felt an annoying muscle knot somewhere in the middle of his back. He got up from behind his desk and straightened himself, twisting his shoulders in an effort to relax his weighty body. It had been a long day and he was tired. Somehow the patients he had seen in the last few hours had been harder to please, less willing to accept his opinion or was he simply getting old. He wasn't sure.

He went to look out the window, thinking that not so long ago Joanne Blake had stood there while he attempted to convince her to get proper treatment. He had failed, and it often came back to trouble him, as it did now. She hadn't had the courage to talk to him personally on the day she left her world behind. She had simply given a phone number to his nurse, asking her not to disturb him. It had upset him much more than he liked to admit. She had robbed him of his last-minute endeavor to influence her decision, and in so doing left him frustrated.

Perhaps it is not yet too late to help, although precious time has been lost. Why not try? Having forced herself to face her misfortune in loneliness she might have mellowed.

"Do you need anything before I go, doctor?" his nurse asked, standing at the door.

Her noiseless entrances were beginning to annoy him for reasons that were not quite clear. "Yes," he replied, turning to face her. "I would like Joanne Blake's file."

"Certainly," she said and disappeared as quietly as she had come in.

A few minutes later, Dr. John Calder was punching the long-distance number. He heard ring after ring. When he had counted ten, he hung up. *Where is she? Has she come back to the city? Perhaps she is out taking a walk, has gone to the store. There is no reason for her to wait by the phone in case someone decides to call.* He copied the number on a small piece of paper, slipping it into his shirt pocket, and made his way to the outer office and the cabinet behind his nurse's desk. He replaced Joanne's file in the appropriate sequence, and locked the cabinet. No patient files were left out unlocked at night. This was one of his long-standing rules.

After checking that the outer door was bolted, he went back to his office, closing the door behind him. From a locked cabinet behind his desk he brought out a bottle of whisky and a glass, pouring himself a generous drink from the half-full bottle. He then leaned back in his comfortable leather chair and enjoyed the quiet.

For the last few weeks, John Calder had been thinking about retiring. He felt he no longer had the energy or the patience for his chosen profession. He wanted time to enjoy some of the good things in life before fate handed him one of the nasty hands it often saw fit to deal people much younger than he. He had seen life snatched away, sometimes without warning, much too often to dream it couldn't happen to him at any time. The incident with Joanne Blake had left him perturbed. It had made him realize that he might no longer have the persuasive skills needed to influence and help patients.

He thought of the advantages of moving to a warmer climate, maybe California, where his oldest son was a vice-president with an up-and-coming software company. That would give him a chance to golf year-round and be close to the grandchildren he hardly knew. Without any professional pressures, he and Janet would be free to visit their other three children in turn, whenever the fancy arose. Financially, they would be comfortable for the rest of their days; he had made certain of that.

Yet, retirement frightened him. He was not quite certain why. *Is it because it is the beginning of the end? Is it because I would have to get to know Janet, my wife of thirty-five years, whom I had relegated to a minor role in my life for so many years, all over again? Is it because there would no longer be any purpose to my life?*

The drink was a comfort as it warmed his stomach and relaxed his whole body. He had looked forward to it all afternoon, as he had every day for many weeks now. It helped him to think and to analyze, but it also removed the burden of Joanne Blake from his shoulders. In gratitude, he toasted the bottle on his desk and poured himself another drink. Tonight it took an additional drink before Joanne, the child, and Joanne, the cancer-stricken middle-aged woman, could be forgotten. He then decided it was time to go home.

Standing up, the walls swayed a little and he held on to his desk for a moment until he could get a clearer picture. He laughed at himself, the laugh of the drunk with no problems to solve, no psychological dilemma to entangle, no fears to face. He managed to put the bottle and the glass back in the cabinet and lock it. Then he removed his white coat, put on his suit jacket and went out to the waiting room where the sight of the couch made him forget that his wife would have dinner ready. He stretched out and in a moment was fast asleep.

An hour later, the woman who cleaned the floor of his building found him snoring. *Poor Doctor Calder must have had a hard day,* she thought. She did not disturb him and went on to clean another office.

The sound of the vacuum cleaner in the next office woke him well after eight o'clock. Except for the squalid taste in his mouth, he decided he felt pretty good. After rinsing his mouth with an antiseptic in his private washroom, he called Janet. An emergency, he said. She understood. She always did. He made another call, this one long distance.

Joanne recognized John Calder's voice immediately: "How are you, Doc?"

"The question is: how are you, JoJo? I was upset that you didn't talk to me before you left as you had promised."

"I did leave my number, didn't I? Listen, Doc, why don't we stop this intellectual seesawing? I know your position: You want me to have medical treatment. You know mine: I want to get through this in my own way."

"JoJo, you can't blame me for wanting to try again, can you?"

"I suppose not, but I'm doing just fine."

"JoJo, this is me. The truth?"

"I had trouble keeping food down last week, but I got over it."

"So you've been taking the pills I prescribed."

"No, Doc, I haven't."

"Then, how have you been able to control the nausea?"

"I've simply been eating very small portions several times a day. It seems to have done the trick." After a moment's silence, she continued. "Doc, I've changed my lifestyle completely. I eat right, I sleep right, I exercise physically and mentally, and I also pray. It has put me on the right road. I know you don't approve, but I'm not lying when I say I'm doing fine. I am, really."

What has happened to my patient? I have totally failed her. Having expected the cloud of depression to be dissipated by the call, John Calder now felt markedly gloomier and he knew it was not solely due to the aftereffect of the whisky. *What dreadful aberration is leading her on such a deluded road that can only end in a hopeless hell? With so many people bent on claiming that doctors and medical methods were little more than quackery, she could have read hundreds of books, heard hundreds of lectures.*

But how could anyone have so adversely influenced the logical, rational, and orderly mind of Joanne Blake? You've handed me a death sentence...*She had been right. I might not have been the executioner, but surely I was the judge...*We've discovered cancer. *What happened to the mind when it had to face an irreversible absolute? Did it search for hope in whatever form it might be offered? Of course it would. Joanne had searched for that hope outside medical management simply because it had failed her by failing her mother.*

"JoJo, all the things you're doing are good. I've always preached the value of good nutrition and exercise..."

"Yet you wanted to put me in a hospital where I would not have had the benefit of either," she interrupted.

"JoJo, you have to be fair. What I'm saying is that these things are good, but by themselves won't bring about a cure. They have to be combined with proven forms of treatment."

"Long, painful forms of treatment. I'm going to try very hard to prove you wrong, Doc, not because I don't respect you, but because I think I can."

Her voice had a determination that panicked him. He had lost. He doubted he could accept it. The mother had died because of the limitations of scientific knowledge, while he stood by helplessly, and the daughter would die, despite the profusion of scientific knowledge. Yet he could only stand on the sidelines. He had only one choice: try to change the situation by using the legal system...*What are you going to do? Get a court order? I don't believe you could do that to me or to my family...*

"Doc? Doc? Are you there?" Joanne asked after waiting a moment for a reply.

"I'm here."

"Are you okay?"

"You know, JoJo, I'm sorry I never learned to swear. I could certainly use it now. Do you think it helps to swear?"

"Doc, don't."

"Don't what? Swear? People who do it probably have the right idea. They get the psychological splinters out before they can leave a scar."

"Doc, please don't do this. You have nothing to reproach yourself. It was my choice and mine alone. You did a lot more than was needed. You cared. Now it's time to let me go. I am not my mother. Doc, listen. Why don't you take a day off and come up to see me as you promised? You could see for yourself how I'm doing."

"I don't see what good that would do. We would only engage in 'intellectual seesawing,' as you put it. Good luck, JoJo. I wish, and I mean that more sincerely than anything I've ever said in my life, that you can prove me wrong."

He hung up before she could say anything more.

John Calder now craved a drink. He fetched the bottle of whisky from its hiding place and poured himself a stiff measure, but he twisted and turned the glass, taking only a few sips of the liquor as he ruminated.

After a while, he poured what remained in his glass out in the sink in his private washroom, rinsed out his mouth again, and called his wife to tell her he would be delayed a little longer.

Roger Blake was working on the household accounts in the family room, half-listening to the television, when he heard the buzz of the doorbell. Seeing Dr. John Calder on his doorstep surprised him.

"Is everything all right, Doc?"

"Of course. I wonder if I could discuss something with you."

"Certainly. Come on in."

They sat in the living room, the doctor declining a drink.

"Roger, not too long ago you came to me for medical advice for one of your cases. Well, now I need legal advice from you."

"Fair enough, Doc. Shoot."

"Can a doctor take legal action to force a patient to get medical treatments that could save his (he had rehearsed his words not to slip up and say her) life?"

137

"Well, I suppose it can be done. It has been done. But it's not something that's easy. It's an emotionally charged issue. I know of one hospital that brought charges against a woman who was trying to starve herself to death because she had some terminal disease or the other. The hospital won because it proved that it could considerably prolong and improve the woman's life. They obtained the right to force-feed her. After all, suicide is still on the books and against the law. But I read about this woman and I bet she'll try to kill herself in some other way, and this time make sure she succeeds.

"What I'm trying to say is this. Is it worth the trouble and the pain? That woman was deeply hurt by the action of the hospital. She argued that since it was her life, she had the right to end it when she wished. She said the law making suicide a criminal offense was based on religious considerations rather than on the principle of fairness for the good of all."

"But it can be done?"

"Yes. Are you thinking of suing one of your patients?"

"Perhaps."

"It would be a big step, Doctor."

"Tell me something, Roger. If you were a relative of this patient, would you approve if his doctor went ahead with an action like that?"

"I don't know. What I'm thinking is that there has to be other ways of bringing someone to get medical treatment, especially if they could save his life. Surely the family could be a big influence. Has the family used the love aspect to the fullest? If I take the patient's point of view, it'd be damn insulting to be sued by my own doctor; it'd be easier to swallow if the action came from my wife or my children. It would show they care a lot for me."

"I see," the doctor said simply.

"What is your relationship with this patient, anyway? I don't mean to pry, Doctor, but at first glance I would assume you're close to that patient in some way. What I mean is this, you've been practicing medicine for what? Certainly over thirty years. Have you ever thought of doing anything like this?"

"Frankly, no."

"Yet, I'd be ready to bet my last penny that over the years you've had other patients who were against getting treated, let's say for cancer. Did you run after them? Did you sue them? If not, why would you want to sue this one?" Roger Blake got up and started to pace as he went on. "A case such as this is bound to attract a lot of attention because, as I said, it's an emotional issue. It's something the media will gobble up because of its human aspect, its life-and-death angle.

"And, Doc, once the media get hold of it, they won't let it die. They'll milk it for all it's worth. They'll want to know your relationship with this patient; they'll want to know the real, quote, unquote, reason behind your action, etc. I'm not trying to dissuade you; I'm only trying to show you that a case of this nature would be a high-profile thing whether or not you like it. Court records are open to anyone, and there are media people whose job it is to check regularly to see what new cases are before the courts and sift out the interesting and unusual ones. You couldn't keep that thing quiet even if you wanted to."

"I see," John Calder said again.

"In short, what I'm saying is that, number one, before considering any such action, you'd have to be damn sure that your motives are very clear, and I mean to you. If they're honest, you'd have to be certain they can withstand the challenge they're bound to get from the media. Number two, you have to consider the patient. Will it drive him...it is him?"

John Calder lied. "Yes, it's a him."

"Will it drive him to more desperate actions? Right now that patient is only refusing treatment, am I right?"

"That's correct."

"There's been no suicide attempt?"

Calder shook his head.

"Could there be if you sued him? As a friend, I'm telling you, that's one aspect you'd have to look at long and hard. Otherwise, the whole thing could come back to haunt you for the rest of your days."

"Somehow, I thought it would be a lot easier than you make out to be," John Calder, said wearily.

"Doctor, we're both professionals. If I were sick, you'd make sure I understood well what actions should be taken and you'd warn me if problems could arise. Well, that's all I'm doing. I want to make certain you know what's ahead, so you can make an informed decision. There's little doubt that you would win the case because the bottom line is that the best interest of the patient comes first. But what about his family? They'd have to be taken into account."

"I understand very well what you're saying, Roger."

"Doctor, why are you taking this burden on your shoulders? There is a family?"

"Yes." *And you are it,* the tired doctor wanted to yell out.

"Why don't you get them to get a court order? In my judgment, it would be much easier on you and the patient."

"You're probably right." Getting up from the comfortable chair, John Calder added, "You've certainly been frank, Roger. I appreciate it. Thank you for your time."

"My pleasure, Doctor. The advice you gave me when I went to see you a few weeks ago was very helpful. I'm glad for the chance to repay you."

Making his way to the hallway, John Calder asked, "How are Terri and Jason?"

"Just fine, but they miss their mother."

"I'm sure they do."

"The worst part is that she hasn't even bothered to write or phone since she left. You'd think she would at least have thought to let her own children know how she is!"

"You told me she went away on business. Perhaps she's just been too busy."

"Very unlikely, Doctor. What bothers me is that it's not like her."

Although he was bound by confidentiality, John Calder had seriously considered breaking his oath where JoJo was concerned, and at that moment, he was tempted more vigorously than at any other time. But, after a second's hesitation, reason prevailed.

"JoJo's a good mother," he said warmly, "I'm sure there's a simple explanation. Don't worry needlessly."

Once in his car, the veil of depression that had been hanging over John Calder's head came down to smother whatever hope might have existed that he could save Joanne Blake from herself. Legal action was definitely out of the question; Roger had made that quite clear. In so doing, he had devastated a man whose only professional fault was to care for a patient to the point of obsession because of the patient still haunting his memory. *I am not my mother....*

Chapter Twenty

Mrs. Lucas had always taken pride in the fact that she worked for Roger Blake. A great deal of that pride was based on her being able to boast to her friends that the handsome lawyer, whose picture they often saw in the newspaper or on television, was her main client. In the last two years she had not bothered to mention the fact that he had moved out of the house.

When Joanne broke the news of her impending departure, Mrs. Lucas was secretly pleased. With lawyer Blake moving back into the house, her presence would be more important, more noticed. Now, with her new routine fully entrenched and accepted, she always waited for Roger to come home before leaving, even when it meant being late for a card game, as was the case this day. The pleasure of having the gorgeous man tell her she was doing a good job made it worthwhile.

The following day would be Terri's sixteenth birthday and, as she had promised Joanne, Mrs. Lucas had earlier taken the gifts out of the spare room closet and put them on the bed in Mr. Blake's room. She was certain this would be very pleasing to the lawyer, since she was not aware of the undercurrents in his life.

Standing in the hallway, Mrs. Lucas said, "Good evening, Mr. Blake," in an infatuated tone Roger did not catch.

"Good evening, Mrs. Lucas. Sorry I'm a bit late. One of my cases is giving me more trouble than I expected."

"No problem, Mr. Blake. Dinner's ready. I made lasagna. It's in the oven. I hope you like it."

"I'm sure we will. Thank you."

"What are your plans for tomorrow night, Mr. Blake? Do you want me to make dinner? I could make something very special if you want."

"For Terri's birthday, you mean? I think we'll go out, but thank you for the offer."

"My pleasure, Mr. Blake."

At that moment, Terri appeared at the top of the stairs. "Hi, Dad. Is dinner ready, Mrs. Lucas? I'm starved."

"Everything's ready. Go tell your brother."

"Okay," Terri said amiably and disappeared.

Mrs. Lucas lowered her voice and told Roger, "The surprise is on your bed. I've closed the door so I'm sure she hasn't seen it. Have a good night. See you tomorrow."

"Good night, Mrs. Lucas," Roger said almost inaudibly, her last remarks leaving him perplexed. He didn't notice Terri had returned until she kissed him on the cheek. "How are you, Dad?"

"Just fine. How was school?"

"Okay."

Jason raced down the stairs, and soon the family was busy eating and recounting the events of the day. Try as he may, Roger could hardly wait to find out what mysterious object was on his bed. During a lull in the conversation with his children, he excused himself and went upstairs. What he saw on the bed behind the closed door made him gasp. He recognized Joanne's handwriting on the card. *Well, she isn't dead*, he thought, exasperated. *She had remembered Terri's birthday, but how did these get in the house*, he wanted to know. *What had Mrs. Lucas said?* The surprise is on your bed. *Fine, but how did the surprise get there?*

He thought of calling Mrs. Lucas at home, but decided against it. He wanted to see her eyes when he questioned her. As far as Roger was concerned, eyes did not lie, and reading them correctly had made him an excellent interrogator. He went back downstairs to finish the meal with his children. "Well, Terri, tomorrow's the big day. How about dinner in town with Jason and your old dad?"

"That'd be great!"

"Good. Any special place you want to go?"

"Whatever you want is okay," she said as she began to nervously fold and unfold her napkin. Knowing that she had something to add, Roger waited patiently. "Dad, can Dave come too? It would give you a chance to get to know him better. He's okay, you know."

"I'm sure he is." Despite his doubts about his daughter's friend, he could not deny her a perfect birthday. "Why not! Tell him to be here around six-thirty and we'll make a night of it."

"Thanks, Dad," Terri said, getting up and hugging her father.

"Will you take me out too when it's my birthday?" Jason wanted to know.

"Of course, Jason. Each your turn."

"Too bad Mom won't be here. Have you heard from her?" Jason was asking as he did almost daily.

"No, Jason, I haven't, but your sister has."

"I have?" Terri said, obviously confused.

"Come on," Roger invited, and the two children followed him upstairs.

"Wow!" Terri exclaimed at the array of beautifully wrapped gifts. As Roger and Jason watched, she slowly removed the envelope on top of the pile and took out the card. She began to read, and Roger saw her expression become a mixture of pleasure and pain. She sat on the bed and looked up at her father, tears in her eyes. Roger put an affectionate arm around her shoulders, and she handed him the card. "It's okay, you can read it," she said softly. Roger read out loud.

My darling Terri,

Sixteen already, and what a beautiful young woman you are turning out to be. You make your father and me so proud! How I wish I could be with you to share this very important day in your life! I pray you are well and continuing to be outstanding in all your endeavors. Your father counts on you while I am away and I know you will not let him down. Keep smiling, my darling. We should be together again very soon. I love you with all my heart and all my soul,

Mom

Roger returned the card to Terri, forcing himself to be jovial. "Your mom's right. You are a nice young lady. Now, come on, open these gifts."

"When did these get here," Jason asked.

"They were delivered today," Roger replied as excitedly as he could.

"Nothing for me?" the boy inquired.

"I'm sure you'll also get a nice surprise in just a few days, Jason."

"I hope so."

"Wow," Terri exclaimed, opening the first gift. "Diamond earrings!"

Roger wanted to protest, but he managed to keep calm. "Now, that's quite a gift for a girl your age."

"Ah, come on, Dad. I'm sixteen," she said, guiding the small studs through her pierced lobes in front of the mirror above the dresser.

"Are they real diamonds? They shine," Jason told his sister.

"Of course they are," Terri replied with certainty. "Mom wouldn't bother with fakes. I wonder what the other gifts are?"

"Well, go ahead and open them," Roger urged his daughter.

As she busied herself with the wrapping, Jason commented, "Now she's going to be on the phone for the rest of the night, Dad. I hope you weren't expecting any important calls!"

"Jason, that won't be a problem as of tomorrow. I'm giving your sister a cell phone for her birthday."

"Cool," Terri said, almost absentmindedly, her eyes on an expensive sweater she had just found in one of the boxes.

Much later, when the excitement had died down and the children were finally asleep, Roger was lying, fully dressed, on top of the thick duvet on the bed. He was angry. *Why had she done it? Why had JoJo seen fit to compensate for her guilt feelings with such expensive, one might even say, ridiculous gifts? And she obviously would have the same planned for Jason when his birthday came in a few days. Was it to outshine me? I doubt it.*

Then, why? Why, JoJo?

Why did she go away at a time when our marriage could, would have worked? There is something she hasn't told me...that maybe she just couldn't tell me or let the children find out.

There was only one answer to that puzzle, and it was one he did not like to even consider. Yet it had to be considered.

Mrs. Lucas was startled to see Roger coming down the stairs as she came in the next morning. "Mr. Blake, you frightened me. I expected you'd be gone."

"I wanted to talk to you, Mrs. Lucas. Please come into the kitchen."

She followed him. "I hope I didn't do anything wrong."

"No, Mrs. Lucas. I just want to ask you a few questions. Please sit down."

She obeyed, and he sat across the table from her.

"Those gifts for Terri, where did they come from?"

"From Ms. Blake," she answered simply.

"I know they came from Ms. Blake," Roger said, making an effort to keep his voice even. "What I want to know is when and how they were delivered."

Mrs. Lucas hesitated for a moment, trying to decide her priorities. A quick analysis told her she should keep Joanne's secret, yet the dear Mr. Blake was right in front of her. She could not risk upsetting him.

"Well, Mrs. Lucas?"

"They weren't delivered. They were here all the time. Ms. Blake prepared them before she left."

"I see," said Roger, somewhat surprised. "And I bet there's a package for Jason as well."

"Of course. She wouldn't give gifts to one child and not the other."

"Of course. She asked you to give them to me when it was time for the children's birthdays."

"She really wanted me to give them to the children, but I thought," and she hoped this would please him, "it would be best if you had them first."

"Thank you, Mrs. Lucas. That was considerate of you. Tell me, were the gifts here in the house?"

"Of course, Mr. Blake."

Of course. Oh, the irritations of life. "Where, Mrs. Lucas?"

"Ha…Mr. Blake, I can't tell you that."

"Why not, Mrs. Lucas?"

"Because there's a package for you also, for your birthday in August. I have to keep it hidden."

"I understand, Mrs. Lucas. You've been very helpful."

"I hope so, Mr. Blake."

"You have. Thank you."

The dinner that night was a great success. Terri was positively beaming, and Roger felt more than a little pride at being her father. "It's my daughter's birthday; make sure she gets good service," he had secretly told the maitre d'.

The atmosphere was propitious enough to even attempt a lengthy conversation with Terri's friend Dave, and, to his surprise, Roger found him passably mature for his age. Despite the fact that he was enjoying the evening, Roger was impatient to get home. He had a search to carry out.

When he was certain the children were both asleep, he went down to the basement. He combed every closet, every corner, every box, but to his frustration found nothing. His thorough search of the first floor was no more successful. Feeling defeated, he made his way upstairs and searched Joanne's closet. Nothing. He missed her laptop computer, which was hidden behind some shoes. Then he remembered the spare room. Of course. It had always been her room, where she could close the door, shut off the world and let her artistic inclinations take over.

Although he knew the room was not occupied, he opened the door cautiously before turning on the light. Its bareness surprised him. The single bed, used from time to time by his mother when she visited from her home in Florida, and a nightstand were the only pieces of furniture. There was something missing. *Where is her easel? Her paint brushes that were usually strewn on a corner shelf are not to be seen. Why would she bring them to Hawaii and then to Japan? Unless she didn't go!*

Don't jump to conclusions, he warned himself. *She might just have put them away.* Slowly he opened the closet door and, behind a few winter coats, the pile of brightly wrapped boxes could not be missed. His son's name in JoJo's handwriting was on an envelope attached to the top package. *What extravagant gifts had she bought Jason?* he wondered.

He looked behind the packages and saw a large box and an envelope with his name on it with a pencil notation of his birthdate in August. He argued with his conscience, but the need for immediate gratification won out. He unglued the envelope as carefully as he could and pulled out the card. JoJo's brief words struck him, not so much by what they said, but by what they implied. They dashed his hopes.

Dear Roger,
Sorry I can't be there to share this day, but I assure you my thoughts are with you. Thank you for the years, but most of all thank you for the memories.
I love you.
JoJo

She ended our love affair without having the courage to face me; I counted so dearly on being with her during the summer, of having her as my wife for the rest of my life. How could she destroy my dream? "Why, JoJo?" he said out loud.

After a long time, he replaced the card in the envelope and put it back on top of the large package. Satisfied that Mrs. Lucas would not notice that he had opened the envelope, he went to bed.

The chirping of birds outside the open window woke him up early after a restless night. Dazed by his discovery, Roger Blake had mulled over an array of possible moves before finally dozing off, his subconscious continuing the process with dreams of horrible and painful discoveries.

He was having breakfast with his children when the phone rang. "Roger? Carol. I hope I didn't wake you up."

"Been up for hours."

"Since you've been putting off my dinner invitation, I was wondering if you and the kids could come over tonight. Sort of a celebration for their birthdays."

His ruminations of the previous night had often brought Carol Ferguson to mind as a possible source of information. She and JoJo had been friends for decades; JoJo might have confided in her. All he would need was the right approach. "Sure, Carol. We'd love to go."

If he went about searching with organized determination, he would find the answer he sought. But part of him dreaded it.

"So, what do you hear from your wife?" Gerry Ferguson asked Roger as they made their way to the dining room at Carol's invitation that dinner was ready. "Carol tells me she really spoiled Terri yesterday."

"More than I approve. It'll be seriously discussed when we go to see her in August, let me tell you."

"Where are you going in August," Carol asked as they approached.

"To Hawaii, to see JoJo."

"That's right. Terri told me when we went shopping. You must all be quite excited."

"Can't wait," Roger said mockingly, much to Carol's surprise.

A huge birthday cake, decorated to include the names of both Terri and Jason was brought out after the meal, with everyone enjoying the festivities. When Carol got up to get the coffee, Roger offered to help and followed her into the kitchen.

"Carol, have you heard from JoJo?"

"No. Not yet. And let me tell you that wife of yours is going to have a piece of my mind when I see her. I sent her many e-mails, but she never replied."

Carol was giving him the cups to carry in, but he put them back on the counter and took Carol's arm so that she faced him. "Carol, I have no idea where JoJo is. I thought you could help me."

"What? You can't be serious! After your trip to Colorado, I understood things had been patched up between you two."

"So did I. What did JoJo tell you before she left?"

"Not much, really. She just seemed upset."

"Upset at what?"

"I'm not sure. She didn't say."

"Come on, you've known her a long time. What do you think?"

"Roger, I don't know. It was like…she didn't want to leave." He let go of her arm, his face noticeably dismayed. "It's just a feeling I got," Carol continued. "She didn't confide in me if that's what you're trying to find out."

"Honest?"

"Honest, Roger. I can tell you're worried. I wouldn't hide anything from you at this point, believe me. Wait a minute. She said something that baffled me. She said that someday I would understand."

"Someday you would understand. Nothing else?"

"No. Those were her last words to me."

He had to fight the mounting panic. *JoJo, tell me it isn't true!*

Chapter Twenty-One

Peter Malton felt a mounting headache. *What in the world is happening around me? It seems that in the last few years, crises can hardly wait to follow each other. No wonder I am getting grayer and my blood pressure is more difficult to control!*

The red-haired man sitting in front of him, a man he had entrusted with the huge responsibility of producing the top-quality medication which identified Scalls-Morton products, was the latest casualty life had seen fit to strike. *How many top employees could the company afford to lose? How would this one be replaced?* JoJo had been replaced quickly although Peter knew to his disappointment, the company had lost a little; the attention to detail had slackened, the unyielding loyalty had weakened. *Are these qualities that have also characterized the long years of Harvey Mack's service doomed to leave with him?*

The longer you live, the more people you know get sick and die. It's all part of the game, someone had told him. But why the good people, Peter Malton mused.

"I can't tell you how sorry I am, Harv. I suspected something was wrong, but I didn't dream it was this serious."

"Neither did I, Peter."

"I know. This letter from your doctor says that you have an incurable disease. Is it cancer?"

"You don't have the right to ask me," Harvey Mack said, his voice irritated and his eyes fiery.

"Harv, I didn't mean to pry. I just thought that perhaps I could help you."

The gaunt face of Harvey Mack was now mocking. "It's incurable."

"Specialists are finding out all sorts of new information about cancer almost every day."

"I didn't say I had cancer," Mack said flatly.

Peter didn't like his production man's attitude, and for a moment got a glimpse of what had been so irritating to JoJo. "I just assumed," Peter managed to say.

"Well, don't. I'm sick, I'm leaving and that's all there is to it."

"Come on, Harv. Let me help you. I know a great many doctors. Perhaps you should get a second or a third opinion. I don't believe there is anything beyond hope. If I did, I wouldn't be in this business."

Harvey stood up, his body now bonier, sneering at Peter Malton. "Yes, there is. I have AIDS. Full-blown."

"What?" Peter exclaimed, his face blanching.

"You want to help me? How do you propose to do it?" Mack laughed a sardonic laugh that frightened Peter. "You didn't suspect, did you? No, Peter, I didn't get it from a transfusion. I know exactly how I got it." He stopped for a moment, his eyes cloudy. "Joanne Blake was the only one who ever suspected...my sexual preference. I don't know how, but she did. I see by your expression that she didn't tell you. Well, I guess she wins."

He sat down again slowly, and after a moment continued. "I suppose it's time for last-minute confessions. I was afraid she would tell you, so I decided to discredit her...and you. I'm the one who started the rumor about the two of you...having an affair." Almost inaudibly, he added, "I'm sorry."

Peter Malton was baffled. *How can people be so vengeful? But there certainly is no point in adding to the defeated man's pain.* He said frankly, "I really don't know what to say, Harv."

"There's nothing to say. I realize I don't deserve it, but I would appreciate if you could see your way clear to not say anything around here. I have been extremely careful. I always wore my mouth mask and my gloves on the floor, and I tried not to touch anyone ever since I found out I had the virus."

"I know how the disease is transmitted."

"Maybe you do, but some people can be quite hysterical about it. I just wanted to tell you, in case you start having second thoughts."

Harvey Mack got up again and went to stand behind the chair he had been occupying. "Thanks, Peter, for everything, and good luck. I'm sure you'll understand if I don't shake hands."

With those words the condemned man quietly left the president's office, leaving Peter unable to utter a comforting word.

In a moment, Peter's secretary was knocking and entering. "Mr. Malton, Roger Blake is at Reception and wants to see you. Does he have an appointment?" She waited for a reply.

Pain, disease, dying. Where did it all end? "It's all right. I'll see him, but first I would like you to get me something for my headache."

"Of course, sir." She left and was back in a moment with two capsules, and poured a glass of water from the carafe on his desk.

"Thanks. Sit down for a second, please."

She obeyed while he swallowed the medicine. At length, he said, "Harvey Mack is leaving today. He won't be back. I want you to arrange a meeting of the executives for five o'clock, and you can tell everyone I'm not in the mood for excuses. I want to see everybody there."

"Yes, sir."

"Another thing, you are not to tell anyone about Harvey until I make the official announcement. Understood?"

"Yes, sir."

"Good. Now please bring in Roger."

Roger was growing impatient. He had been waiting for more than twenty minutes and it was adding to his irritation. He knew he should have made an appointment, but he counted on the element of surprise working in his favor. At last Peter Malton's secretary approached.

The company president extended his hand. "Nice to see you, Roger. What can I do for you?"

"I'll get right to the point, Peter. Where is JoJo?"

Fuck. Why today? He managed to reply, "In Hawaii, Roger."

"Peter, don't lie to me. I'm not in the mood for nonsense."

"You're not in the mood?" Peter chuckled.

"What the hell's so funny?"

"You barge in here without calling while this company's in the middle of a new crisis and you expect me to make some sort of revelation about JoJo. What exactly do you want me to say?" Peter asked, his voice sharper than he would have liked it to be. He hoped it would hide his uneasiness.

"I want you to tell me the truth."

"I have, Roger. Hasn't she been in touch with you?"

"No, she hasn't, and I want you to tell me why." Roger voice was cutting.

"Hell, probably because she had to throw you out on your ass two years ago when you cheated on her. Or don't you remember?"

"We worked things out before she left."

"So what do you want from me?"

"She works for you. You have to know where she is. I want an address."

Peter lowered his eyes. Ever since JoJo had left, whenever Peter had seen Roger, it was with Mary and the children, and a vague answer had been easy enough. Now, he was stumped as to how to reply. He would always be loyal to JoJo over Roger. There would never be any question in his mind. He had to think quickly. "She asked me not to give it to you."

"I don't believe you."

"It might not be easy to accept, Roger, but that's the truth."

"You never did approve of me marrying JoJo, did you?"

"Damn it, Roger. My office's not a nursery.'"

"What the hell is that supposed to mean?" Roger asked, angrily. He was the better interrogator and he would cut Peter Malton, who had patronized him for so many years, down to size.

"It means I don't have time for nonsense. If and when JoJo wants to get in touch with you, she will. I can't force her to do it, can I?"

"I don't believe she's in Hawaii. I think she's hiding out because she's pregnant and she'd be ashamed if the children knew."

"What?" Malton almost yelled. "Roger, your imagination's working overtime."

"I don't believe so. She had decided to go away before we went to Colorado, but she made sure that we made love before we even left, so she could claim I'm the father if something went wrong. Isn't that right? Who is the father, Peter? Maybe it's you and that's why you arranged this little…business trip."

Peter's face was now red with annoyance. "Get out of my office right now, Roger, or I'll call security."

"What for? Because I had the courage to tell you the truth! Don't make me laugh."

Peter Malton was exhausted. *Why did Roger have to show up today of all days with such an unlikely scenario?* He didn't know the man in front of him well enough to dislike him. Over the years the two men had on occasion disagreed, but it had mostly been about politics. That JoJo would be the subject of an angry encounter between the two of them was totally baffling to Peter.

Quietly, he said, "Roger, how can you even think such a thing? I understand that you feel hurt because she's not been in touch, but that's no reason to go crazy and insult me, but most of all, insult JoJo."

"Then, once and for all, tell me the truth."

"She's been in touch with Terri for her birthday, hasn't she?"

"Yeah. She made arrangements with the maid before leaving to make sure the gifts would be taken out of the closet on the right day. Not exactly personal. And she's got a pile ready for Jason, and one for me for my birthday in August. I found it and read the card. She has no intention of coming back."

"What makes you say that?"

"By what she wrote. Damn it, Peter, I love her. I don't want to lose her." He stopped for a moment and leaned back in the chair across from Peter's desk. "I'm sorry about what I said…about you and JoJo. I just wanted to force you to say something. Anything. It didn't work." He sighed deeply before continuing. "I'd be willing to take JoJo back under any circumstances…even if she is pregnant, and I won't ask any questions. Please tell her that for me."

"Roger, where in hell did you get the crazy idea that JoJo's pregnant? She's not."

"It seemed like a plausible reason for her disappearing."

"She has not disappeared. She's away on business."

"I don't believe that, and I'm going to find out where she is come hell or high water."

With these words, Roger Blake left Peter Malton's office, slamming the door behind him.

So JoJo forgot to mention that she and Roger worked things out in Colorado. Doesn't she realize that Roger will not accept not knowing where she is? Or did she plan it all? Peter rubbed his temples. It had been a hell of a day, and it was not half-over yet. He needed a pleasant interruption. He picked up the receiver on his telephone console, punched the familiar number and talked to his wife.

Chapter Twenty-Two

On leaving Peter Malton's office, Roger walked resolutely and made his way to his wife's former office. Peggy saw him approaching and smiled. "Well hello, Mr. Blake."

"Hello, Peggy. How're you doing without my wife to give you orders?"

Peggy smiled. "I always liked working for Joanne. I'll be glad when she comes back. Has she gone away like she planned?"

His suspicions were confirmed. Joanne had not gone on a business trip. "You mean she hasn't even sent you a postcard?"

"No. I expected she'd be in touch once she figured out what she was going to do. Where is she anyway?"

"She's in Hawaii."

"Really!"

He bent down and in a low voice confided, "She's seen Kevin Costner who's filming there."

"No!"

Roger nodded and smiled.

"Some people have all the luck," she said. "When you talk to her, tell her I'm hurt that she didn't get in touch."

"I will, Peggy. You can count on it. Take care."

He made his way to the elevator, pleased with himself. He now knew for certain that JoJo had taken a leave of absence. *But why? Despite Peter's protests, she has to be pregnant. That is the only explanation.*

In the elevator he continued his assessment of the situation. *Peter will never change his story if he has given JoJo his word. Of that, I have absolutely no doubt. The relationship between my wife and Peter Malton bugged me at times, although I was never sure why. Is it that, because she worked for Peter, because she spent so much time with him? Is part of me jealous? Yet I know there is no reason to be. Perhaps I have an obsessive need to be the only man she needs.*

Probably, he concluded.

By the time he reached his office, Roger had arrived at the conclusion that the only person who would know if his wife was pregnant was John Calder. He called his nurse and was given an early appointment the next day.

Miles away in a country house near a lake, a dog named Red was agitated. The woman he had taken a liking to, who talked to him, who fed him, was lying on the floor near the toilet and wasn't moving. He had licked her face, but it hadn't helped. He sat on his hind legs for a moment, softly whimpering. Soon he was licking her again, but she didn't move. He went to sit on hind legs again, this time by the door, but didn't stay there long. He was restless. He needed to do something. Anything. He again approached the woman and put a paw on her arm. She moved a little, and he began to wag his tail and bark softly.

Joanne slowly opened her eyes, and her hands went to the pain on the side of her head. "Red, what happened? Oh yes, I remember now. I felt sick, came in here and then everything went blank."

She got up slowly, her head throbbing. In the mirror she saw a nice-sized bump just above her temple. "Boy, I guess I hit the toilet on my way down. That hurts."

Red followed her into her bedroom and saw her stretch out on the bed. He jumped up, curling up close to her. "What would I do without you, my friend," she said, caressing the animal's head. "I wonder why I lost consciousness. I bet it's because I don't eat enough. I don't, you know, but if I eat a normal meal, I

156

feel nauseated. What's the solution, my friend? I can't give up now. I've got to keep on fighting! Are you going to help me?" she asked, petting him.

Some time later, she slowly made her way to the kitchen. There she ate half a pear and washed down a vitamin-supplements tablet with fresh carrot juice. It was the most she had eaten at one sitting since the start of this latest series of nausea attacks. She went back to bed. Once comfortable, she guided her mind into an imagery trip. This time the object was not to destroy cells, but to calm her stomach and force it accept the food. Her capacity to control mental patterns and crafty machinations had sharpened, and the mental plan was quickly carried out. She repeated the process several times, finally letting herself sleep.

When she awoke an hour or so later, she felt rested and knew that she would not vomit again soon. She decided that she should replicate the mental exercise every time she ate until her stomach has no other recourse than to submit to her mind and obey its wishes.

Later, Joanne was busy working at a painting of Red on the porch, when Agatha Wheeler walked up the driveway. The animal was stretched out peacefully in the sun, taking in the scenery, and Joanne was so totally absorbed with the progress of her brush strokes that she did not see her visitor until she was within a few feet.

"I wouldn't want to disturb ya," Agatha said frankly.

"You're not disturbing. I need a break anyway." Seeing the curiosity in the woman's eyes, Joanne invited, "Want to see my latest venture?"

"Yes," Agatha replied with an intonation that assured Joanne of the pleasure her words had provoked. "You're very good," the older woman said, looking the painting over. "That sure's Red. I never knew a painter before."

"Would you like to have one of my paintings?"

"Sure," Agatha said, her voice once more elated.

Joanne went inside and came back with a small canvas of Triton Lake, the first one she had completed after her arrival. "Do you like this one?"

"Yeah! That's the lake there. Real nice."

"It's yours."

"I got to pay you. How much?"

"It's a gift for you and your husband." As Agatha began to protest, Joanne said quickly, "You've been so kind to me, getting my groceries, showing me how to prepare a fish, your husband plowing the garden…"

"Was nothin'. Folks in the country help each other." Still examining the painting, Agatha added, "It's got your name. Blake. That's nice. Thanks."

Joanne, who was feeling stronger, smiled at the older woman's delight. The painting would be a great source of joy in her life and, no doubt, the object of envy on the part of her friends. It gave Joanne a sense of satisfaction.

"Thanks," Agatha repeated. "What happened to the side of your head?"

"It's not serious. I just fell."

"Ya could have hurt yourself bad. I always said it's no good for a woman to live in the country alone. Well, you're gonna have a new neighbor soon."

"A neighbor?"

"Yeah. The fellow who rents the house there," Agatha said, pointing to the old wooden structure, now partially hidden by the large leaves of the trees, "is gettin' in earlier this year. One of the girls at the bank told me. Should be here soon. Be company for ya. He's a nice fella. Writes books."

"I know, your husband told me." Joanne was not thrilled at the news. She liked her life the way it was. She had Red to keep her company and Agatha for the occasional conversation. She did not need anyone else in her life right now. She changed the subject abruptly. "How long do you think it's going to be before the vegetables I sowed in the garden are ready to eat? They're up already."

"It goes pretty fast. Ya should have things like lettuce and beans soon. Tomatoes and corn, things like that, ya won't have for a while." Agatha was up and running. At Joanne's invitation, she sat down and continued her discourse on gardening for some time.

Roger arrived early at the medical building, hoping John Calder would see him before his first appointment. Old man McBride had called a meeting for ten, and Roger didn't want to be late. The previous day, the venerable senior partner seemed more absentminded than usual. To Roger it was a definite sign that an important or front-page-type case was in the offing. He couldn't be delayed, yet as luck would have it, the doctor was late.

Roger tried to read a dated news magazine, but he found it impossible to concentrate. He looked at the nurse making an appointment with a patient on the phone, and observed that a lot of time could be saved if he simply went to the filing cabinet, took out JoJo's file and read Calder's notes. He would quickly know if she had a pregnancy test and whether or not it corresponded in any way with her hasty departure.

At last John Calder arrived and asked Roger to give him a couple of minutes. Once inside his office, he replaced his suit jacket with a white coat and went to his locked cabinet to take out the bottle he realized only too well had become a crude crutch to abate his sense of inadequacy. He did not bother with a glass, putting the bottle directly to his lips. He eagerly gulped down a couple of swallows and waited. In a few moments the liquor warmed his stomach as it made its way to his bloodstream. It would support him until lunch. He went to his washroom and rinsed his mouth with an antiseptic.

"So, Roger, is this a professional or a personal call?" the physician asked, once Roger was seated.

"Personal."

"What's the problem?"

"There's nothing wrong with me, Doctor. I just want to ask you a question. When was the last time JoJo came to see you?"

The question took Dr. Calder by surprise although he had half-expected it would come sooner or later. The liquor gave him courage. "Not so long ago you were telling me that we're both professionals. I believe we still are, so I'll make believe you didn't ask me that question."

"Come on, Doc. We're not talking about some stranger here. We're talking about my wife!"

"That still doesn't give me the right to breach my obligation to respect…"

"Doctor, I don't need a sermon. I simply want to know if JoJo's pregnant."

John Calder hoped beyond hope that his eyes did not reflect his bewilderment.

"Roger, isn't that something that the two of you should be discussing?"

"I can't very well do that when I don't know where she is, can I? I know she hasn't gone away on a business trip. I think she's hiding out because she's pregnant."

"Roger, I won't tell you anything. You're wasting your time."

"I'll take that as an affirmative answer."

"Take it any way you want." John Calder was angry, angry that his position did not allow him to ease the burden of the young man in front of him and to bring a family together in the short time left. Angry and tired. *Why don't I just announce my retirement and put this absurd dilemma out of my mind!*

"That's your final answer?"

"Yes, Roger. I'm afraid it is. I'm sorry."

"Not quite as much as I am, Doctor." With these words, Roger stood up. "Another of JoJo's men I'll never shake," he conceded, leaving Calder baffled.

On his way out, he took a moment to talk to Calder's nurse while examining the filing cabinet behind her. Nothing was impossible if one was motivated enough.

By the time Roger got back to his office, a plan was brewing in his mind. He was mentally studying its ramifications as old man Joseph McBride addressed the meeting.

"Unless there are some strong objections, we intend to take on this case. I have known Charley Bristol all my life, knew him when he was a lad, saw him grow up. I don't believe he's guilty. But we're going to have to work hard, look at all the angles. At first glance the evidence seems cut and dried, but it is not irrefutable, although we're going to have to, as I say, do our homework."

Roger did not like the sound of the announcement. Charley Bristol's father had been mayor for as long as Roger could remember until his death a few years earlier. Throughout his long tenure, he made certain his son Charley would follow in his footsteps. His dream came true three years earlier when Charley was elected mayor with an overwhelming majority, the voters certain the impassioned and spunky leadership of the father would be perpetuated by the son.

Voters had not been disappointed. Charley was eager, but he was also outspoken, and soon a strong opposition began to emerge. Now he was being accused of improprieties with a female assistant.

As far as Roger was concerned, Charley was probably good for the city, at least as good as anyone else. What made him uncomfortable was that Joseph McBride would undoubtedly be fanatical in his handling of the case, despite his advancing age. And because of that advancing age, would expect his colleagues

160

to push themselves to the limit. There would be no reprieve until Charley Bristol was irrevocably cleared.

"Roger," McBride was now saying, "I would like you to do some of the legwork for me. I have a few ideas in mind which I want you to follow up on."

"Of course," Roger replied simply, disappointed that he probably would have to put aside, at least for a while, his own plan of finding out JoJo's whereabouts, a mystery he was determined to solve.

Chapter Twenty-Three

The ringing of the telephone was insistent. Dazed, John Calder shook his head in the hope of obliterating the confusion. It did not. The liquor he had been consuming would not allow him to think clearly, but he was alert enough to know that answering the ring would be a mistake. His patients should never know that he had been baited into a road traveled by the weak and the inept.

At last, the service picked up and the noise stopped. *Could have been Janet*, he thought. She seemed less tolerant of his lateness these days. In his private washroom he let the water run very cold before splashing it mercilessly on his face. Drying himself, he sensed that he was sobering up, and seeing his image reflected in the mirror, he wondered why he had let himself become so vulnerable. The Joanne Blake disappointment was certainly part of the problem. It had made him question his competence, which had always been above any and all reproach. It made him think of retirement, although he knew he wasn't ready to take that step just yet.

For now he would put everything out of his mind, go home, have a good, hot meal and later—when the intoxication had fully faded—attempt again to sort it all out.

Making his way out, an outline began to appear through the thick, frosted glass of the door where his name was written in large black letter. He stopped. There was no light in his waiting room and he saw the silhouette, a man, turn the handle a few times and then try a key that failed to unbolt the door. The figure disappeared quickly. Calder rushed to unlock the door from the inside and came face to face with the cleaning woman who was approaching with her gigantic ring of keys.

"Oh, Dr. Calder. I thought you were gone. There was no light."

As she talked, he looked up and down the corridor, but no one was in sight. "Did you see someone in the hall just now?"

"No, Doctor. I just came out of Dr. Bell's office." The door leading to his office was exactly across the hall. "Why do you ask, Doctor?"

"I thought I saw someone."

"I didn't hear anything. The door downstairs is locked at this time."

"It's supposed to be," Calder said. Pointing to her numerous keys, he added, "Does anyone ever ask you to open a door at night?"

The cleaning woman thought for a moment then said frankly, "I never open a door if I don't know the person. Last week Dr. Rosen asked me to open his office door for him. When he got to his car, he saw he had forgotten his keys on his desk."

"If he had forgotten his keys, how did he open the door downstairs?"

"I asked him, and he said he got in when someone was going out."

Dr. Calder thanked the woman and walked to the elevator. He knew the liquor had not totally crippled his mind. He had not hallucinated. *What would anyone want in my office? There was no money, no valuables. No doubt an enterprising thief, who got in when one of the last patients of the day or one of the doctors was leaving, was taking a chance that some of the offices would be unlocked, hoping to find something.*

Calder mused that the cleaning woman coming out of the office across the hall had made the would-be thief run away. Robberies were after all a daily occurrence, but since there was nothing of value in his office, he decided he wasn't going to worry needlessly. He would, however, pass the word around the next day; some of the doctors had valuable collections: stamps, coins. One even had a signed sketch by Picasso in his early years. Why they didn't keep those things at home always puzzled Calder. Before leaving the building, he double-checked that the front door was well bolted.

Veiled by one of the potted evergreens that lined the street, Roger Blake saw John Calder make his way to the parking garage next door. He took a few deep breaths in an effort to negate the rush of adrenaline he had just experienced. He had been unnerved when the door of the office across the hall from Calder's opened, but even more so when, from the behind the staircase door, he heard Calder's voice. It was a miracle he had not been spotted.

Right there and then, Roger Blake decided that he was not cut out for this type of investigation. He would leave it to someone with nerves of steel.

Agatha Wheeler had walked in the warm sunshine to the end of her garden to inspect the growing crop of vegetables, which she was pleased to see looked very healthy. She was assessing what weeding needed to be done when she saw a medium-size white sedan turn into Joanne's driveway. Agatha had waved at Joanne just a few minutes earlier as she left for her long morning walk and jog with Red. Knowing that she would not be back for some time, Agatha decided to be neighborly.

Arriving at Joanne's hideaway, she saw a well-dressed woman coming out of the house.

"Oh, hello there," Mary Malton said.

"Good morning. Ya lookin' for Joanne Blake?"

"Yes. Do you know where she is?"

"Just left on her walk. Goes every day. Won't be back for maybe an hour. "

"She walks an hour every day?"

At the surprised look of the visitor, Agatha said, "That's in the mornin'. Walks fast, I guess ya could say. Does it at night too, now. Joanne a friend of yours?"

"Yes, she is. I came from the city to see her. She's well, then?"

"She's skinny, but looks healthy to me. When she first come up, she didn't look good. Somethin' was botherin' her, but she got over it, I guess."

"I'm glad," Mary managed to say, somewhat stunned by what she was hearing. She had expected to convince her friend, most probably hardly able to move, to get medical attention in the city. "By the way, I'm Mary Malton."

Agatha introduced herself and invited Mary to sit on the porch and wait.

"That would be nice. It's so lovely here."

"Sure is. Joe, that's my husband, and me, we've been here since we got married. Goin' to be forty-two years this summer."

Agatha accepted Mary's congratulations and was soon happily relating the history of the region. So few people to talk to in the country. She was still talking when Joanne came up the drive, puffing, Red in tow.

"Mary, how nice to see you," she managed to say between quick breaths.

"Are you okay, JoJo?"

Agatha did not miss the affectionate expression. *Something new to talk about in the village!*

"Of course. I've been jogging for a while. I'm just out of breath." Agatha excused herself, leaving the two friends to talk.

"You're sure you're all right?" Mary asked Joanne when she came back to the porch with two glasses of well water. "I mean, should you be doing all this jogging?"

"I don't jog all the time. I walk fast, jog a little, walk fast, jog a little. What should I be doing?" Joanne asked, sitting herself on the railing of the porch. "Feeling sorry for myself? Mary, I'm getting better."

"JoJo…" Mary began, extending an arm in the direction of her friend, "you've got to look at this realistically."

"And what exactly is realistic, Mary? The accepted way: hospital, treatments, the whole shebang? I firmly believe I've taken the right step and I'm going to stick to it. How's everybody?"

Mary knew everybody meant Roger and the children. "They're all fine. The kids were really crazy about their birthday gifts, let me tell you, although Roger feels that you gave them outrageous things to make up for the guilt of going away."

"He's right."

"They're still asking Peter for your address, by the way."

"What does he say?"

"He gets around it somehow." Mary wanted to tell Joanne about the heated exchange between Roger and Peter, but she felt unable to spoil her friend's good mood.

"You know, Mary, I didn't realize I would be imposing on Peter so much."

"Don't worry about it, dear. He didn't get where he is by being intimidated by petty problems. He has more important things on his mind."

"How are things at the old rat race?"

"There's been a whole reorganization of personnel since Harvey Mack left."

"Harvey's gone? I can't believe it. His work was his life. What's he doing now?"

Mary hesitated a minute then decided that the direct approach was best. "He's dead, JoJo. You remember Peter telling you Harvey did not look well?" Joanne nodded. "Well, he left quietly a few weeks ago after telling Peter he had AIDS." Mary saw Joanne's face pale. "Peter's the only one who knew why he left. It was a shock to Peter; he relied a great deal on Harvey as you know."

"I know," Joanne said quietly. "Poor Peter. He ends up with everyone's problems. But, if Harvey died so quickly, he must have been quite ill when he left."

"He committed suicide the day after he left the company. Wanted to spare his wife and his daughter, I suppose. You knew Harvey was gay, didn't you?"

"I suspected."

"Is that why you didn't like him?"

"Of course not. It was his attitude toward me," Joanne said, her mind taking her back to her office and her last encounter with Harvey. She suddenly felt very sorry for the man she knew had never been really happy. There had been no hope for him, not even false hope. The hand that had been dealt her colleague was so much more cruel and vicious than the one she had been handed.

In her agony there had always been a ray of hope, at times very dim and feeble, but hope nevertheless. And while it grew brighter and brighter for her, Harvey Mack had had to face hopeless torture. Joanne was certain that, more than anyone, she fully understood the love that had guided Harvey's last conscious heroic act. She hoped the heavenly slate listing his flaws and frailties was erased when life deserted his body. He deserved it.

"I'm sorry I'm the one who had to tell you the news," Mary said.

"I'm glad you did. Puts life in perspective, doesn't it? Well, tell me, is Roger still talking about going to Hawaii in August?"

"He didn't mention it lately. He's quite busy defending the mayor these days. He was on the six o'clock news again last night."

In answer to Joanne's questions, Mary related all she knew about the case against Mayor Bristol. "Roger's working too hard, I think. He spent all of last Saturday and Sunday in meetings related to the case. Peter and I took Terri and Jason out." Before Joanne could put in a word, she added, "We really enjoyed it. Peter took Jason golfing while Terri and I went shopping. It was fun. Children have a way of making you feel younger, don't they?"

"When I'm better, I'll make it up to both of you."

"JoJo, there's no need for any such thing. Don't worry about anyone but yourself."

"Mary, deep down, do you believe I can do it? Cure myself, I mean?"

"Truthfully, I didn't expect you to be doing so well. I have to concede you must be doing something right."

"I'll make it, Mary. I will."

Later, when Mary Malton drove away and waved back, Joanne was feeling good. She was certain now that there was hope. And definitely not a false hope. She would again see all those she loved.

The warm June sun was touching everything in its path with brightness. Dressed in cotton shorts and a loose top, Joanne had made herself comfortable on the porch. A palette in one hand and a long brush in the other, she was concentrating on the colors she was mixing to obtain the perfect hue needed to finish the painting of Roger. She was working from a photograph pinned to the top of her easel, a picture she had carried in her wallet for a couple of years. She rested her brush and pushed her stool back to examine her effort when Red, who had been sleeping at her feet, stirred.

Joanne looked up and saw, coming up her drive, a plumpish man somewhere around fifty with short legs and a funny walk. She couldn't determine whether the problem originated from a defective gene or from the wrong style of underwear, and smiled. Red went to the man and, after sniffing for a moment, came back to the porch, satisfied that the man was not a stranger.

"Hello there," the man said in a friendly voice. "I'm going to be your neighbor for a while. My name's Michael Dunbar. I'm told you're Joanne Blake and that you live here by yourself."

"Is that a problem for you, Mr. Dunbar?"

"Not at all. I just find it unusual. It's a pretty remote area for a woman alone."

"You live alone, don't you, Mr. Dunbar?"

"Sure, but I'm a man and it's only for a few weeks. I'm a writer, a novelist actually, historical novels. Perhaps you've read some of my works?"

"Sorry. I can't say I have."

"Your loss," Dunbar said, still standing near the porch, now a crooked smile on his face. "I come up here because I find the solitude helps me put my thoughts in order. You're a painter?"

No, I'm really a pianist and what you're seeing is only an illusion, she wanted to tell him. Aloud she said, "Strictly a hobby, Mr. Dunbar."

"Please call me Mike. May I look?"

"I would prefer if you didn't."

He was taken aback by the reply, but continued. "I see Red's still around, just like when old man Wheeler was alive. I don't care much for dogs myself. I suppose it has something to do with the fact that I never had one as a child."

Beware of men who don't like dogs, someone had warned her once. Perhaps the saying was true, because there was something about Dunbar she found obnoxious, although she wasn't quite certain what it was.

"Red and I get along very well."

"Glad to hear it." He paused for a second, looking around. "Since we're two lonely souls out here by ourselves, perhaps we could have dinner together soon."

"I don't think so. I don't go out. Thank you anyway."

"I meant at my place. I'm a gourmet cook; it's been my hobby for a number of years. My personal recipes have appeared in some of the more popular magazines."

"How interesting."

"So, what do you say? How about tomorrow night? I make a marvelous duck l'orange."

"At the risk of offending you, I must refuse. For reasons that I cannot explain, I am not a very sociable person. Welcome to the neighborhood. If you'll excuse me, I want to get back to my work."

She transferred her attention back to her painting, leaving her visitor totally bewildered. He was, after all, a famous author, not at all used to being shunned. He knew some women in New York devised all sorts of wild plans to ensure an invitation to one of his celebrated private dinners. The skinny woman whom fate had determined would be his neighbor for the next two months would be a challenge, but not an insurmountable one.

Chapter Twenty-Four

Roger Blake didn't remember ever being so tired. Ever since old man McBride had committed the firm to the defense of Mayor Bristol against the indecency charge, Roger had had little time to relax. There had been numerous meetings, people to interview, facts to verify, always with Joseph McBride not far behind to check on every little detail.

As Roger had feared, the work he had to put in on The Case, as it was known around the office, was proving taxing when combined with the work to be done for his own clients. He was frustrated that he had little time lately for personal pursuits, including his children. More often than not he got home too late to share dinner with Terri and Jason, and he had to rely heavily on Mrs. Lucas and Mary Malton to oversee some of his parental duties.

Taking his attention away from the report he was reading, Roger rubbed his eyes. Drained of energy, he looked forward to the weekend, which would be free of any and all work. He needed rest, but he also needed to execute his personal plan: Find out why JoJo had disappeared and where she was.

His phone buzzed. Mr. Derek Hughes had arrived. Going to the reception area without bothering to put on his suit jacket, Roger brought the visitor back to his office where they sat at a round table in one corner.

Derek Hughes was a tall man, probably around six-foot-four, Roger judged, with a massive build. His crooked nose, the result of a clash with an unfriendly man who did not take too kindly to having his lifestyle scrutinized, made him appear more unsympathetic than he really was. While people found him menacing, which was helpful in his investigative work, Derek Hughes was mostly an amiable man.

"So, what do you have for me, Derek?"

"Well, as you requested," he began, "I followed the lady for almost two weeks, and there's nothing to report." Hughes took out his notebook, and began to recite in a monotone. "After work she goes home, has dinner with her parents and then spends most evenings sewing or watching television. On Saturdays she helps her mother clean the house and do the grocery shopping. On Sundays, they go to church, read, and in the evening, the older sister comes for dinner with her husband and their two sons. I'm telling you, Blake, it's like a sad Victorian vignette."

"I don't like it."

"And her co-workers are sticking by her; they say she's telling the truth."

"The next thing you're going to tell me is that she's about to be canonized!" Roger said irritably.

"Just about from the looks of things. I went through her room one day when the parents were out."

"How in hell did you get in the house."

"I know how to work a lock, you know. Don't worry, nobody saw me."

"We can't risk…"

"You hired me because I'm good, remember?"

"Go on."

"Well, I didn't find anything. I looked through everything, let me tell you. If she was paid off by the mayor's enemies, the money's not stashed in the house."

"Doesn't the whole thing strike you as rather weird? Here we have an attractive twenty-six-year-old female. You agree with me that she's attractive?"

"I certainly do!"

"With no boyfriend, no social life."

"My gut tells me it's too clean."

"Right! Much too clean. She did live on her own for a while. Why did she go back to live with her parents?"

"She told her colleagues she found it too expensive to live in an apartment while her parents had this large house," Hughes said. "On the surface that makes sense. A lot of young people are moving back home or living at home for as long as they can nowadays. It's a trend, but let me tell you they don't give up their independence. What's odd here is that this girl seems to have come home to devote herself to her parents. She was obviously born late in their marriage, but the parents are in good health and still active. It's like going back in time and it doesn't sit."

Roger got up and began pacing. "What about relatives?"

"The father comes from a farming family. He was considered a bit of a black sheep for coming to the city—years ago, of course—to become a fireman. His two brothers stayed on the family farm until they got married. Then they got their own farms, next to each other, near Triton, not far from that new prison. The oldest brother died a little over a year ago and the other one's still farming his own place, plus his brother's place. Basically, good, quiet people, the whole lot of them."

"No one in dire need of money?"

"Not as far as I could find out. The girl's father has a decent pension after all his years of service; his house's paid for. The uncle, the farmer, is not rich, but he seems to do okay."

"Going on the assumption that Sarah Wheeler was paid to discredit the mayor…"

"The money had to be good," Derek interrupted, "I mean, not just a small temptation."

"Enough to fulfill a dream," Roger said, sitting down again. "We've got to find out what that dream is."

"You're sure the mayor's clean in this?"

"I have to defend him. I have to believe him, and I see no reason not to. The guy is basically okay. I'm convinced he was not stupid enough to risk his career over a girl, no matter how pretty she is. If he was attracted to her, I don't believe he'd have made crude advances in his office. He's just not the type."

"What do you want me to do?" Hughes asked.

"We have to find either a paper, an agreement of some sort, or the money. Where would that be? In a safe-deposit box?"

"You think she insisted on a sort of contract?"

"Let's say it would fit."

"I'll get right on it. If I find anything, I'll yell."

"No illegalities, Derek."

"I know my job, Blake."

With these words the tall man got up and left the office.

Derek Hughes was the best in the business, but Roger worried about his methods. On occasions when they had worked together, Roger had often refrained from asking him how he had managed to obtain evidence. This time, with McBride right on top of things, Roger could only hope nothing would come crumbling down.

The next day, when Sarah Wheeler left City Hall at lunch time, she stopped about midway on the steps to check something in her purse, but the big man with the crooked nose, seemingly waiting for someone across the street, did not miss her surreptitious glances. *Is she checking for reporters?* Derek Hughes's gut told him something different.

She casually walked down the remaining steps and got in the first cab in a line of taxis waiting for fares. Hughes got into the next cab and followed at a proper distance. Some ten minutes later Sarah Wheeler was walking into a crowded restaurant. Shortly after, so was Hughes. He was seated at a small table near the door and ordered. The attractive girl sat at the other end of the room, her back to him. She remained alone throughout her meal. Derek Hughes had expected her to lead him to a bank, not a restaurant. He was baffled until the waiter deposited her bill on the table. She immediately covered it with her hand, and Hughes saw what most people would have missed: with a quick covert movement, she slipped an envelope into her purse. After paying her bill, she left the restaurant. Ten minutes later she was back at her desk at City Hall, ably punching computer keys.

The next day was the last weekend of June. The sun was hot as Derek Hughes, dressed in shorts and a T-shirt, drove north in a small, inconspicuous sedan. The large beige car he was following was not far ahead.

As per her usual schedule, Sarah Wheeler had stayed home the previous evening, but Derek knew in his gut something was in the offing. He left his surveillance post early and was back on duty soon after the sun was up. His intuition had been right. Shortly before nine, Sarah and her parents got into the large car the older Wheeler had owned for a number of years, and made their way to the highway, Sarah at the wheel, driving slowly.

After a while the car stopped at a filling station. Hughes continued on because he was sure of the Wheelers' destination. He had made good time when he reached Triton. He filled up his gas tank, took time to visit the washroom and then ambled to the grocery store. After he had chosen a few items, the big woman cashier appeared a little frightened to see him. He smiled.

"Came up here to do a little trout fishing. I understand it's pretty good in these parts."

She relaxed a little while he smiled even more warmly. He went back to his car to start on the cheese, crackers, fruit, and pop. His large frame couldn't go without being fueled with food until he got back to the city. He was finishing a second banana and a can of soda when he saw the large beige car come up the main street and turn off. He waited a few minutes before following.

When he reached Joe Wheeler's house, the large beige car was parked under a large maple tree. He kept on driving. He had been intrigued at seeing an expensive car parked near the house that he assumed belonged to the deceased Wheeler brother. Perhaps the place had been recently sold. He decided to find out.

Joanne Blake was picking large ripe strawberries in a small patch near her growing garden when she saw the small car pull up and the tall man get out. She immediately wondered how he had managed to get into the vehicle in the first place. Red greeted Derek Hughes with sharp barks, surprising Joanne. She told the dog to stop as she went to meet the man.

"Hi there. I'm looking for Mr. Wheeler."

"You have the wrong place. You'll find Joe Wheeler at the next farm down the road," she said, pointing.

"I'm not looking for Joe. I'm looking for his brother who used to live here."

Joanne eyed her visitor inquiringly. "He's been dead for a while. I live here now."

"I see. There's no name on the mailbox. Have you been here long?"

The massive figure in front of Joanne made her uncomfortable. "If you want information about Mr. Wheeler, just go and see his brother. I'm sure he could answer all your questions."

Derek Hughes smiled. His line of work required a good memory and he was certain he had seen the small woman with the shiny brown hair before. What bothered him was that he wasn't sure where or when. "I used to come fishing here. Haven't done so in a few years. I just assumed Mr. Wheeler would still be around."

"I'm sure his brother can take you."

"Thank you, ma'am. You've been most helpful."

With those words, Hughes bowed slightly and went back to his car, but not without first noting the license number of the parked car. Her face was familiar and he would satisfy his curiosity.

He drove his car past Joe Wheeler's farm and parked it on the side of the road several hundred yards away. The trees blocked the farm buildings, but he had a clear view of the two posts marking the entrance driveway. He leaned his seat back and waited, sipping on another can of pop.

The afternoon sun was high and the temperature still soaring when Joanne saw Michael Dunbar coming her way. She had set up her easel close to the road and was working on a painting of the fields and trees in front of her. She was slightly annoyed at being interrupted, especially by this man.

"Doing a scenery now, are you?"

Actually I was hoping you'd come by so I could paint your ugly legs. "Trying."

"I hope I'll get to see all your paintings before I go back to New York."

Don't count on it, buddy. "My paintings are for my own personal viewing only."

"You gave an exquisite one of the lake to Agatha Wheeler. I was very impressed by its quality, its magnetic surrealism. What would I have to do to get one?" he asked, his lips curling up in a smile to show brilliantly white teeth.

You'd have to move to the moon. "Agatha's been very kind to me. It was a token of my appreciation."

"I'd be willing to buy one from you. Who knows, with my connections in New York, I could establish an impressive demand for your paintings."

174

"I don't think I'm quite ready for that just yet."

"Fair enough, but do keep it in mind. I'm not as bad a fellow as you seem to assume. I was very impressed with your painting, and I'm serious when I say I could open doors for you. You could have a very lucrative career, instead of just a hobby."

Joanne became aware that her mouth was open, and closed it. The man might be sincere; she had to give him a chance. "I'll think about what you said if I ever decide to sell my paintings."

"Fair enough. I can't ask for more. That invitation for dinner still stands. I don't bite, you know."

Joanne smiled, not so much at Dunbar as at the fact that someone was approaching. Red had gone past them to go greet a slim, attractive young woman in a cotton sundress coming from the direction of Joe Wheeler's place, carrying a large straw bag.

"Mrs. Blake?" the young woman inquired as she approached. "I'm Sarah Wheeler. Joe's niece."

"Nice to meet you. Your aunt's very proud of you," Joanne said, extending her hand, smiling. "This is Michael Dunbar."

"Oh, I know. We've met before. How are you, Mr. Dunbar? Still enjoying this part of the world."

"Still love it, Sarah. Always will, I'm sure. I saw your picture in the paper. Quite a case from what I understand."

Sarah looked down and appeared embarrassed. "I'm just doing what has to be done. I just couldn't keep quiet about a thing like that."

"Quite noble of you. I do admire women who stand up for themselves. Hope you win. Well, ladies, if you'll excuse me, I have to get back to my manuscript. Nice to see you again, Sarah. Joanne."

"What can I do for you, Sarah?" Joanne asked as the two women looked at Michael Dunbar ambling down the road.

"I was wondering if you would mind if I went to look into an old trunk in the basement?"

"Of course not. Did you used to live here? Come on in."

The two women walked toward the house, and Sarah explained. "This was my uncle's place, but I spent a lot of time here with my cousins when I was a kid. I kept my toys and things like that in a trunk. I want to look through them if it's okay."

"No problem. I'm just renting the place as you know."

175

"I hope that trunk has not been in your way? I can take it out if you wish."

"I haven't been in the basement once since I've been here. No reason to go, I guess. Anything you want to leave there is certainly not in my way."

"Thank you. Do you have the key?"

"Oh, yes. It's in the kitchen. Come." Sarah followed Joanne into the kitchen where the key was hanging on a nail. "I think your uncle told me that was the one."

"Yes, it is. I'll put it back in its place before I go."

Sarah went out the back door, with Joanne following. When the girl had unlocked the padlock and opened the double doors to the cellar, Joanne went back to her painting, unaware of the large man who had been watching the action from behind a bush.

Chapter Twenty-Five

Roger Blake pulled out his cell phone and punched one of the numbers in the memory listing. He hoped Derek Hughes would have at last returned home; he was tired of hearing the monotonous greeting of the answering machine after having decided that it'd be wiser not to leave a taped message. After a few rings, Hughes answered.

"I was just about to call you, Blake. I have some news," he said in reply to Roger's greeting.

"Great. Can you come over? I want to talk to you about something else."

"Be right there."

No lock has been invented that I can't beat, Derek had once said. Roger hoped he had meant it. *It is imperative*, Roger mused. Both children were out, Terri at a party and Jason at a baseball game with Peter Malton, and Roger was grateful to have the house to himself.

"I hope you had no problem finding the place," Roger said as Derek came in.

"Of course not. I know this city inside out. Besides, I was here one night to give you some papers, a couple of years ago."

"That's right. I had forgotten. Come in and sit down."

Hughes accepted a beer and the two men made themselves comfortable in the family room. Daylight was fading and Roger turned on one of the table lamps. The central air conditioning provided a low hum that would insure privacy. One could never be too careful.

Derek related the activities of Sarah Wheeler the previous day and her trip to the country. Roger listened, intrigued. After a while he said, "You believe she's hiding the money in the basement of the house where that woman lives?"

"It's one possibility that must be looked into. One way or the other, I'm going to find out. I'll go back up there this week and look in the basement for myself."

"If that woman lives alone, she'll hear you."

"You worry too much, Blake."

"But why would the girl hide money up there? There could be a fire. Don't you think she would have put it some place where it'd be safer?"

"She got some kind of payment yesterday at the restaurant, of that I'm sure. She never went near any bank, then drives out to the country and rummages in her late uncle's basement. It fits that she hid it there."

"I hope she did."

"I'll do my best to find out."

Roger twisted the glass of beer in his hands for a moment, then said, "Derek, I want to talk to you about another job. This one's personal, and it would have to remain strictly between us."

"No problem there. You know I always keep my mouth shut."

The tone of Derek's last remark prompted Roger to say, "Of course you do. I didn't mean to offend you."

"What exactly do you want me to do?"

"Break into a doctor's office and let me read the file on one of his patients."

"You mean, you want to come in with me?"

"Yes."

"Sorry, Blake, but the answer is no."

Roger's back stiffened.

Derek continued, "I'll do it for you, but alone. I've always worked solo and I'm not ready to take on a partner at this point of the game."

"I understand," Roger said slowly.

"When do you want this done?"

"Tonight."

"Tonight? You're lucky my girl's out of town for the weekend, " Derek said with a teasing smile. "This is Saturday night."

178

"That's why I thought it would be a good time."

"Tell me where and what file you want."

"Dr. John Calder's office." Roger gave him an address and indicated the location of the office in the building. "The lock on the door is a bolt. Is that going to be a problem?"

"I'll look at it. Whose file do you want?"

"My wife, Joanne Blake."

Derek's arm, which was lifting a bottle of beer to his mouth, stopped dead in its track. After a moment, the visitor took a sip and waited.

"It's quite simple, Derek. My wife supposedly left on an extended business trip months ago. I have reasons to believe she went away because she's pregnant. Not by me; we'd been separated for two years. I simply want confirmation. Her doctor won't tell me anything. I want the date and reason of her last visit."

"I don't mind telling you I don't like it. I do what I do because it gives me the satisfaction of helping bring people who deserve it to justice. That's why when I work for you, like on the Wheeler case, I'm willing to bend things a little. No one should be charged for things they haven't done. Here, I wouldn't be helping anyone; you just want to satisfy your curiosity."

"I have the right to know. She's my wife, and I have to think of our children's future."

Hughes remained quiet for a long time, starting on a fresh beer Roger got for him.

"I know I'm imposing on you, Derek. It being Saturday night, and it's at the last minute. I'd be willing to double your usual fee. What do you say?"

The big man looked at Roger for a long moment, then finally said, "Very well, but let me warn you that if you ever mention to anyone I was involved in this, I'll destroy you, so help me God. You'll have no career left, Blake."

Roger was taken aback by the words and the tone of voice. "You know damn well I'll never implicate you, whatever happens."

"As long as it's well understood." Hughes looked at his watch and said, "I'll do it now. Be back in a couple of hours."

"I'll go with you and wait in the car."

Derek Hughes got up and looked down from his height at Roger with an expression that made it quite clear it would be wise for the lawyer not to push the point. The investigator let himself out of the house quietly.

The warm, clear night had brought a crowd of people of all ages to enjoy a Saturday evening out in the restaurants and nightspots that lined the street adjacent to where Dr. Calder's office was located. The large tiered parking next to the medical building was nearly full. Two happy couples who were about to cross a quiet intersection against the light in front of a patrolling police cruiser were waved through by the two policemen. The officers' job was to make certain undesirable types were kept at bay; regular folks out to enjoy the evening were forgiven insignificant carelessness.

Slowly, the blue and white car moved toward the main artery, and the patrolmen didn't see the big, tall man making his way to the front door of the medical building.

Derek Hughes had scrutinized the door earlier and he knew he would have no problem. He walked at a regular pace, stopping at the door. Working as if he belonged there, his deft hands skillfully plunged a long tool into the keyhole. After many long seconds of expert maneuvering the lock gave way and he was inside the building before anyone on the street had time to notice. He took the stairs up with surprising agility.

The door to Dr. Calder's office proved more frustrating than the front door. In the dark corridor, Derek used a small flashlight held in his teeth to expertly manipulate a long magnetized hooked instrument for some ten minutes before the lock surrendered. He paused a moment for a sigh of relief before going in quietly.

He easily found the filing cabinet and overcame the lock in a few seconds. In the dim light he began his search. When he had located Joanne Blake's file, he sat down at the nurse's desk and began reading. He could not decipher all of Dr. Calder's handwriting, but he read enough to be troubled: Carcinoma…refused treatment…persuasion ineffectual…moving to country…prognosis terminal.

Hughes mentally recorded that the dates of the notations went back to the beginning of the year. Digging under the top pages, he read the copy of the letter attesting to Joanne Blake's condition. The next few pages were what appeared to be detailed laboratory reports, stating that the patient had stomach cancer.

Derek closed the file after failing to notice the noted telephone number. He stared in the dark for a moment.

Because of the experience he had accumulated over the years, Derek Hughes rarely took anything for granted. In many instances, people he was certain were innocent had, by their actions, proven their guilt beyond the shadow of a doubt. Even in his current work for Blake on the case against the mayor, he had not lost sight of the possibility that the mayor might be guilty. Even if his gut had told him Sarah Wheeler was not what she appeared on the surface, only when he had seen her secretly accept that envelope in the restaurant, had he known for sure there had been a conspiracy against the mayor.

Roger Blake had told Hughes his wife was pregnant and Derek had accepted that fact. It had been a mistake. He should have looked at the other possible reasons for her extended absence. If he had, he might have refused the assignment, and would not now be facing the decision of whether or not to tell Roger Blake what he'd learned. *Of course, since a payment was agreed upon, I have little choice. Yet do I dare lie and tell my client that his wife is indeed pregnant? It is, after all, what he wants to hear. Roger Blake wants a simple and clean confirmation. He is not expecting anything else.*

Slowly, Derek replaced the file in its correct order and locked the cabinet, wiping everything he might have touched with a large white handkerchief. He made his way out of the building, locking doors behind him. Once outside, instead of going to his car, he walked for a while then stepped inside a crowded, noisy pub. He sat at the bar, nursing a beer, while he weighed his options. More than an hour had passed by the time he reached a decision.

Approaching the Blake house, Derek saw an expensive sedan come to a stop. He parked a few houses away and waited. Soon, a boy got out of the car and Roger came out to greet him and exchange a few remarks with the driver. Soon, the sedan pulled out and Roger went back inside. A few minutes later, lights went on in a bedroom upstairs. Several minutes after the room went dark again, Derek Hughes walked to the front door and knocked softly.

"My son was out at a baseball game with a friend. He's gone to sleep now; he won't hear anything upstairs. What did you find out? It took you so long, I was worried," Roger said nervously.

The two men were again in the family room.

"Blake, you're not going to like what I have to report. I've thought about it a lot. I mean, I considered not telling you the truth, but I've come to the decision that you should know."

"She's pregnant and you found out who the father is."

"No. She's not pregnant." Derek paused for a moment, and looking straight into Roger's eyes, forged ahead. "I'm very sorry I have to tell you this." Again, a pause.

"Damn, Derek. Spit it out already!"

"Your wife has gone to live by herself. It didn't say where, because she was diagnosed with stomach cancer."

Derek saw the overwhelming shock in Roger's eyes, but nevertheless continued. *I have to get it over with as quickly as possible.*

"The doctor wrote that she refused some sort of laser treatment and that she went to live somewhere by herself. There was a copy of a letter with the heading To Whom It May Concern, which confirmed her condition. I had trouble reading some of the doctor's notes, but I understood the prognosis to be less than a year. You don't know how sorry I am, Blake. This is the hardest thing I've ever had to do."

After a long silence, Roger said in a voice Derek could hardly make out, "Thank you for telling me the truth. I appreciate it."

"What are you going to do? Can I help?" Derek's offer was sincere.

"I don't know yet. There was no indication of where she went?"

"None that I could make out. I'm sorry."

"Could you find her, Derek?"

"It might be difficult. Surely someone at her work might know."

Indeed, Roger thought. Aloud he said, "Let me write you a check right now, Derek. It'll give you a chance to put this whole thing out of your mind."

Roger got up and came back a minute later with his checkbook.

"Blake, this one's on me."

Chapter Twenty-Six

Terri came home past her curfew, but Roger lacked the mental strength to reprimand her. Besides, she was too excited.

"Want to know what happened tonight? We stopped at Susan's house after the party, and her father told me he was looking for someone to answer the phone at his nursery. The girl that worked for him had a car accident yesterday and won't be back at work for a long while, maybe all summer. He offered me the job and I accepted. Isn't that cool? My first job. Susan wanted it, but she'd already told the people at the tennis club she'd work there. Besides, I think it's better not to work with your parents, don't you think? I mean, if I worked at your office for example, I think it'd be hard."

"That's true, dear," Roger replied evenly. He remembered what JoJo had told him about seeing her mother die. Suddenly, he felt very sorry for his daughter. Soon she would have no mother, Jason would have no mother, and he would no longer have a wife.

"Are you okay, Dad?" Terri asked, pouring herself a glass of milk.

"Just a little tired. You'd better get to bed. Congratulations on the job."

She kissed him on the forehead and said, "Thanks. Goodnight, Dad."

Roger went upstairs shortly after Terri. He was proud of his daughter, and he was glad she was so thrilled at the prospect of a summer job. It would help her mature and maybe, just maybe, she would be able to weather the pain that was just ahead. He stretched fully dressed on top of the comforter, trying to understand why JoJo had chosen to face her horrible destiny alone and why she had refused treatment. *If there was hope, why hadn't she grabbed it?*

He did, however, understand the reason that had made her turn to him after their lunch in his apartment months earlier, and he was grateful for the memories of Vail. *They will have to last a lifetime. Why, oh God, why her? Why are you taking my love away from me? From the children?* Tears began to roll down his cheeks.

He understood so many things now: the evasive excuses for her departure, the tears in her eyes on the eve of their separation, the extravagant gifts for the children, her remark to Carol Ferguson, "Some day you'll understand," the missing paint and brushes from the spare room, her weight loss. But he didn't understand why she had not wanted to confide in him, why she had not let him help her. *Is it to protect me? It is unthinkable that she should be suffering alone. I have to find her, be with her for the last few months of her life. I have to. Peter Malton will tell me where to find her. I will get it out of him.*

Roger slept only intermittently, nightmares filling the minutes of escape. He got up early and made strong coffee. The previous evening he had been devastated; this morning he was angry. Angry at life, angry at JoJo, angry at John Calder, angry at Peter Malton. There had been a conspiracy against him which he found difficult to accept. At eight-thirty, he dialed Peter Malton's number and a recorded message answered. It added to Roger's anger. There was so little precious time left.

Although he did not feel up to it, Roger took his children swimming at the lake just outside the city as he had promised them earlier in the week. The sea of people on the beach bothered him as well as the humidity, which became more and more oppressive as the day wore on. Terri and Jason met some of their friends, and watching them enjoying themselves, Roger wondered how he would manage to be both a mother and father to them. He had relied so deeply on JoJo. He would be forever lost.

Later, as part of his promise, Roger took his children out to dinner. As they were walking into the restaurant, he stayed back a little and once more punched Peter Malton's number on his cell phone. He swore again at the recorded message. *Where are Peter and Mary Malton? Peter had not mentioned anything the night before when he was dropping Jason off, but then again, why should he? He is JoJo's friend, not mine, and I don't have his cell number.*

After Terri and Jason had gone to bed, Roger poured himself a scotch on the rocks. He drank it much faster than he would have under normal circumstances and quickly followed it with a refill. By the time he reached his bedroom, his head was buzzing. He let his body fall on the bed and in a moment escaped into salutary sleep.

Derek's first order of business on Monday morning was a visit to the office of motor vehicles. The crushing humidity had not relented, and he was grateful for the cool air inside the building. He made his way through a maze of corridors and entered an office with no indication on the door of who worked inside.

"The man himself," an attractive woman about thirty years old sitting behind one of only two desks in the room said as a greeting.

"Good morning, sweetie."

"You're calling me sweetie. You want something, right? What am I saying? Why else would you come in this office reserved for special investigations? What is it this time, and will I lose my job because of it?"

"You're a servant of the public, right? Well, I'm Joe Public and I want to know the name of the owner of a license plate."

"I should throw you out, Hughes, but…only because you're Maggie's friend."

"I appreciate it. You know I do."

As he read the letters and numbers of the plate belonging to the mysterious lady at the Wheeler farm, the woman punched them in. In a few moments she had an answer. "Joanne Blake, 450 Maplegrove Avenue."

At Hughes' look of panic, the woman said, "That's not the name you wanted to hear, is it?"

He composed himself quickly. "Thanks, sweetie." Reaching in his pocket, he pulled out two tickets. "For Saturday's ball game."

"Well, very nice. Come in again."

He left the office quickly. So that's where he had seen the woman. Right in Blake's house. She had answered the door when he delivered documents to the lawyer, certainly over two years before. He had not forgotten the pretty face, but he had forgotten where he had seen it. Now, condemned to die, she had taken refuge in a remote farmhouse without telling her husband. Derek Hughes sat in his car for a while, thinking.

He was under no obligation to tell Blake of his discovery because he had, in fact, simply been satisfying his personal curiosity. By reporting the information he had unearthed in Dr. Calder's office on Saturday night to Roger Blake, he had more than fulfilled his obligation. It was now up to Blake to find his wife. *But,* Derek thought, *there is the unfinished business of the Wheeler case.* He had to go back to Triton, and it suddenly displeased him. Getting into the basement would be easy enough, what bothered him was having to go on the property, knowing Joanne Blake's secret. *Should I warn her that her husband has found out the truth? She would want to know how, and that would mean a lot of questions better left unanswered. Laws had, after all, been broken, but given the circumstances, could that not be forgiven?*

No. I have to resist the temptation. The pretty lady faces enough pain. I have no right to complicate her life. I have done my job and the matter should no longer be of any concern to me.

That muggy Monday morning, Roger Blake was late getting to his office. He had overslept, his body fighting to recoup the hours of lost sleep. He also had a mild headache aggravated by the stuffy inside air. He had never understood why, especially in periods of high humidity, tenants of the building did not force the owners to keep the air conditioning operating on weekends. Or at least turn it back on Sunday afternoon so the air could be acceptable for the start of the work week. He would have to endure a few more hours of stale, humid air, and it did nothing to improve his mood.

An early meeting had been called by Joseph McBride, and Roger reported his progress on unmasking Sarah Wheeler. Everyone, especially old man McBride, received the news enthusiastically. If suspicions proved right, and Roger hoped they would in the next few days, the whole messy trial of Mayor Bristol could be avoided. It would spare an innocent man further indignities, not to mention bring a new wave of heightened recognition for the firm. Joseph McBride was indeed pleased. So pleased that he did not accept Roger's attempts at excusing himself from having lunch with him and the mayor.

When he left the meeting, Roger's mood had not improved. His plan to confront Peter Malton that very morning had been torpedoed and his anger was mounting. But he decided that he needed to control himself in order to avoid antagonizing his co-workers. By lunchtime, he had rescheduled appointments and felt marginally better; he would be free to pursue personal matters the rest of the day and the following day if necessary.

He silently prayed that the lunch with the mayor would not turn out to be interminable.

Joanne Blake rarely made use of the small radio she had brought with her to the country. She didn't want to hear newscasts. She had no desire to find out to what degree of madness the world had progressed, how many people had found it necessary to kill fellow human beings, or how much devastation the latest natural disaster had caused. However, on occasion, she did listen to classical music on a station that catered to music lovers rather than to those who yearn for endless chatter.

This Monday morning was such an occasion. She was stretched out on the sofa in the living room and the music was an anodyne for her body and her soul as she guided her imagery to new heights and new victories more quickly and more effectively than at any other time. For a long time, she heard neither the music nor the hard rain hitting the roof with unvarying regularity.

The mugginess of the previous days was beginning to abate with the driving summer downpour. It went on for nearly an hour before it lost some of its vigor and began its retreat as a fine sprinkle. Joanne felt the cooler air being pushed into the house through the screens on the front and back doors, and was grateful for the relief it brought.

Red had been waiting for the rain to end stretched out on the front porch. He got up abruptly and sat on his hind legs for a moment. When he was certain he had not misinterpreted the sound that had reached his ears, he jumped up and made his way around the house to the closed doors leading to the cellar. There he began barking furiously. When the man opened one of the doors and attempted to go up the concrete stairs to make a quick getaway, the sight of Red ready for action and the alarming growl made him stop.

Derek Hughes had driven up to Triton soon after visiting the motor vehicle office when he saw the sky was darkening. He reasoned that the sound of the heavy rain after the burdensome heat of the last few days would mask any sound that could draw attention to his presence. The rain had started when he was on the highway. It had slowed his trip, and by the time he had hidden his car and made his way on foot to Joanne Blake's hideaway, the rain was subsiding.

With music reaching his ears through the open windows, he had quickly mastered the padlock and gone down to the basement, noiselessly closing the door behind him. The furnace in the middle and the large oil tank in one corner could easily be seen with the light coming in through the small windows. He used a flashlight to inspect the rest. There were a dozen or so wooden boxes piled up against one wall. On a crudely made shelf, there were a small boat motor and an old toolbox. Near the wall that he judged to be the front of the house, there was an old metal trunk on top of a few planks. *Eureka!* he thought. In an instant, he had managed the lock. Inside the trunk were old dolls and an assortment of childhood toys and souvenirs.

He plunged his hand under everything and his fingers touched something interesting, very interesting indeed. He pulled out a metal box containing a few envelopes. He didn't need to open the white ones to know they contained money because his agile fingers had felt it. A larger brown envelope was sealed with several layers of heavy tape. He had done his job. He would report to Blake and it would be up to the lawyer to make certain the authorities were informed.

Noiselessly, he put everything back in place and locked the trunk. As he was making his way out, he hit an old piece of pipe lying on the floor. Because he was wearing sport shoes, the sound had not been loud, but it had been high-pitched. He waited a moment. Not hearing any footsteps above him, he continued toward the doors only to be confronted by Red.

How could I have forgotten there was a dog? My discovery of Joanne Blake's identity clearly had more of an effect on me than I realized. I failed to be prudent.

Red's unrelenting barking and growling put an end to Joanne's mental exercises. Stepping into a pair of sandals, she went out the back door in the light rain. The sight of Derek Hughes in her cellar frightened her, an emotion she had not experienced in months. She tried to not show it.

"Don't tell me. You were looking for fishing rods," she said.

Red was still objecting to the man's presence.

"Please call off your dog and I'll explain."

"And I bet it's going to be a beaut." Joanne found it amusing that such a large man would be scared of Red but, she had to admit, the animal really looked menacing. "One command from me and he'll go straight for your throat."

"I won't make any sudden moves."

"You'd better not!" To the dog, she said, "Red, sit. It's okay, but do keep an eye on him." To Hughes, "Okay, come up on the porch. I want to get out of this rain."

The dog had stopped barking, yet continued to growl for a moment as Derek came up the stairs and preceded Joanne to the porch. She sat in an old rocker, a few feet from the man who did not appear comfortable in a flimsy lawn chair. Red, now quiet, came to sit on his hind legs, close to Joanne, intent on keeping an eye on things.

"What's your story, Mr...?"

"Hughes. Derek Hughes. I didn't come here to harm you. I was looking for something in your basement."

"And pray tell what were you looking for?"

"Something Sarah Wheeler put there yesterday."

"I figured your story about fishing with Mr. Wheeler was a bit cockeyed. Are you a policeman?"

"Sort of. I'm a private investigator. I followed Sarah Wheeler up here and since I had reason to believe she hid a large sum of money in your basement, I came to check it out."

"Money? Did she?"

"Yes. I have to warn you the police will be coming up here with a warrant, probably very soon."

The rain was spent. Only a few occasional drops rolled off the porch roof. Red got to his feet and went to meet Agatha Wheeler who was coming up the drive, folding an umbrella.

"Hello, Agatha," Joanne said.

"Are ya okay? I see ya got company. I was worried that somethin' happened because Red was really barking up a storm there. Not often he does that."

"He didn't like this gentleman from the looks of things."

"Oh. Is he a friend of yours?"

"No. Mr. Hughes came up to look for a fishing spot."

"Mister, ya can't just come and use the lake just like that. Ya have to go with one of the farmers up here. My husband can take ya if ya want. We live just down the road there," Agatha concluded with a wave of her arm.

"Thank you. Perhaps another time," Derek said.

"Want to sit down, Agatha?" Joanne inquired.

"Can't. I was makin' lunch. Better get back to it. Sure there's no problem?"

"I'm quite all right, thank you. I'm sorry you disturbed yourself."

"I just thought I'd best check, just in case."

"Thank you again, Agatha. I really appreciate it."

The older woman took one last look at Dereck Hughes before heading back. Joanne was grateful she had come to check. It might prove very useful in case of an accident or if the disease got the better of her.

"Thank you for not mentioning the purpose of my visit to Mrs. Wheeler."

"You know who she is, of course, which means you know Sarah is her niece. I didn't think it would be appropriate." With Red back at her feet, Joanne continued, "Mr. Hughes, you said the police would be up here. What has Sarah done? Has she stolen money? She mentioned something about a court case."

"Sarah has not stolen money, but we have reason to believe that she has been paid handsomely to discredit Mayor Bristol and ensure that he will not be reelected. I was hired by the mayor's lawyers to follow Miss Wheeler."

Joanne remembered her conversation with Mary Malton and panic struck her. "Who exactly hired you, Mr. Hughes?"

"Roger Blake." His face did not betray what he knew.

"I hope there won't be a bunch of lawyers coming up here or I'll have your hide."

"No need to worry, ma'am. This is a matter for the police now. I would just ask you not to tell them that I searched your basement."

"Then, how are you supposed to have found out about the money?"

"I followed her and I saw her go into your basement."

"In other words, you've broken the law with the blessing of a lawyer, and you want me to keep quiet about it. The end justifies the means and all that."

"In this case, ma'am, the end is the career of a good man. I cannot force you not to tell anyone that I broke into your basement; however, it could prove very embarrassing not only to me, but to the law firm as well."

"I'll think about it, Mr. Hughes. Now I suggest you leave before Red gets impatient and decides not to wait for my signal."

"Yes, ma'am." Hughes got up and walked away, certain that Joanne Blake would keep quiet. She couldn't afford to be in contact with her husband, not after all the trouble she had gone through to be alone. Derek could only hope she would have enough sense to give a false name when the investigators came around.

Joanne watched the tall man walk away, and a feeling of panic resurfaced. *Why did I have to be thrown into the middle of Roger's case? What will I do when they, whoever they would be, come to search my basement? Maybe they'll recognize me.*

She had to get away for a while, and let the Wheelers handle the police. Sooner or later they would have to know about their niece.

Chapter Twenty-Seven

In his well-appointed office, Peter Malton was studying a financial report for the previous month, pleased by the figures. He took time to savor them. In the last few years, the company had had its share of problems, but because it had faced adversity head-on, it had emerged the better for it. More recently, the personnel changes that had been necessitated by the departure of two of the top people had required an adjustment, but Scalls-Morton was thriving and confident.

Peter's mind wandered to the previous day. He and Mary had gone to their oldest son's summer cottage and, with their children and grandchildren around them, had indulged in the simple pleasures that made life worthwhile and the problems of the company more bearable.

Suddenly, his door was pushed open and quickly slammed shut again.

"You goddamned bastard! I want to know where JoJo is and I want to know now."

Peter Malton could not believe the outrage he saw in the eyes of the man in front of him. "Roger, please get a grip…"

Reinforced by the liquor he had lavishly consumed at lunch, Roger Blake approached Peter, interrupting in a loud voice as his angry fist his the desk. "My wife is dying and you kept it a secret from me. Who in the hell appointed you God?"

Peter was frightened at the thought of what could happen. Somehow Roger had found out and his anger would know no bounds.

"You heard me, Malton. I want to know where JoJo is. *Now*." His voice had reached a volume that shocked Peter. "You knew from the start what was wrong and where she went. How could you all the while pretend, in front of the children and me, that everything was all right. She's my wife, not yours."

The door opened quietly and Peter saw the questioning look on his secretary's face. He motioned her away. "It's okay." The door closed again.

"Roger, please sit down," Peter said in a low voice.

"No. I won't."

"Then do keep your voice down. This is an office, not a cheap saloon." With Roger's eyes piercing him, he asked, "How did you find out?"

"None of your damn business. Where is she?"

"I can't tell you, Roger. I had to promise her I wouldn't. You may not believe it, but we argued because I wanted you to know. I wanted her to tell you, but she was very adamant about it. She did it to save you and the children from the pain of seeing her die because she loves you so much.

"I'm sure you remember she saw her mother die when she was a child. I was there. I know how much it took out of her. She didn't want any of you having to go through the same thing."

"Whatever the reasons for her decision, now that I know, I want to be with her. I'm not going to let her die alone. Where is she?"

"I repeat, Roger. I can't tell you. I have to keep my promise to JoJo."

"You never liked me, did you, Malton? And this was your chance to have the upper hand. Well, it's over, buddy." As he uttered the words, Roger came around the desk and grabbed Peter's tie and pulled. "Are you going to tell me or am I going to have to kill you, you fucking worm. You didn't have to comply with JoJo's wishes. Not in this case and you know it. I thought you loved her. If you did, you would have forced her to get treatment, instead of letting her waste away by herself. It's absolutely insane. She might have had a chance, did you ever think about that?"

"More nights than I care to mention. Both Mary and I tried time and time again to get her to change her mind, believe me!"

Roger pulled again on the tie. "Well, you should have tried harder. Where *is* she?"

"Roger, I can't tell you."

"You mean you won't. If you don't, I'm going to choke you right here, so help me God."

Peter was looking at the eyes full of anger, but he also saw overwhelming pain. Unexpectedly, Roger released his grip on Peter's tie and went to stand by the window behind the desk, his hands going up to cover his face.

Peter gave out a silent groan, undid the top button of his shirt and rubbed his neck. "I know how you feel, Roger, believe me," he said in a compassionate tone.

"I don't think you ever could." Roger's voice was low and tearful now. "You would have to be in the position I'm in right now." He turned to face Peter Malton again, his eyes red. "Peter, I have to go to her, don't you understand that? Think how you would feel if the roles were reversed and Mary was ill?"

"I have thought about it more times than I care to mention. I was against the idea of JoJo going away from the start, but she's stubborn. You know that more than anyone. I couldn't get her to change her mind, and I guess in the end, I bought the argument that she had the right to choose how and where she would spend the rest of her life."

"You do know where she is?"

"Yes. Why don't you sit down, Roger? I'll make you a drink."

Roger sat down wearily. "One thing I don't need is a drink. I've already had quite a few."

"I suspected as much."

"You've been seeing her?"

"Not as much as I would have wanted. Mary saw her not too long ago though and she was very impressed by the way she looked."

"Really?"

"JoJo's convinced that she can will herself to overcome the cancer with some sort of mental exercises. She's also been very active physically and eating only certain foods. By the looks of things, it's helping."

Roger's shoulders relaxed. "Do you think it could work?" he asked cautiously.

"Frankly," Peter spoke slowly, "I'm of the opinion that she's probably in a remission period. What she's doing is no doubt beneficial, but I don't think it can cure her. I think it's a lull before the storm. I'm sorry, Roger."

"Peter, please tell me where she is. Please! I have to be with her. Can't you see that?" Roger said, his voice sadly low.

Peter thought for a moment. Ever since JoJo's shocking announcement, he had considered telling Roger the truth many times. He knew it would be the only fair thing to do, especially since they had reconciled their differences, yet he had never been able to bring himself to break his promise to JoJo. *Should I do it now that circumstances have changed? After all, isn't JoJo's first concern that Terri and Jason be spared the pain? The children could still be shielded while Roger supported his wife in her supreme effort.*

Peter had often discussed JoJo with Mary late at night when he had trouble falling asleep. He knew his wife would support any decision he made now and would understand that the breaking of a promise could be much more important than keeping it, especially if it brought together two people who desperately needed each other.

JoJo would understand that he had no choice. It was also reasonable to assume that she might even thank him for having the courage to go against her wishes. Peter had never questioned why JoJo had chosen to marry Roger Blake, and there had never been any doubt in his mind that she loved her husband very deeply, just as the reverse was also true. *Who indeed has appointed me, Peter Malton, God? By what superior power could I be the master puppeteer dangling lives at the end of a string, keeping them apart? Is the script mine and mine alone to write and perform? I have assumed a role I saw as mine, but perhaps my glasses need polishing.*

"Roger," he began, "I will take you to her."

"Thank you," Roger said softly, sighing with relief, "but I think I want to face JoJo alone. I have to convince her it was all my doing. Just tell me where she is."

"I would like the opportunity of explaining to JoJo face-to-face the reasons behind my decision."

"You can do that when I bring her back. First, I need some time alone with her. Please."

"I suppose that's only fair," he said at length. "Very well." Peter Malton took a large pad from the corner of his desk. "On one condition."

"Shoot."

"That you don't tell Terri and Jason. JoJo wanted so much to spare them."

"I have no intention of telling them anything."

"Good. She's in the country about an hour's drive from here. I'll draw you a map." When he finished explaining the location of the Wheeler house, he gave the paper to Roger, who folded it and put it in his pocket.

"I'm sure I'll have no trouble finding it. Thank you." Roger hesitated for a moment, then said, "I'm sorry, Peter, for the…outburst. I have known since Saturday and when I couldn't reach you, I guess I just went sort of crazy."

"I understand, Roger. Your anger needed a target and I was it. I'm glad you got it out of your system before facing JoJo," Peter Malton said, ineffectively trying to smile.

"Yeah," Roger said simply. "Peter, you know a lot of doctors…"

"If you can get her back here quickly, I'll get her to the world's top specialists."

"Thanks again, Peter," Roger said, extending his hand.

Peter Malton shook the hand that was offered, and felt a deep sympathy for the man JoJo loved so much. "Get your tail up to Triton, Blake. We've all lost too much time as it is."

Derek Hughes drove as fast as the law allowed, at times faster, to get to the city. He had called Roger Blake's cell phone, but it was turned off. He called the law office only to be told Roger wasn't expected back until the next day. He stressed the importance of his call, and the receptionist promised to try and reach the lawyer. The news Hughes had for Blake would take his mind off his personal problems, at least for a while.

Hughes had been most impressed at how cool and collected the lovely Joanne Blake had proven to be. But then, how could he have expected anything else from the woman who, stricken with a terminal disease, had seen fit to face it alone, away from everyone she knew. She had appeared unperturbed by the news that he, Derek, worked for her husband. He had not seen the slightest hint of surprise in her eyes, and considered that the best actors were not all on television or movie screens.

When he reached the city, Hughes drove directly to Maplegrove Avenue, arriving just in time to see Roger Blake get into his car. He parked and quickly ran to catch Blake as he was backing out of the driveway.

"I've got great news for you. I've…"

"It'll have to wait, Derek. I found out where my wife is. I have to go see her right away."

"Great. But listen, Sarah Wheeler had stashed the money in the basement of the house. I saw it."

"I was sure you would. Why don't you go and see old man McBride and give him all the details. He can follow it up."

"So he can ask me how I got in. No, thanks. I only deal with you."

"Fair enough. But it can wait. I'll call you in a day or so."

Derek tried to object only to see Roger Blake continue to back out and put his car into drive.

Hughes needed to push the face of the pretty Joanne out of his mind. He got into his car, drove downtown and went to a movie.

Soon after Derek Hughes left, Joanne Blake put a few clothes into a small suitcase. She had no idea how long it would be before the police came around asking questions, but she knew she had to leave as soon as possible. *Hughes doesn't know my name; at least I didn't tell him, but as an investigator he could easily find out. If he does, will he tell Roger?* She decided he would not. *He owes me.* She had to gamble that if she was away during the search of her basement, her name might not even come up at all.

She went into the kitchen and gathered a few of the bottles of vitamin supplements when she noticed Red following her. She stopped and bent down. "You know I've got to get away, don't you? Sorry, my friend, but I can't bring you with me. I don't even know where I'm going! But I'll be back in a week or so." She hugged the animal. "It'll go by fast, you'll see. You can go to Agatha when you're hungry. I know she'll feed you. Okay?"

The animal looked at her with watery eyes.

"I tell you what. When I'm all better, you can come with me to the city and we'll come up here during the summer." She hugged Red again and went back to her packing.

After locking up, she got into her car, hoping it would start. She had used it only a few times to go to the village soon after her arrival. Lately, since Agatha so kindly got the groceries she needed, there had been no need for transportation. She pressed the gas pedal and turned the key. The motor purred and Joanne smiled. She waved to Red who, sitting on the edge of the porch, would, she thought, have cried if able to.

At the sound of the car, Agatha came out to meet Joanne.

"I'm going to the city for about a week. Here's the key to the house," Joanne said, handing it to Agatha. She wanted to add that she knew where the key to the basement was should the police be around. She didn't. She also wanted to tell the kind older woman about Sarah, but wisdom won out.

"Do ya good. Gonna see your family?"

"I'll visit a lot of people. Do you think you could feed Red? I think he's going to be a bit lost."

"Don't ya worry about Red. Been 'round here a long time. I reckon he'll manage. When I see him, I'll be sure to feed him."

Joanne thanked Agatha and waved back to her new friend after turning onto the road. In Triton she stopped at the bank for some cash, and soon she was on the highway, heading north with no definite plan. After about a half hour, she exited and drove through a quaint-looking town. On the outskirts, a recently built motel with a swimming pool attracted her attention. She checked in.

Chapter Twenty-Eight

Roger Blake easily recognized Joanne's rented house from Peter Malton's description and was impressed as he turned into the driveway. She had indeed chosen a lovely spot. In a moment he was knocking at the door with mixed emotions of fear and happiness. When he heard no sound, he repeated his rap and waited, his nervousness heightening.

Suddenly, a sound from the side of the house facing the lake made him turn. Of course she would not be inside. With the air freshly cleansed by the rain, she would be enjoying nature at its best. He was sure his heart skipped a beat at the thought of seeing Joanne again at last, but as he rounded the corner, he only saw a dog.

Red sniffed the visitor, and when he did not bark, Roger was assured of his friendliness. He bent down and petted the animal before heading around the house and trying the back door. He looked around calling JoJo's name, made his way into the barn through the small door and walked down to the lake. He was coming back when he saw a car slow down on the road.

Inside the car, Agatha Wheeler told her husband, "We best stop. I don't like strangers 'round."

"Could be a friend of hers."

"Still, we've got to tell him."

Joe Wheeler stopped the car and backed it up. In a moment, he had parked it next to Roger's vehicle.

"Hello there," Roger said, coming to Agatha's side of the car. "Do you live around here?"

"Yeah. Just up the road."

"Good. Then perhaps you can tell me where my wife is. My name is Roger Blake. I'm Joanne's husband."

Agatha was taken aback. *Why in the world would anyone choose not to live with such a handsome man? Had Joanne run away because he was one of those wife beaters she had heard about on television? Maybe an alcoholic?* Agatha wished she had pried more.

"Gone to the city," Joe replied.

"She has? When?"

"Left a couple of hours ago. Said she was goin' to visit people," Agatha managed to say.

"Oh. For how long?"

"A week she said."

"Thank you. Thank you very much. I'll see her there, then," Roger said. He quickly got into his car and left, waving to the Wheelers.

"Why do ya reckon she didn't want to talk about him?"

"Now, Agatha, don't get all worked up. It's none of our business."

Roger made it back to the city in record time, all the while his mind trying to determine what had made JoJo decide to come home. *Has she finally come to her senses and returned to get the help she needs? How happy Terri and Jason would be at seeing her, although it is imperative they not know about the illness. Certainly not yet. Maybe after she got treatments.*

The sun was still high in the sky when he brought his car to a screeching stop in his driveway and ran inside. Mrs. Lucas was about to leave. "Mr. Blake, you're back already?"

"Yeah," he said absent-mindedly. "Where are the children?"

"I fed them early, then they both went out. They said you knew where they were going."

"Yeah, I know. Nobody else here?"

"No. Were you expecting someone?"

"Yes, I am."

"They didn't get here yet. Do you want me to stay and get you some dinner? There's some stew left. I could warm it up in a jiffy."

"Don't worry about it, Mrs. Lucas. It's okay." He managed to smile.

"Well, goodnight, then, Mr. Blake."

Like a madman Roger went through every room in the house, hoping JoJo had somehow managed to come in without Mrs. Lucas noticing. After a fruitless search, he sat in the living room, despair momentarily overcoming him. *Has she come to the city to see someone else? Why had she not come home? He wasn't supposed to know, so perhaps she had gone directly to a hospital. Dr. Calder would know.*

Roger found the physician's personal number in the small directory in the kitchen filled with numbers they used more or less regularly. Janet Calder answered, telling Roger her husband was at the hospital on an emergency. He thanked her and said he would catch up with him there.

John Calder had indeed been called to the hospital on an emergency. One of his patients had suffered a heart attack and he had gone to see if there was anything he could do. There was not. The patient had died en route. He spent some time consoling the widow before making his way to the doctors' washroom. There, in front of urinals, only a few doors from where patients often died, he opened his black bag, took out a small bottle of whisky concealed inside a box that had once contained medical gloves and hurriedly downed numerous swallows before anyone came in. He put the bottle back and used a mouthwash spray, clumsily, against the roof of his mouth before stepping out into the large white corridor. Some of the spray had hit his lips and he could feel the sting. He was going to his car when he saw Roger approaching the emergency door.

"Is anything wrong, Roger?"

"No, I just wanted to talk to you. Your wife told me I'd find you here. Do you have a minute."

"Sure. Why don't we go inside?" John Calder invited, his words slightly slurred.

They sat across from each other on straight-backed, uncomfortable chairs in one of the empty examining rooms. "Is this a medical problem, Roger?" Calder asked.

"Yes," Roger said, momentarily noticing the smell of the whisky and the redness in John Calder's eyes. It made him feel uncomfortable. "I'll get right to the point, Doc. I have found out about JoJo having cancer."

Slowly, the doctor said, "Oh, I see."

Roger thought that somehow the doctor looked relieved. He said, "I know she didn't want to get medical treatment, at least at first."

"What do you mean, at first?"

"Well, she came back this afternoon. I assumed that you arranged for her to go into the hospital."

"No, I didn't." He looked strangely at Roger for a minute and then picked up a receiver against the wall. "Admissions, please...This is Dr. Calder. Was a Mrs. Joanne Blake admitted today? ...Thank you." Putting the receiver back, he said as coherently as he could with the liquor circulating in his bloodstream, "Are you sure, Roger, that she came back here? If she had decided to get treated, she would have come to me...I was in touch with a doctor in New York...he uses a new laser technique with a high rate of success...she was aware of that, and she also knew I could get her into the program quickly. I'm sure she'd have come to see me."

"Then where did she go? I don't understand what she's trying to do," Roger said, slumping in the chair.

"She was adamant that you should not know. That's why I didn't tell you the truth in my office. I hope you understand. How did you find out?"

"That's not important now, Doctor. What's important is for JoJo to be treated. Do you think she can make it?"

"I don't know, Roger. I haven't seen her since...she left. I don't know what her condition is...I could only tell you after tests." He put one hand clumsily on Roger's shoulder and it slipped off. "Find her and we'll help her."

"What's wrong, Doctor?"

"What do you mean?"

"I mean I wonder...You look drunk."

"You're right, Roger, I am drunk, but I know what I'm saying."

"You're treating patients drunk?"

"Not all the time, my dear boy. Only since JoJo..." John Calder's eyes closed.

Roger was suddenly terrified. "You mean, you've been drinking since you found out that JoJo had cancer? For months now? Why?"

"You wouldn't understand. It's between me and JoJo's mother."

"What in the hell are talking about? You're an alcoholic. In my book that makes you a physician with no more ability to treat people than an animal!" Roger said, his voice low, but strong with anger.

"Wrong, Roger. Animals don't have feelings. I'm drunk because I have feelings. Do you know how hard it is to see people die all the time, especially those you love? JoJo happened to break the camel's...or is it my back."

"How can they let you practice? You're not fit to be a doctor, and certainly not fit to care for JoJo. No wonder she didn't want to be treated!"

"Now just a minute," John Calder said, suddenly surprisingly alert. "I'm very competent and I've always done my job well. I only drink on my own time. To forget all the pain. Do you understand that, Roger?"

Before Roger could reply, Calder went on. "Only it doesn't work. I lost my nerve when JoJo decided it was easier to die alone than to fight. She didn't listen to me, to anything I had to say. Such a waste, Roger. She had a good chance then. Now...In the old days, sometimes we couldn't do much for people like her mother. She was such a nice, gentle woman. And beautiful. I could never forget her. And I guess what finished me," he said, his voice now angry, "was that JoJo, your stubborn wife, didn't want to lift a finger to help herself when there was time. It was just too much for me to accept."

For a long time, the small room was eerily silent.

Roger saw deep lines of fatigue in the old doctor's face. Somehow he understood what the doctor had been trying to say. Having cared for a family over many decades, it was understandable how he could have become emotionally attached to them. It was not supposed to happen, someone had decreed, but it did. Roger accepted that fact. He had to. It had happened to him.

He had broken his marriage vows because he had gotten emotionally attached to one of his clients. He knew it had not been love, but there had been a unique openness and an easy frankness he had wanted to cherish and nurture. It got him into trouble because he had misread the signals. Two years later, the feelings of close friendship were still there and he now understood them very clearly. It made him appreciate the old doctor's struggle.

"I'll never touch another drop if she comes in, you know," Calder was now saying, his voice clear. "I never drank before all this business, so don't worry. I'm not an alcoholic. I'm merely a weak human being. I'll help her with all I can muster." The doctor put a hand on Roger's shoulder. This time it was steady and strong. "Find her, Roger."

Dr. Calder and Roger Blake walked out of the hospital together. Before parting, Roger asked, "You will let me know if she contacts you?"

"Of course, Roger."

"Don't tell her I know. I'll break the news to her."

John Calder did not start his car immediately. Normally, he would have stopped in a bar on his way home, but not tonight. *Never again. JoJo has from all indications seen the light, at last. Maybe, just maybe, there would still be time.*

Silently he gave thanks.

Chapter Twenty-Nine

When Roger got home, the thought that fate was scheming to goad him, probably laughing at his plight, made him feel mentally exhausted. It had been a hell of a day. He had found his wife, only to lose her again. He had antagonized and threatened to kill a man he admired. He had heard the confessions of a drunk, but basically honest doctor who could not accept his limitations. And now, he had no idea where to start looking for JoJo. Perhaps her friends could shed light on his dilemma.

Before getting busy with phone calls, he made coffee and, realizing that he had not eaten dinner, heaped some ham between two slices of bread that he didn't bother to butter. He was about to bite in when the phone rang.

"Roger? How did it go?" Peter Malton wanted to know.

"She's not there any more. Have you seen her?"

"What are you talking about, she's not there? Where did she go?"

"That's what I don't know. A neighbor told me she had gone to the city to visit people. I thought she might have gone to Dr. Calder, but he hasn't seen her? Do you have any ideas?"

"Not really. Have you tried her friends?"

"I was just about to call around now."

"I don't know how you found out about JoJo, but is it possible that she's aware that you know about her condition and has run away?"

"There's no way, I assure you." He wanted to add, *Derek Hughes is the only other person who knows what I found out and has no idea where to find her.* "Peter, if you should hear…"

"Of course, Roger. There'll be no more secrets, I promise." After a moment, he added, "Roger, try not to worry. She's come this far, there's got to be a simple explanation. Do keep us informed."

After hanging up, Roger munched on his sandwich while perusing the small directory that was still on the kitchen table, and checked off a few names. First, he dialed Carol Ferguson's number, managing to keep his voice casual as he inquired about the family and their activities. After a couple of minutes of conversation, he asked casually, "By the way, have you heard from JoJo lately?"

"No, I haven't."

"Just between you and me, Carol, I have reason to believe that she's back here."

"Really? When did she get in?"

"Some time today I believe, but since she hasn't come home…"

"That's not like her, Roger. She would have rushed home if she were in town."

Carol was right, of course. JoJo had told the neighbor she was going to the city, but was it the truth? He had accepted the news at face value, yet JoJo had lied so very expertly before her departure. "I suppose you're right. If you hear anything."

"I'll let you know right away, and," she emphasized, "I'm not going to tell her you're looking for her. I wish I knew what's going on?"

"My sentiments exactly."

Roger decided against making other calls. Carol was her dearest friend, the one she'd run to. The others were not nearly as close.

If she hasn't come to town, where could she have gone? New York was a possibility. Dr. Calder must have told her the name of that doctor with the laser treatment. She could have gone there. Almost instantly, his spirits rose at the thought. She was getting care and after a while would contact the Maltons. He sighed with relief. The future had suddenly taken on a new, more rosy perspective when his children came in.

The next day, Derek Hughes was called in by Roger Blake. "Did you find your wife?" the big man inquired.

"No. She wasn't there. Right now I'm not sure where she is, but I suspect she's gone to New York to get some treatments."

"I hope she gets better. Today, medicine can work miracles."

"Thank you, Derek. Sorry about my being abrupt yesterday."

"No need to apologize."

"So, tell me exactly what happened at the Wheeler place."

Derek recounted what he had found in the basement of the house, omitting that he had talked to Joanne.

"The woman in the house didn't see you?"

"There was no one around."

"Good work. Now give me the exact location of that farm, and we'll see to it that Sarah Wheeler becomes very talkative."

Derek had spent most of the night wondering how he could get around that question, finally conceding that he couldn't. He wanted to kick himself for not taking Blake's advice to see McBride with the information, but hearing the lawyer say he had found his wife had been a shock. He had taken a decision without thinking. Not good in his line of work. But, he philosophized, sometimes things had a way of working out. Blake already knew where his wife was hiding; he just didn't know Derek also knew. Hughes wrote the address and matter-of-factly described the rented house.

Roger was unmistakably startled. "That's the Wheeler place? That's where my wife has been living!"

"You mean it was your wife I saw talking with Sarah Wheeler last Saturday?"

"Had to be. How did she look?"

"Well, in fact, very well. She was painting outside."

"She was painting? Good. I always thought she should devote more time to painting. She's pretty good, you know."

Hughes wanted to change the subject. "I guess that does it for this case, Blake. You'll take it from here?"

"Yeah," Roger replied, preoccupied. "Thanks, Derek."

Walking toward the elevator, the investigator felt a deep sense of relief. He had worried that Blake would bombard him with questions about his wife. *If that had been the case, what would have been his duty?* he wondered. Not an easy decision because he was aware that at another time, in another place, in difference circumstances, he would have exerted a great deal of effort to befriend the lovely Joanne. Now he could only hope his mind would soon stop focusing on her face.

Confronted with the evidence against her, Sarah Wheeler confessed to having been paid to bring charges against Mayor Bristol. Yes, she said, the money was in a trunk in the basement of the house that had belonged to her late uncle, along with an agreement she had insisted be signed by the two men who had approached her. It had taken them two years and a great deal of money, along with the promise of more, to convince her.

Sarah had seen the potential of the farmlands around Triton Lake. With the money, she saw an opportunity to buy some of the farms and, with her cousins, work at having the zoning in the area changed. She would then own valuable recreational land. Roger was very impressed, if not by her methods, certainly by her ambition. Yes, she would go with the police to the house on Triton Lake and get the money and the agreement. Roger was clearly disappointed. He had hoped the girl's revelation would afford him an excuse to go back to the house and perhaps get inside.

But as the work week was ending, he didn't need an excuse to go back to Joanne's hideaway. He would simply go up and see what he could find.

As week's end, Joanne was bored in her small motel room. She had been jogging along the road daily, but disliked the strange looks she got from drivers. She had used the pool every day, but she desperately missed the lake. She missed the scenery, she missed having Red curl up at her feet at night, she missed Agatha's chats, she missed her painting. But she hesitated going back until she was certain the search of her basement had been completed, yet she couldn't be sure when that would happen.

Jogging early on Saturday morning, she decided to check out to get back to her hideaway for the weekend. Surely no one would be working on a long summer holiday weekend. If need be, on Monday she would find another place to hide for a few more days. Entering the small lobby of the motel, the front-page picture of the morning newspaper caught her eye. With the mayor was with his lawyer, Roger Blake, under big black letters: Mayor Bristol Cleared of Charges, Assistant Confesses Payoff. Joanne bought a paper and, while the manager was adding up her bill, started to read the article.

"Quite a story," the man behind the counter said. "The girl had stashed the money at her uncle's house in Triton. That's not far from here. I guess you just never know."

Joanne settled her account and rushed back to her room. She got comfortable on the bed and slowly read the whole story. *There is no longer any need to worry. It is all over.* She let her body lie back and, in a few minutes, all her muscles relaxed while her mind went to work. The imaginary weapon hit several of its targets in succession and a smile appeared on her lips. She was certain total victory was near.

When she opened her eyes again, she was very hungry.

She packed the few things she had with her and was soon behind the wheel of her car. Before reaching the highway, she stopped at a small restaurant where she ate fresh fruit and a bowl of hot cereal which she topped with a glass of milk. *What would Dr. Calder say about me now being able to eat so much without any problem?* she thought. She considered driving to the city to see him, but she knew it was too soon. She would wait a few more weeks. The scale at the motel, if it was accurate, had confirmed that she weighed one pound more than the last time she had weighed herself prior to her departure from the city. That was not yet enough. She would let the rest of the warm summer encourage her into a diligent recuperation.

On Saturday morning, as he had done daily since Monday, Roger phoned the Maltons. Again, they regretted to inform him that they had not heard from JoJo, the same reply he got from Dr. Calder the previous evening. The only thing to do was drive back to Triton. She had said she would be away a week, but perhaps in the house he would find a clue as to where she had gone and be reunited with her that very weekend. The thought excited him, and his mild elation was not lost on Terri.

"I guess you're glad it's all over," Terri said as she came down for breakfast. She caught him by surprise. "What?"

"The whole thing with the mayor, silly. You certainly look less uptight."

"I guess I am. Do you want me to drive you to work?"

"No, it's okay. Susan's father's picking us up."

Roger watched her munch on cereal. He asked, "Still enjoying being part of the working class?"

"I get to talk to a lot of people. It's fun."

Jason made his entrance, yawning.

"You better hurry up, Jason," his sister warned. "We're not going to wait for you, you know."

Roger poured his son a glass of juice. "Do you want some eggs?"

"Sure," Jason replied, and Roger got busy.

"Remember, Jason, to be extra polite. That's the way to make lots of tips," Terri put in.

"I know what to do, don't worry."

"The only reason you got this job is because I work there already, so don't drop things when you put them in people's cars."

"You think I'm a klutz or something?"

"Okay, guys," Roger said. "Terri, I'm sure Jason will do just fine." He was cracking eggs. "My two children working. Boy, it makes me feel old."

"Dad, it's just a weekend job," Jason remarked, amused.

Roger was grateful both Terri and Jason would be busy all day. Their summer work, even if it was only on Saturday for Jason, had come as a blessing all around. It kept his children occupied, while relieving him of worry and freeing him.

Soon he was driving north on the highway.

Chapter Thirty

Even though the sun was warm, a cool breeze made the air pleasurable when Roger, exhilarated, arrived at Joanne's rented house.

Getting no answer to his knock, he walked to the back, checking the windows. One of them had been left opened a few inches and he saw how easy it would be to cut the screen and lift it up all the way. He was contemplating this strategy when he saw Red come up from the barn. "Hi there, buddy. Anybody else around? I guess I'd better find out," Roger said, petting the animal.

He checked the barn and walked down to the water where a couple of men were rowing in a small boat farther down the lake. He saw no one else. On his way back to the house, he took time to inspect the large garden and thought that JoJo had not wasted her time while in exile.

Michael Dunbar had spent more than an hour trying to console Agatha Wheeler though she was inconsolable. She couldn't understand what had made her lovely niece turn bad. It could only be all those gangsters in the city. She would never be able to live it down, not the way people talk in the village, she told Dunbar. He reminded her that people have short memories, but it was of little help. She was still crying when he left.

He was walking back to his house when he saw Roger in the garden. "Hi, there," he waved. Getting closer he added, "Don't I know you from somewhere?"

"I don't know. My name's Roger Blake."

"Of course. You were the mayor's lawyer. Wait a minute! Blake? You're related to Joanne."

"Her husband."

"I see. Nice woman. But why are you here? She's gone to the city for a while."

"Did she say when she would be back?"

"She didn't talk to me a whole lot. Keeps very much to herself, doesn't she? Agatha, that's the lady at the farm there," he said, indicating with his hand, "Agatha Wheeler told me…"

"That's Sarah Wheeler's uncle and aunt there?"

"Yes. To say they're upset, would be putting it mildly. You should have seen them when Sarah came up with the police this week! Good thing your wife was away." Dunbar lowered his voice. "If I were you, I wouldn't hang around here too long. Joe and Agatha are good people; they don't need to be reminded, know what I mean?"

"Of course. Do you know if there's a key to the house hidden somewhere? I'd like to get in."

"You don't need a key. When old man Wheeler, that's the other uncle who used to live here, was sick, he'd lock the door all the time, but I'd get in. Let me show you," Dunbar invited.

Roger followed the burly man as he sauntered to the back of the house and looked around on the ground for a moment. "Ha, there it is," he said and picked up a piece a metal lying in the grass. He proceeded to slide it along the edge of the framed screen, which, Roger saw, led into the kitchen, and in a minute frame and screen were in Dunbar's hands. "Now, you simply lift the window."

Luckily, Roger thought, *Dunbar doesn't look too menacing. If he did, Joanne would not have been too safe in her house.*

"By the way, my name's Michael Dunbar," he said. "Let me get in and I'll unlock the door."

Before Roger could say anything, the man was halfway in. In a moment the front door was opening.

"I'm glad you came along. It gives me a chance to look at your wife's paintings," Dunbar said as he examined the half-dozen oils propped up against one of the walls in the living room.

"She's good. Really good. She wouldn't let me look at them. That one of you is especially superb, don't you think?"

Roger who had been silently surveying the room joined Dunbar, and was so awed by his portrait that he had to struggle to speak. "Excellent."

"I agree with you. I told your wife I could arrange a showing in New York if she wants. I hope you can convince her. She has talent, no doubt about it," he said, picking up a canvas on which his house showed through a scenery of trees. "I would like to buy this one," he told Roger. "Would you ask Joanne to keep it for me? I'll pay a good price—within reason, you understand."

Roger thought the man was sincere. "I'll ask her."

"Good. Well, I must get back. Just be sure you lock up before you leave."

Roger went through every room in the house, trying to feel JoJo's presence. He flipped through her books to understand, as much as he could, what she had been trying to do. Mental exercises, Peter Malton had said. Roger prayed they had helped. He was sitting on the sofa, taking it all in when he heard the car.

Joanne Blake smiled at the sight of her adopted home and quickly turned in. She was halfway up the driveway before she spotted Roger's car. *Shit. How had he found out? Hughes, of course,* she thought. *It is too late to turn back.* Besides, something inside her made her want to accept this twist of fate. She parked her car and was getting out when she saw Roger stepping out. Her heart began to pump quickly.

He approached her slowly as she stood still. In a moment, his strong arms were circling her body. She was unable to control the tears.

"Do you think it has helped?" Roger asked. He was seated on the sofa beside his wife still holding on to her hand, as he had been doing for the past hour, while she explained her life, her struggle, and her mental efforts of the previous months.

"It certainly hasn't done any harm. I've gained a pound. Not much, but still something to be proud of. I can keep food down, something I couldn't do just a few weeks ago. I feel I'm getting better each day. I know I'm getting better."

"I'm glad, but don't you think that it might be time for the laser treatments Calder wanted you to have?"

"How do you know about those? Did Dr. Calder tell you I was sick?"

"No, JoJo, he didn't."

"Then, how did you find out? Peter?"

"No. Neither of them would tell me anything. But Calder seemed surprised, if that's the word, when I questioned him."

"Questioned him? But why?"

"I thought you had gone away because you were pregnant."

"What?"

"Forgive me, JoJo, but I had to find some sort of answer as to why you would leave your family without ever getting in touch. It was so unlike you. I knew something was wrong and that Calder and Malton had information I didn't. I felt there was a conspiracy against me. And I was right," he added, a hint of false hurt in his voice.

She smiled briefly. "How did you find out, Roger?"

"I broke into Dr. Calder's office."

"My God! And read my file?" She took her hand away from his. "How could you do such a thing?"

"Try and put yourself in my shoes. I was desperate. Try to understand?"

After a while, she had to concede. "I guess I do. I realized too late that your investigative mind would not rest until you found me. I almost called home a few times, but I was too worried that if I heard your voice or those of the children, I wouldn't have the strength to lie adequately."

Roger's arms circled her shoulders. "You fool," he said, kissing her temple lightly. "I wish you'd had more faith in me instead of going through this all by yourself. In any event, let's put it behind us." He continued with urgency in his voice. "But now is the time to go forward. How about those treatments? Don't you think it's more than time to combine them with your own efforts?"

"I don't know, Roger. I couldn't stand…"

"JoJo, remember, you're talking to a lawyer. I'll get a court order if necessary."

"You wouldn't!"

"Want to try me? When I want something, really want it, I can get it. I've proven it."

Joanne Blake smiled broadly and it felt good. She was no longer alone in her terrible struggle.

The sun was starting to go down when they stopped talking. Giving in to Roger's arguments, she finally agreed to see Dr. Calder and go on to New York. The children would not be informed, at least for now. If she didn't need to be hospitalized, she and Roger would escape to the Wheeler house on weekends.

"And another thing. Don't even think about going back to work when you get better," Roger said, attempting, but failing, to give his voice a firm tone.

"I had no such intention, although Peter'll be disappointed. I'm thinking of becoming a full-time artist. I've been offered a showing of my paintings in New York, you know," she said in a pseudo-haughty tone.

"I'm glad you'll be taking Dunbar up on his offer."

"Is there anything you don't know?" Joanne exclaimed.

As a reply, he took her in his arms, nearly choking her.

"Listen here, buster. I'll run away again if you don't ease your grip," she said, kissing his ear.

"And I'll just find you again."

As darkness fell, they were sharing a bond of passion that would only partly ease their desire for each other. All the while, Red was stretched out on the porch across the front door, his head on his front paws, his eyes alert, guarding. He would let no one intrude.

Epilogue

Energized, John Calder walked to the arrivals area with other deplaning passengers, his thinning gray hair unruly after a relaxing nap on board the plane. He started a slow run when he saw Roger.

"My boy, I don't know how, but…Why don't we go over there and talk," he said indicating rows of empty seats. They sat against the far wall.

"What happened, Doctor? Tell me everything. I should have gone to New York with her."

"And do what?" Motioning the unimportant remark away with his hand, Calder continued. "They did all the tests and somehow, I don't know how, in the last few months the cancerous cells have not spread, as should have been the case. I've never seen anything like it. It's as though they were stopped in their tracks. The doctor, the one who's going to do the laser treatments, was very impressed by her condition. I have to admit she wasn't all wrong. Anyway, they're going to start giving her the drug tomorrow and then the laser therapy. If all goes well, she'll be able to come home in between. It's very hopeful, Roger. I would say her chances are more than excellent. This is when I wish I believed in God. I would give thanks for giving us stubborn people like JoJo."

Roger Blake did not take his vacation in August as he had planned. He postponed it until October when he took his wife to Hawaii. There, in the cool breezes under the tropical sun and amidst the beauty of paradise, Joanne Blake welcomed the fifth decade of her life with a new vitality. The milestone that had so frightened her was greeted with gratitude that she had now been given hope, real hope, by the medical staff.

She would no longer waste precious time on counting years. She would devote herself to the future where love, tested by the ultimate trial, would bloom for decades, and all the while, both husband and wife would bask in the mysterious satisfaction that only those who have managed the depth of crushing despair can ever know.

The End

Printed in the United States
94880LV00007B/428/A